# THE THRESHING FLOOR

**CONTENT WARNING**

This novel includes body shaming, sexual situations, references to infertility, child loss, eating disorders, persons with disabilities and sicknesses being cured, a non-explicit, brief reference to the sexual abuse of a child, and non-explicit references to suicide. A rabid dog is euthanatized off-page, and a wild animal dies.

**Reader discretion is advised.**

Copyright © 2024 Steph Nelson

This book is a work of fiction. Any references to historical events, real people, or real places are used fictitiously. Other names, characters, places, and events are products of the author's or artist's imagination, and any resemblance to actual events or places or persons, living or dead, is entirely coincidental.

All rights reserved. No part of this book may be reproduced or used in any manner without the prior written permission of the copyright owner, except for the use of brief quotations in a book review.

Edited by Maddy Leary
Book Design and Layout by Rob Carroll
Cover Art by Olly Jeavons
Cover Design by Rob Carroll

ISBN 978-1-958598-49-8 (paperback)
ISBN 978-1-958598-72-6 (eBook)

darkmatter-ink.com

# THE THRESHING FLOOR

STEPH NELSON

DARK MATTER INK

*For my heart baby, Evelyn Hope*

*February 23, 2009–March 7, 2009*

"Then the iron, clay, bronze, silver, and gold broke to pieces at the same time.

They became like chaff on a threshing floor in the summertime;

the wind blew them away, and there was nothing left."

Daniel 2:35

# NOW

**BLOOD THRUMS LOUDLY** in my ears. My head hurts, but I have to keep going, keep pushing farther down this dark corridor. Turning back isn't an option.

It's cold blackness all around, like an abyss yawning to consume me whole. I blink a few times to confirm my eyes are open. There's no difference, but if I could see anything, it'd be the white fog of my own breath. I shiver and tuck my hands inside my oversized sweater to drum up some warmth.

I'd hoped this basement would have a window to climb out of. Maybe even a door to the outside. It's a fucking mansion, after all. But I've been moving down this pitch-dark hallway for what feels like hours, rushing as fast as I can. It has to lead somewhere. Preferably somewhere I can hide.

When the pressure in my skull becomes a vise grip, I slow down to walk, keeping a sweatered fist against the wall for support. With only socks on, the soles of my feet feel numb as I move across the polished concrete floor. It's like sneaking across a Home Depot. Or a prison.

Smooth drywall gives way to rough brick with sloppy seams of grout. It snags my sweater, so I push my sleeve back and feel as I go.

The concrete floor ends abruptly in a sudden drop. It would be nothing in the light, but since I don't see it coming, my footing falters, and I hit...dirt?

What the hell?

It's like I've entered some part of the corridor where they gave up on making it look nice. Probably assumed nobody would see it anyway.

A tentacle of fear snakes up my neck at that thought. What the fuck is this basement for?

I finally turn a corner to see something ahead.

A red light cuts through the darkness, radiating from a razor-thin gap below a door.

But the power is out in the whole building. How is it possible for one light to be on?

And why?

I pause to watch for shadows moving on the other side of the door. A brush of dark to punctuate the crimson line. Evidence that someone is inside.

There's nothing.

Somewhere behind me, footsteps thump down the stairs leading to the basement.

Leading toward me.

Panic flushes through my body. If someone comes down this corridor, they'll crash right into me. I need to find cover or I'll be pinned here, and that's not an option.

I reach the door, expecting it to be locked, but with hardly any force, it creaks open an inch.

My gut drops. Unlocked.

This is probably a trap, but I have no choice.

The red light goes off. Then it flashes in long strobes.

Red. Dark. Red. Dark.

The dark is so much longer than the flashes of red, and it messes with my eyes.

The door is heavy when I open it, like steel, and holy hell, it's got to be five inches thick. The smell of rot and shit assaults my nose, and I gag. I can't go in there. I can't.

Feet tap polished concrete behind me, and my pulse spikes again. Sure, they haven't reached the dirt yet, but they're close. Way too goddamn close.

I walk into the room. The putrid smell is *so* much stronger inside. I gag again and nearly vomit. I step toward the wall, trying to orient myself. I have to get as far away from the door as possible. Perhaps find an exit, or a closet to hide in.

Underfoot, I feel a squish and a crunch. I flinch back, and now my sock is wet.

*What the hell?*

My mind goes right to dead animals, which would explain the smell. That thing felt about the size of a squirrel. Or a rat? Could be a rat.

"Who's there?" A female voice cuts through from deeper inside the flashing red darkness. It sounds like she just woke up.

Chains jangle.

I freeze, breath hitching in my throat. Someone's down here? Chained up?

*What the actual fuck?*

"Help me." The voice is a breathy whisper.

I strain to see, but the strobe effect is aggravating my head, making it hurt worse than it already did. I have to help, but terror tightens around me like a straitjacket.

I don't want to go any further.

I must go further.

*Move forward. Just take a step.*

I move, hugging the wall so I don't trip again.

"Where are you?" I whisper, raising one arm in front of my face, protecting it from whatever I can't see in the dark.

Another soft crunch underfoot.

*Shit.*

More icy wetness squidges through my sock and between my toes. The taste of bile rises, but I swallow it and keep moving.

"Toward the back," she says.

My hand collides with some sort of metal hanging along the wall. I finger it until I realize it's a chain attached to the ceiling. It doesn't sway easily, so I can tell there's something bulky at the bottom, but with the doses of red light so short, and my eyes so night-blind, I have no idea what it is.

When I go to grip the chain and move around it, something scrapes my hand. I gasp and bring my hand close to my eyes, straining to see during the blinks of red. But all I can make out is a substance, wet and warm.

My palm is covered in blood.

# TWO MONTHS EARLIER

# DALICE

**I'VE ONLY BEEN** on the phone with my sister for a few minutes when I stick my head out of the bedroom to get eyes on Cash. Minutes are all my two-year-old son needs to wreak havoc.

Especially in our dinky apartment.

Something thumps in the bathroom, so I rush in there where, yep, he's pulling toilet paper off the holder. When he sees me, he laughs maniacally, bouncing on his bum. It's like he knows it drives me bonkers, but Cash has a knack for taking advantage of moments when I'm not paying attention. He still can't walk, which means he can't run. But that doesn't mean he's slow. The kid has perfected speed crawling and lightning-fast troublemaking.

"Are you listening to me?" My sister Brandy's strained voice comes over the phone.

With the iPhone smashed between my cheek and shoulder, I wrestle Cash into my arms and rip toilet paper out of his clenched fists. He uses them to push against my chest, shouting "No!"

I kiss his forehead.

"Yeah, sorry, Bran. Cash was TP-ing the bathroom again."

She doesn't laugh, which is so on-brand for her.

"I asked if taking on a second job right now is really a good idea."

I plop Cash down on the living room floor, turn on the TV, and navigate to Netflix. With his short attention span, and his mind on his toilet paper project, it'll only buy me another five minutes, tops. I need way more than that to clean up the mess and get ready for my shift, but I tell myself he'll sit for longer, because you never know. Miracles happen.

"We've talked about this," I say to my sister, hustling back to the bathroom to clean up the mess. "I'm only doing…Pig Out Place…for the insurance."

Reaching down to scoop armfuls of toilet paper is surprisingly aerobic, and I'm unsurprisingly out of shape, so I'm winded in two-point-five seconds. I should roll the toilet paper up and reuse it. Save money. But by the time I think of it, most of it's in the trash.

I stand and take a deep breath.

"Weekends flipping burgers in order to cut Cash's medical bills in half is a great trade-off." The words all pour out fast before I take a breath.

Pig Out Place is a local chain restaurant. Like if Red Robin and Denny's had a baby. It offers insurance benefits to part-time employees, which is irresistibly compelling because I work full-time during the week as a house cleaner. Self-employed, hence no insurance.

"Don't you guys qualify for Medicaid?" Brandy asks.

She already knows the answer to this one. But I feel like she knew the answer to the last one, too. I press my lips together and squeeze my eyes shut to channel all the patience.

"No, we don't. I make just over the limit, but with my school loans, Cash's medical bills, and the credit card debt I've racked up trying to feed us while paying for all the things, it's still not even close to enough to live off. This job is *for the insurance*."

Can't she take a hint and stop asking the same stupid questions over and over? I don't want to be even more blunt with her. It'd start a fight.

"Why don't you cut back on clients? Bring in less from cleaning houses so you can get on Medicaid?"

Oh my God. My head drops back, so I'm staring at the ceiling. Maybe I can find some patience up there somewhere. It's worth a try.

My sister believes I seek out the hard way of doing things. As if it's my preference to let life beat me up to learn lessons. And in doing that, I'm punishing her.

That's why she makes these oh-so-easy suggestions. But *she's* not the idiot who waited to go to college until she was thirty-two, then got pregnant just shy of graduating.

Nope, that was me.

She's not the one so bad at being pregnant that she had to quit school to carry the baby full term.

Also me.

And she's not the dingbat saddled with three years of student loans now in repayment, forcing her to leave Seattle, a city she loved, and move home to Spokane where she could afford rent. She's not the one without a college degree that'd help her find a job to pay off all that debt. That was—guess who?

Me.

Me.

Me.

Cherry on top? That child I could barely carry to term has a life-threatening medical condition, which is why I'm willing to work at Pig Out Place—the same spot I worked as a twenty-something, for God's sake.

"Oh right, I should just make *less* money," I spit out. "Genius! Why didn't I think of that? Jesus, Bran. I'd rather take on *more* houses than work at some stupid restaurant with an embarrassing name. But it turns out, with only twenty-four hours in a day, I can't clean enough houses to afford out-of-pocket expenses for Cash's care. I need insurance."

It's a damn good plan, and I wish Brandy would tell me that instead of trying to come up with scenarios I've already thought of.

People who aren't in your shoes don't realize how little bandwidth you have for discussing all the issues surrounding being in your shoes. Or see that since this is your reality and not simply a conversation over the phone, you've already thought of and ruled out every single one of these ideas on the first day of problem-solving. Plus, talking about it is wasted time you could instead spend getting food on the table, keeping the collectors away, saving up for your son's heart transplant, and, if possible, making the kid smile. That last one's extra credit, though, when lined up against whether you'll be able to afford it when his heart taps out.

"But Cash also needs his mom around," Brandy says. Her tone is defiant, like she's so certain she's right. And of course, she is, but there's way more to it.

I clench my teeth as a reminder not to speak and instead take a deep breath.

Brandy doesn't get it. A mommy-and-me date with Cash can't fix this shithole I hand-carved for us. She sees my life through her own lens—a younger, married woman without children. Everything is so goddamn easy for her.

"Well, I'm trying," I say.

"Of course you are, but I want to see you and Cash together more often. Not having a dad... He really needs his mom."

What I want to say is *I don't fucking have a choice!* Instead, I say, "Thanks. I'll see you in a few," and end the call before she officially sends me over the edge.

I've gravitated back into my bedroom without realizing it, and once again, I don't know where Cash is. The abandoned TV blares *Cocomelon* in the living room, and there's no trace of him.

"Cashy! We gotta go see Auntie Bran," I say, hurrying toward the bathroom again.

Ta-da! There he is now, shirtless.

The huge, pink vertical scar on his chest is the first thing I see. Proof of his past two open-heart surgeries. Cash grips a fresh roll of toilet paper that he must have gotten from under the sink. At least he didn't get into the toilet bowl cleaner thinking it was a melted Slurpee or something.

"Broken," he says, handing the roll to me for help. He can't get it started.

"Yeah, it's totally broken, bud. That's why you shouldn't play with these. They break so easily." I smile and shrug, like that's an actual answer, and go to set the roll on the counter, but there's no real estate.

I shove aside my face wash, a flat tube of toothpaste, concealer, and three toothbrushes. Why three? No idea. An open eyeshadow palette goes sliding into the wet sink, where my tweezers have already made a home. Whatever.

"Cashy, we have to get going. I'll pack you some fishy crackers for the road. Sound good?" I carry him to my bedroom and try to fit his arms through a shirt while he flails, fighting me.

I win and place him in his crib. He screams, but I need a hot second to get ready without worrying about what he might get into.

No time for a shower now, so I grab a towel off the bathroom floor, get the corner wet, and wipe yesterday's makeup from under my eyes. A whiff of stink hits my nose, so I run the towel across my underarms and put on deodorant.

When I turn to leave the bathroom, I notice a huge flyaway, like a massive duckbill coming out of the back of my head. Damn this short hair. It's so easy to take care of when you shower every day, but skip one and it's total bedhead.

Not the good kind, either.

I stick my head under the sink and get it so wet that my light pink strands turn dark. I have blonde hair, but it's almost never blonde. It's a fine shade, I guess, but I get bored with it, and hair is such a non-committal way to change my look. I snag my fingers through it and towel off so it's not dripping. Add a little hair paste, and it'll have to work. I can do my makeup in the car.

Back in the bedroom, I get Cash out. He's hot from crying.

"Sorry baby, I'm still here."

I brush my hand around the inside of the crib for his pacifier. Brandy will bitch about this too, because he's too old for it.

*You think you're broke now? Wait until you're paying for orthodontia to fix that binky mess in his mouth.*

She never runs out of fresh ways to skewer me.

# DALICE

**EVEN THOUGH BRANDY** is my little sister, you wouldn't be able to tell by looking at her. She's thirty-one yet acts like an old lady. I mean, she's still beautiful and, as always, thin. She's blonde like me, although I don't think she's ever colored her hair. It's not that she physically looks old, it's everything else. Her clothes, her mannerisms, her choice of home décor. We're only four years apart, but it might as well be worlds. She's super smart, but dumbs herself down to act like the perfect *wifey*, which her husband, Hank, doesn't hate at all.

Brandy lives far north of Spokane, up the Newport Highway and toward the Idaho panhandle. She always wanted to be out this direction because she likes all the pine trees. Houses in her neighborhood have, at a minimum, five massive pines in each yard.

Hank hates the trees. Hates the pine needles and how they pile up on the grass. He says it's nothing like raking leaves because you have to pull needles out of the rake to get them into a container. They stab, even if you're wearing garden gloves. Not sure why he has such a strong opinion on it because Brandy does all the raking anyway. She does everything around the house.

Hank is older than Brandy, even older than me. He's newly retired from the military, which doesn't say much since he retired at, like, thirty-seven, but all he does is watch the news.

He's young enough to start a second career, but instead, he skipped right to the sedentary lifestyle of a seventy-year-old man. Hank says he's earned it, and maybe he has, but if so, why choose an armchair and Fox News as a prize?

Brandy wanted to be this far north to fulfill her ultimate dream of living in a foresty neighborhood. I'm pretty sure she fixates on this one thing to ignore all the ways her life hasn't turned out how she wanted.

When I pull into her driveway, Cash starts wiggling in his seat.

Brandy's house is immaculate, probably because she doesn't have kids. As fate would have it, Brandy's biggest disappointment in life also happens to be the one thing I have.

A kid.

She always wanted children, but wasn't able to have any, and since they moved so much with Hank in the service, they decided not to adopt. Brandy's quick change from desperately wanting children to accepting the life of a kid-less military wife was so very her, ever the pragmatist. Or, at least *public* Brandy. I know my little sister, and I don't buy that she's as peachy as she seems.

Their house is a nice two-story place, built in the seventies but totally remodeled. It's got that split-level thing going on, along with lots of light, hardwood floors, and an open kitchen. Downstairs, Hank has set up his command center: huge-screen TV, computer at the ready in case he needs to jump on Facebook to defend his political views.

I shouldn't be so judgmental, but my mom used to say "Idle hands are the devil's workshop," and that's what I think of whenever I see Hank. He's the picture of privilege, to be able to spend his days this way. It's a privilege I don't share. No time to stay caught up on which charlatan is pulling what shenanigan right now. Anyone who has gotten that far in government is already rotten anyway. Brandy views the obsession as Hank's thing, a hobby of sorts that she doesn't share, and she's happy he's not up in her grill all day.

"Hey, Cashy!" Brandy answers the door after one gentle knock and zeros in on him.

He doesn't give her the time of day. Cash is single-minded whenever we come here, and he squirms for me to put him down. Once his hands and knees touch the floor, he speed-crawls up the stairs toward his playroom. Brandy's got it stocked with every toy he doesn't have at home, which might bother me if I wasn't so grateful that he has at least one place where his childhood can be magical.

"*Hi Brandy*," I say with emphasis to point out that she hasn't greeted me.

"He doesn't even have boots on," Brandy replies.

"Good to see you, too. I'm doing fine, thanks."

She ignores my comment. "I literally called you this morning to remind you to bring his coat."

"He has a coat." I hand her a gray zip-up hoodie.

Brandy rolls her eyes. "That's not a coat, Dal. I need to run errands today."

"We don't live in the Arctic. This coat is fine."

"It's almost winter!" Brandy yells.

I raise my eyebrows. She's extra mad. Over a coat? I mean, yeah, it's October, but it's not snowing yet.

Little red lights flash in my brain: *Warning. This isn't about the coat.*

Brandy is the classic stuff-then-explode type. Lots of passive aggression until the volcano builds up enough pressure to erupt. I rarely see it coming until it's much too late, but I'm getting quicker at recognizing the signs since she's been watching Cash.

I need to diffuse this, whatever this is. Because if it's one of those erupting moments, I don't have time.

"You could pick him up a coat," I say, forcing a smile. "Some boots too, if that makes you happy. Thanks in advance." I reach for the doorknob to leave, but my comment doesn't land as a diffusion. It's my tone. I can tell as soon as the words leave my mouth that I'm a little mad, too.

"I wish you'd listen to me sometimes!" Brandy yells. "That you weren't so goddamn stubborn. You're not always right, you know. It's like you crave learning everything in the most difficult way possible."

There it is.

Her old standby gripe about my life. As if I chose this. Like I wanted to be alone, raising a child with special needs in my mid-thirties.

Now I'm officially pissed.

"You'd think being a single mom busting ass in order to give my kid the best chance possible at life would inspire more support."

"Whoa!" Brandy says, defensive as if *I've* picked this fight.

I should hold my tongue, but it's too late now. I'm invested.

"It's not like you have time for anyone. I've asked you to hang out umpteen times and you're always too busy. Doing what, Brandy? What makes you so busy you can't hang out with your sister?"

*Shit.* I'm adding more fuel to the fire. And it's stuff that's unrelated to her original complaint. I'm turning this little campfire into a forest fire. Sure, it's true. I'd love to be closer to Brandy, and sure, I'm right that she's always so busy with nothing to show for it. And she never listens to *me*, either. But still, timing!

"Well, if you think I'm too busy, it's probably because I'm always watching your son," she says through clenched teeth.

*Fuck.*

I walked into that one.

"I gotta go," I say, and rush down the driveway.

"Am I putting him to bed tonight?" Brandy shouts from the porch, annoyance still clinging to her voice.

At my car, I turn and sigh, because despite what she says, how she treats me, all my wounded expectations for our relationship, she's still here, taking care of my son day after day. I love her for that. "I promise I'll be back before bedtime. And…thank you for watching Cash. I don't know how I'll ever repay you." Tears pinch, threatening to roll freely, but I swallow them down. She can't see me cry.

It's so weird how you can be pissed at your family in one breath, and in the next breath, be so grateful for them without compromising even a shred of that deep anger. It's like a bottomless well that'll always be there to tap. Simmering on low but standing by and ready to fight another day.

Brandy's body deflates, and she stands still, like she might concede.

Maybe she sees how tired I am. How hard I'm trying. Maybe she feels bad about constantly picking on me, and this is the point where she drops the walls and we start up a true friendship. Maybe she'll go out with me for drinks, or on a walk like we used to with Mom. It's been so long since she took any interest in me beyond being a project. Not since Mom died.

But no, Brandy waves me off like a bad idea and goes inside.

# 1992

REVA PREHNER IS nine years old on a hot summer day in Spokane. She chases after her eleven-year-old brother, Shane, yelling "It's not her fault!" as if these words have some magic power to change his mind about their dog.

Shane ignores her and walks past Grandpa's Oldsmobile, which is parked behind their trailer. It's an early-model black Cutlass with a red interior and a blue tarp draped over it. It's the car Grandpa died in years ago when he accidentally fell asleep with it running in his garage.

Shane says he killed himself, but Mom says it was an accident.

Reva catches up to Shane as he heads toward the woods at the edge of their mobile home park. He pulls on Fish's leash with one hand, alternatively yanking the dog along and dodging her when she gets too close. Her mouth sops wet with drool, and Dad's old .22 hangs from a loose strap across Shane's back.

Reva can't take her eyes off it.

"Don't follow me. She's dangerous," he says.

"It's *Fish*! She won't hurt me," Reva sobs and tries to stop Shane, tries to convince him that this doesn't need to happen even though she knows she can't. He doesn't change his mind once he decides something.

"This isn't Fish anymore." Shane turns and faces her, keeping one eye on the dog. His cheeks are wet, like hers. The few freckles scattered across his nose stand out the most when he cries. Sweat soaks his brown curly hair and it hangs down his cheek.

Shane has been different since Dad left last year. Older, as if it's been many years instead of just one. Right now, Shane should be out playing soccer, listening to his Nirvana and Pearl Jam tapes, or jumping off docks into the lake with his friends. He has a lot of friends, unlike Reva. But here he is, putting down their beloved dog instead.

"She has rabies," Shane says, picking up his pace toward the woods. "Fish will absolutely hurt you if she gets the chance."

"But she's not foaming like the Carpenters' dog was. And she's calm."

"They don't always act crazy like in the movies."

But Reva didn't say the movies. She said the Carpenters' dog. It was really foamy, nothing like Fish is now. And either way, Fish wouldn't hurt her because, despite being Shane's dog, Fish likes Reva best.

Dad got the dog for Shane's birthday years ago. She has stubby legs, a short brown coat, and a white mark on her forehead. Dad said the Lord told him to take her home for Shane, and the markings reminded him of the Jesus fish. Reva always had a hard time seeing those white blobs as a fish. It was just two fat circles—one big, and one smaller. And even though she never said it out loud, she decided that Dad meant to bring Fish home for *her*. Secretly, Fish was Reva's dog, a gift from Dad that nobody else knew about. Not even him.

Fish is her only friend. The dog doesn't think it's weird that Reva is so quiet. She doesn't expect Reva to say all the right things, to have the right clothes, or to be pretty. As far as Fish is concerned, Reva's red hair is the best color, and her face is perfect, like Cindy Crawford's.

It's not, of course.

She's sure her crooked teeth and freckles keep her far away from pretty. The point is, Fish doesn't care. She always wants to play and never laughs when Reva says stupid things. She always snuggles up to Reva, which is a lot more than Mom does.

"Can't we take her to the vet? They can make her better."

"We don't have money for that. And anyway, I think they'd put her down too." Shane's voice breaks on the last word.

"But it's not her fault!" Reva wails. Her legs are like jelly. They haven't walked very far, but the worries bearing down inside her are making her a little floaty.

It's not fair. It's not Fish's fault she got sick, and she couldn't help acting out. The sickness made her do it.

"It doesn't matter. She's not in control of herself anymore, and the longer we put it off, the more chance there is she'll hurt someone. She already killed the Normans' cat."

"Stray cat." Reva corrects him as if being a stray lessens the blame for Fish. That mangy animal wasn't technically the Norman family cat. They only set food out for it now and then so it wouldn't go hungry.

"Still, she killed it. She's never been aggressive, and so we can't risk her hurting anything—or anyone—else."

"What if she won't? What if she can change?"

"Some things *can't* change, Reva," Shane says, turning to stare at her. He wipes his nose with the back of his hand. "They are what they are. Doesn't matter how much we want them to change or how much they want to, either."

"Dad says we can always change with the Lord's help."

"Dad isn't here anymore though, is he?" Shane glares at her.

He's right. Dad disappeared as if they meant nothing to him, and that's when they had to move out of their home and into Trailer Trash Town, as Mom used to call it before they lived there.

She hasn't called it that since.

Dad had been a pastor at a small church, so they never really had money, but the church paid for the house they lived in. Then some super bad thing happened with him and Mom. Reva's not sure what, but it was so bad that he stopped being the pastor and left in the middle of the night. Didn't even say goodbye.

"Can we pray for Fish? I think God can heal her," Reva says.

Shane exhales hard and closes his eyes. He's losing patience. She's surprised he hasn't yelled at her yet. "You pray for her right here while I take her into the woods. Don't follow me."

This time, Reva tries to do what he says, but it turns out she can't pray. All she can do is watch them get smaller and smaller until Shane's gray tee shirt and acid-washed jean shorts slip into the vertical brown lines of pine.

Now her hands are hot.

This weird sensation pulls her away from thinking about Fish for a second. They're not hot like when they get sweaty because of summer, more like she's holding them up to a wood stove. She opens them and stares down through the wall of tears in her eyes.

Gold.

Her palms are covered in gold, like some statue. She can move them—they're still her hands—but what is this weird layer on them? It reminds her of gold dust, like pieces could flake off. She tries to rub it off on her shirt, but nothing happens. No gold comes off.

Then the crack of a gunshot in the woods startles her back into the moment, and she sobs even louder.

# DALICE

I'M NOT THAT late for my shift at Pig Out Place. Five, maybe ten minutes, but Kelly, my manager, is there to offer me a wordless glare anyway. I went to high school with her, and it's more than a little humbling to be her employee now. Especially since we worked here together so many years ago.

Pig Out Place is closer to where Brandy and I grew up, south of where Brandy is now. We lived in a small 1940s tract house near Franklin Park, in walking distance from NorthTown Mall. Even though by the time I was old enough to be interested in the mall, the only real reason to go there was the movie theater. Our mom talked about the mall as a bustling place to hang out during her teen years. She and her friends would meet up and try on prom dresses even though they were only thirteen.

Back when Macy's was still there.

When it was actually The Bon Marché, and before that, Frederick & Nelson. Before that, it was The Crescent.

Spokane has real issues with keeping stores and restaurants around. Pig Out Place has been lucky to last this long. Mom used to say it was because of the economy, but I never got why this city was like a black hole of failed businesses, even when cities around us thrived. It's still that way. Every time I drive around, I'll catch some place where I can rattle off at least three other businesses that occupied it before whatever this new one is. I should be grateful, because this is the reason I can even afford my apartment at all. Thanks, Spokane economy!

Ryan stands next to Kelly, being his tall and skinny self. He's young—early twenties—but an old soul. I forget he's not my age.

"Dalice, you're with me today," Ryan says.

I furrow my brows because I thought I finished training with him. He makes this face that I think means *Just go with it*, but I'm not sure. I follow him to the kitchen anyway, and when I glance back at Kelly, she's still glaring.

"What's her deal?"

He shrugs. "She hates when people are late. And by late, I mean even seconds."

"Won't happen again. I thought I was on my own today, though. Didn't we finish server training last week?"

Never mind that I don't even need to train. Serving here is like riding a bicycle. Only thing I really need to learn is the new menu, so I can't help but feel like Kelly made me go through training just to put me in my place.

"You are technically done, so you owe me one for distracting her from your tardiness."

"She probably knows the schedule and what you were doing." The truth is, Kelly's a bitch, but she's not dumb.

"She'll overlook it. I've done her lots of favors lately."

I get what he means, but I can't pass up the chance to tease him. My eyes grow big and I whistle, then nudge him. "Favors, huh? But I thought you were…"

"Into men? Yeah, I am, and that wasn't supposed to be a sex joke. I'm just saying I've made her happy enough *in a professional sense* lately that I can take a hit. Get your mind out of the trash." Then he says, "You sure you're ready to go solo today?"

"Yes. Believe it or not, this isn't the most difficult thing I've ever had to do."

"Well, that's good news, because guess who showed up in your section? It's the after-church crowd. The absolute worst.

Although I see one real hottie in the group. He's serving up big Zac Efron vibes. Might make it interesting for you."

Ryan doesn't point, but throws a chin in the air and goes back to scooping fries into a basket. He's right. It's probably fifteenish people. All adults, mostly my age. And he's also right that there's one guy with them who is, like, celebrity-hot. I push it aside and focus on the other thing Ryan said.

"What do you mean the 'after-church crowd'?"

I don't remember this from my years working for the Pig. Then again, I rarely worked on Sundays.

Ryan hands me a basket of fries, grabs my shoulders, and spins my body, aiming me at them. "Why don't you go find out?"

"But they haven't ordered these yet."

"Oh, trust me, they'll want them."

My stomach sinks when I'm only a few feet from the table because I recognize one of them.

Michaela Jansbury. Another girl I went to high school with and haven't seen in over a decade. She was the quintessential popular girl. Absolutely stunning still, I see, although she's gained some weight. I shouldn't gloat inside about this, but to my shame, I do.

"Dalice Carter?" Michaela says within the first one-point-three seconds.

"Hey Michaela, long time no see."

"Oh, call me Mickey now."

I give a flat-lipped smile and steal a peek at the hot guy. He's watching us from across the table, but it's so loud in here that I doubt he can hear what we're saying. I turn away quickly, but not fast enough to avoid waking up some butterflies in my stomach.

While I ask for orders, I accidentally look at him again, and shit, he's still watching me. Very comfortably, I might add. Like he's confident he can get away with staring. My stomach upgrades to aerial flips.

His lips draw up at the corners into a smile.

I break eye contact quickly. I need to focus. Insurance for Cash. That's why I'm here. The only reason I'm here.

Turns out Ryan's right about the *after-church crowd*, though, and I get a crash course. Two basic burger orders and free French fries for days. Basket after basket of them. Ryan laughs from the kitchen, watching it all go down, but I watch in horror as they pound fries.

They want more water.

They want more ketchup.

They want their fries to arrive at the table faster.

To be hotter.

They stay for two hours and leave a one-dollar tip (in change) with a note on the receipt that says "Where will you spend eternity?"

Good Lord, please don't send me another table like that.

Once I'm pretty sure they're gone, I return to the table and use a finger to guide the coins off the table into my palm. But I sense someone behind me, so I turn.

It's the hot guy.

He's a few inches taller than me, but I'm five-nine, so he's no shrimp. He's got a fringe of dark eyelashes framing icy blue eyes, a light spray of freckles, and brown hair. It's styled well. Short, but longer on top, and brushed back into this curly quiff. I spy a few gray strands, but not many. He's got to be my age, maybe older, because he also sports crow's feet and smile lines around his mouth.

Hot Guy reaches out with two twenty-dollar bills. "Sorry about my friends. Most of them don't have jobs. They're fresh from hard circumstances and trying to get their lives back on track, you know?"

No, I don't know.

And it's too much money for a tip, so I feel like I have to refuse it. God, can this day get any more annoying?

"They paid the bill." I push his hand that's holding the money back toward him. He looks up like the touch startles him. I felt the charge of energy too. He blinks furiously.

"It's for you," he says. "Please take it."

His sincerity is interesting, because I expected him to be a useless asshole like the rest of his table. Like I remember

Michaela—I mean Mickey—being. But I couldn't tell for sure because he was so quiet the whole time.

I give a resigned nod and take the bills, putting one in my pocket, then straightening my arm out so the other twenty is right in front of him.

"All right," I say. "Consider this a loan. Should be enough to cover a round of drinks for us later."

God, what am I doing? Last thing I need in my life is a dude to manage. And when would I even have time to go out?

"I don't drink, sorry," he says and pushes the bill in my direction. His warm hand covers mine for a nanosecond, and I want to gasp at the electricity I feel again. What is it with this guy? It's like coming alive every time we touch.

I make a show of putting the cash into my pocket, trying to distract from this sting. It's not disappointment, exactly. More like embarrassment. I certainly don't make it a practice to pick men up, but the times I've done it, nobody has shot me down like this.

"Shane, bruh!" some guy shouts from the lobby. "You comin'?"

"Be right there."

When he turns to face me again, something about his smile forces my mouth to say words when I should walk away. I swear to God, it's not my fault.

"Shane, huh?"

He nods. "What's your name?"

"Dalice, like the city in Texas, but spelled fancier. Or at least my mom thought so." I reach into my apron for a slip of paper. "And this"—I scrawl with a short pencil—"is my number. You turned me down once already, so now you owe me coffee. Or tea. I don't care, it could even be pop, which I hate. Just text me."

What the hell am I doing? It's like I'm possessed by a flirting demon. I need to get control of myself.

He opens his mouth to say something, but soon Mickey is by his side. He shoves my number in his jeans pocket so fast it surprises me. Almost like he's trying to hide it from her. Are they a thing?

"Dalice and I went to school together. Class of '06!" Mickey says, bouncing like a teenager.

I steel up inside because she's signaling my age to him. God, she hasn't changed. I mean, Shane's probably older than me. Not like I'm trying to pass as young or anything, but being older is sexy in a guy—not so much in a woman.

Shane nods like it doesn't mean a lot to him. "Cool."

Then it's awkward. Mickey doesn't touch him, but something about the way she's standing there feels protective.

"Hey, Dalice, can I get your number? It would be fun to catch up over coffee or something," Mickey says.

I turn to Shane, half-expecting him to tell her he has my number and he'll share, but his eyes grow large, and he looks away. Weird.

"Sure."

She gets out her phone and I recite it to her while she types it in.

"We should go," Shane says, and Mickey nods, then turns to walk away. He hesitates like he wants to say something else. Instead, he smiles and walks out.

I wonder if he'll text. Probably not, but that's alright, because the farther I get into my shift, the more the thought of him fizzles out and my reality settles back in.

Broke, single mom, Cash's heart condition, student debt, goddamn credit card balance.

Then I practically blink and it's time to wrap up my shift.

Cash is on my mind as I walk to my car. I need to get him home and in bed, but at least I'll have time with him in the morning for cuddles and breakfast before I take him back to Brandy's and clean my first house. Ooh, I'll surprise him with banana chip pancakes. Cash loves those.

I plug my dead phone into the car charger, and when it finally powers on, a text message comes through. Then another, and another, then missed calls and voicemails galore. All from Brandy.

*Something's up with Cash. Wondering if I should take him to the doctor. Call me.*

THE THRESHING FLOOR 37

The first text is harrowing enough, and scrolling through, they only get more frantic, so I don't bother reading another. Until the last one catches my eye.

*At the St. James ER with Cash. Come when you're off work.*

# DALICE

**I CALL BRANDY** on my way to the hospital, but she doesn't answer, so I set my phone on the passenger seat. I'll get the details at the hospital.

*The hospital.*

The words alone fill me with dread because of my history with Cash. And how expensive it is to be there. I shouldn't think about the incoming ER bill, but anxiety still clamors in my mind, mingling with the geyser of emotion I'm barely keeping back. I must keep my cool until I know what's going on.

I sit at the red light to turn off the highway and onto Francis Street, near the mall where St. James is located.

Seems like it took forever to get to here, but I don't really remember the drive. I feel like I'm in a mental fog. It's dark out. My shift ended at seven, and I vaguely notice my stomach growling. I can't hold back the fear anymore. It pushes out a huge exhale of breath. Tears sting as they wet my eyes, and my nose runs as if on command. I wipe it with my hoodie sleeve.

*Breathe, remember to breathe.*

I know all of this way too well. I lived it for months on end after Cash's initial diagnosis. It rears up every time something might be wrong with him, every time he has a surgery or a cath procedure. Best I can do is keep it at a low level of numbness; it's like a robot-mode I go into.

Except that I still cry. I'm a leaky Tin Man who never rusts.
But I've also found that this neutral emotional space helps fight the mental battles that always come. They're pounding at my heart, trying to throw elbows into my mind.

*Didn't Dr. Sonora say the next thing would be a heart transplant?*

*What if he's too sick for a heart transplant?*

*What if he gets so sick while waiting for a heart that he'll never have a chance at a normal life?*

And then the alpha question bullies its way in: *What if my baby dies?*

I rarely let myself go there, but I'm too weak right now. Too worried.

The light turns green, and I pull into the hospital parking lot.

The nurse takes me right back.

Brandy stands when I walk into the room. Her eyelids are red and her face is blotchy. "I'll pay for the ER visit. Don't worry about that," she says.

She knows me. That I'd be worried about money even now.

"What happened?" I ask, already at his side, smoothing his blonde hair back from his forehead. He's asleep.

"He'd been sleeping all day, which seemed strange, but you know, some days he's more tired than others. I could barely keep him awake for meals, so I called you. When you didn't answer, I called Dr. Sonora's line, the number you gave me. It was a pager, and she called me right back. She said that it was probably fine to wait until I got ahold of you, but also that if I couldn't get ahold of you in the next hour, to take him to the ER. But it's hard to know what's an emergency and what's not. Plus, I can overreact about things like this. Hank says I do, and especially with Cash. I don't even tell you all the times I worry about him. But Hank came upstairs tonight to get something from the kitchen, and I had Cash in the portable crib in the living room because I wanted to monitor him. Well, he stopped in his tracks and said, 'His lips are really blue, babe.' That's what Hank said. And if Hank thinks it's something, and it's not just me, oh God, Dal, maybe I should have—"

"You did fine," I interrupt her monologue, still staring at Cash. He's wearing oxygen tubes. I push aside the deluge of emotion she's throwing at me and focus on the details instead. "You did what Dr. Sonora said, and that's exactly what I'd do."

"Okay, I need to run."

"What?" I get whiplash from how abrupt she is.

"I have to go."

"Please stay." My voice cracks. It's yucky to be this open with her. To show my glaring need.

Brandy folds her arms, crumpling her green North Face puffer coat. "I can't. Not tonight. But keep me posted on what the doctor says. I'm sorry."

Fucking hell. Sure, Brandy and I don't hang out, but this seems extreme. I turn away so she can't see my tears, and the door snicks shut.

I pull up a chair to sit by Cash. Hank is right. His lips are bluer than normal. He's always got a slight tinge of blue, but this is so much more dusky. And I know what that means. Oh God, do I ever know. His heart is struggling, and he's not getting enough oxygen in his blood.

The doctor comes in and updates me on Cash's situation. He's stable. The pulse oximeter reading was scary low when he arrived, so they gave him oxygen. He leaves, and a nurse comes in and fusses around Cash's bedside. I don't move from the cold plastic chair, and I don't stop touching my boy, trying to show him how much I love him. That I'm here.

A rush of everything he and I have gone through in his two short years cascades over me until I can't stop shaking.

The open-heart surgeries he's already had, all the times I didn't know how things would turn out, the days logged overnight in the NICU at first, and then the PICU when he got older.

The fact that he's a little developmentally delayed because I didn't catch it early enough.

That he lived for a month with half a heart, and only survived that long because of a secondary heart defect—a hole that allowed blood to flow well enough to make up for the main heart condition. But still, it was me who didn't catch on to the fact that he was underweight because he couldn't stay awake to breastfeed. It was me who didn't listen to Brandy the very first time she mentioned that his coloring seemed a bit off.

The ultrasounds didn't catch it either, but there was that one scan, the last one at twenty weeks, when the tech said she didn't think she'd gotten the best pictures of his heart. She wanted me to come in for another one.

I didn't call and schedule, because whatever—all the reasons. Too busy working and trying to get straight As in school. I thought if they were truly concerned, they'd call me back for a follow-up, and they never did.

As far as I knew.

After the pediatric cardiologist diagnosed Cash's condition, I called my OB's office to see what had happened, trying to dish out blame somewhere else besides squarely onto my own shoulders. But they had records of calling me and leaving messages repeatedly, asking me to come in for another scan. Somehow, I never got them.

Whenever my brain goes here, the next thought is *I caused this.*

I'm the reason Cash's heart is so fucked up.

"You need something, honey?" The nurse puts a hand on my hunched shoulder once she's done tending to Cash.

"No, no. I'm fine, thank you." I sniff loudly, trying to make the tears stop, and she reaches over for a box of tissues.

She can't tell me it'll be fine, or any variation of *It's all going to work out.* I know that by now. It was the only thing I wanted to hear when Cash was first diagnosed, but I learned quickly how adept medical staff are at giving information without a hint of optimism or promise. Still, they can make it feel like some semblance of encouragement. It's a magic trick I haven't figured out.

For the record, nobody has ever told me Cash would be fine.

Next, they move him out of the ER and into the PICU, our home away from home. It's creeping up on midnight and I've forgotten about my growling stomach. It pipes up again to remind me it's there.

The doctor on duty comes in to talk to me. "I called Dr. Sonora, and she'd like him to stay overnight. We did an echo and sent it to her, but she wants to come by first thing in the morning and do one herself."

Another echocardiogram.

If I close my eyes, I can see the precise contours, the misshape of Cash's heart, from how many times I've stared at it on a black-and-white screen. What's enlarged, and what's missing.

What will they find this time? Dr. Sonora wants to do another one, and that isn't good news. It means she doesn't like what she saw tonight.

"Is she worried?" I ask, even though they can't answer that.

"Not sure, but she thinks it can wait until tomorrow, so that's something. She'll update you on the next steps soon. Try to get some rest."

It's *something*. See how they do that? It's not "a good sign." It's not "hopeful." It's "something." The word *something* is non-committal and open to interpretation.

Even though it's super late, I text tomorrow's clients and push them to later in the week. I'll have to work longer days, but at least I don't have Pig Out Place again until Sunday. I also text Brandy and tell her about Dr. Sonora coming to do an echo tomorrow. She doesn't reply. Probably already asleep. A flash of anger rises in me again. She should be here, even if we'd be fighting the whole time. I don't want to be alone right now, but she rushed out so fast. I want someone here to tell me it's going to be fine, especially because the doctors can't. Everyone needs a voice of reason in their life. Or a good liar. I'm desperate to find either at this moment.

I set my phone on Cash's bed, and it wakes up, vibrating with a text message from a number I don't recognize.

*It was good to meet you today. Hope to see you again.*

My first thought is that hot guy, Shane. But I gave Mickey my number too. It could be her. Although, the text says "meet you." I certainly didn't meet Mickey today.

*I'm sorry, I don't recognize this number*, I type.
*Shane from Pig Out Place.*

My insides do a little happy dance. Text bubbles appear, disappear, then appear again. He doesn't know what to say next.

*Oh, hey! Good to meet you too*, I text.
*When can we grab that coffee?*

His text appears at almost the same time as mine goes out.

Well, well. I'd love to get coffee with him. But meeting Shane, Pig Out Place, shuttling fries to that table—it all feels like a hundred years ago. I'm still in robot-mode, and I'll be here until we get an answer about Cash. Depending on that information, it could be a while before I'm ready for an actual date.

But this wouldn't be a date, right? It's a distraction. I text him back, because it's not like I can do anything for Cash right now. It's a waiting game until I talk to Dr. Sonora.

*When are you thinking?*
*Well, it's almost one. Maybe around ten?*

Whoa, horsey. He might be joking, but it's so hard to tell over text. He has to be joking.

*Are you serious?*
*Yes, but only if you're interested. If not, then no, I'm definitely joking. Haha.*

I let out a little puff of a laugh and shake my head. He's got a sense of humor, so that's something. I start typing a rejection, because I really can't have coffee with him tomorrow—I mean today, this morning. I was originally thinking I could make next week work at the soonest. But I don't want to turn him down, and it's nice to have something light to focus on. Someone to talk to.

That doesn't mean I should jump on it, though.

I could always let him in on my life to see if he's worth my time. Let fate decide when we will have coffee, if at all.

Yep, that's it. Toss the guy into the deep end and see if he wants to swim.

*I would, but I have a doctor's appointment for my son tomorrow. We're at the hospital right now. Another time?* I type.

This way he finds out that not only am I a single mom, but I also have a kid with medical issues. God, I'm smart.

*You have a son?*

And there it is. Dreamy Shane's prelude to an adios. My heart plummets even though I expected nothing more than this. I'm about to type some version of goodbye when another text comes right through.

*What's his name?*

That's unexpected. Cash's dad would have bailed at the first mention of a kid. In fact, he did bail at the first mention of his own kid, so…

*Cash. He was born with a heart condition. He's two,* I type.

*Oh wow. I'm so sorry. Is he ok?*

Tears well up again at this one kindness from a stranger. Of course he's not okay, but it feels really good to have someone ask.

*I don't know yet. We're here until his cardiologist can make it over tomorrow to examine him.*

I'm telling him too much. Being too open. Brandy always says I overshare. That I plunge into things with my eyes closed. He didn't even ask about Cash's age or his condition, and I spilled that. Am I so desperate for a friend that I'll gush my problems to a rando hot guy I just met? Still, it feels fantastic to not be totally alone in this for a second.

*So you're there waiting for the doctor?* he texts.

*Pretty much.*

*This might sound weird since we don't know each other, so absolutely no pressure, but what if I brought you coffee now? Unless you need to sleep.*

Sleeping is out. I've already made peace with it.

And actually, a coffee would be amazing. But it *is* a little weird. I know why I'm not sleeping tonight, but why isn't he? Is he too eager? Should I be more guarded? It's not like anything is going to happen here in the PICU. I'd be in absolutely no danger. And I'm not afraid to tell him to leave when I'm too tired for company.

*If you want to. I'm at St. James,* I text.

*What's your poison?*

*Honestly? Bourbon straight up right now. But since you're talking coffee, I guess a caramel macchiato works. Hot.*

*Lol. Hungry at all? Grab you a muffin or something?*

God, yes. So hungry. Part of me wants to say no, be the girl who doesn't need to eat. But I've already come clean about being a single mom. So what if this guy finds out I actually eat carbs like a normal human being?

*Yes, please. A muffin would be amazing.*

*Done. See you soon.*

This is probably dumb, but there's no way I'll be sleeping tonight. Might as well pass the time in a way that keeps me from compulsive and useless worrying over Cash. And at least I'll get a muffin out of it.

# SHANE

**WHEN I GET** to St. James, I realize I don't even have Dalice's last name, let alone where her son's hospital room is. It seems like a moment of clarity telling me I should forget the whole thing. I don't know her; she doesn't know me. She really shouldn't know me. But it seems like she needs a friend, and that's something I can be.

*You need a friend too. Someone separate from them. Someone not even she knows about.*

"Every good and perfect gift comes from God."

"Render to Caesar that which is Caesar's, and to God the things that are God's."

*Tell Dalice about her. It's selfish not to.*

A cascade of intrusive thoughts comes at me, so I squeeze my eyes in a quick succession of blinks and imagine placing a road sign that says STOP. This has been happening a lot lately. This back and forth in my mind, Bible verses and demands that *She with a capital S* would make. They war with my gut instincts. Luckily, the blinking works as usual, and my mind clears.

Once I'm through the automatic doors, I greet Ned, who works nights at the St. James ER. He'd tell me where Dalice is, but I don't ask. I'm still hoping to keep my meeting with her a secret. So, instead, I text her and find out they've moved from the ER to the Pediatric Unit.

I have the hospital's layout down by heart, so I make my way to the elevator and down the hall to the left. When I come around the corner, I see her sitting on one of the gray vinyl cubes in the main waiting room. She sees me and gives a little smile and wave that takes my breath away. Her short pink hair accentuates a perfect neck. She has big brown eyes and pillowy lips. Her skin has this golden tone that makes me think she probably tans well. She's got on a gray hoodie, and when she stands up, I see she's wearing a pair of perfectly fitting black pants. A little black collar under her hoodie pokes halfway out.

Right, her uniform. She's probably here straight from Pig Out Place.

Really, though, it's not just that she's gorgeous. It's something else. Not sure what, but the fact that I just met her and we already have this connection—it's unlike anything that's ever happened to me.

Dalice leads me through the hall and into the PICU, past a bunch of sliding glass doors made private by pulled curtains. She stops at the last one and I follow her inside, then hand her the coffee and a small paper bag holding a blueberry muffin.

"Thanks for this," she says, holding up the bag. She pulls the door shut and draws the curtain.

All I can say is "You bet," because I get distracted by the little boy. He lies there, covered in tubes and wires in a bed that seems to swallow his tiny frame, even though the bed itself is small. His lips are a shade of night. My heart sinks to the floor. How can I keep him from what *She with a capital S* could do to help him?

"I'm so sorry. This must be incredibly hard," I say.

Dalice wipes a tear and clears her throat. "It is. We've been dealing with his heart conditions almost since he was born, but everything has been going so well, all things considered. His doctor didn't expect him to need another procedure until a transplant. That wasn't supposed to be until his teens at the earliest. Others like him have made it into their early twenties before needing a transplant. The longer he can go without it, the better." She stops abruptly, as if she's trying to silence herself, and takes a sip of her coffee. She makes a sour face.

"Is it cold?" I ask.

"A little." She laughs softly.

"Oh dogs. Sorry."

"Dogs?" She laughs again.

I wave the comment away. I hate explaining that I don't cuss because of my faith. I also make a mental note to retire *Oh dogs*. Next time I'll go with *Oh man* or *Yikes*, or something.

"Well anyway," she goes on. "Thank you for coming. I knew I wouldn't get any sleep tonight."

"I don't sleep very well a lot of nights, so this is a nice distraction for me, too. I'm glad I could be useful. Or, useful *in theory*." I point to her coffee and scrunch up my face to show once again that I'm sorry about the cold drink. Dalice takes a bite of the muffin. "So, you're here alone all night?" I ask.

She shifts her weight in the chair, then swallows, and I realize how stalker-like the question sounds. "I mean, do you have anyone to take a turn sitting up with him so you can get some rest?"

"No. It's just me, flying solo with this little dude for the past two years. It's how we roll. I mean, I have my sister, and she takes care of Cash during the day, but otherwise, she's not really..." Dalice's voice trails off and she swallows hard.

"Sisters." I roll my eyes, trying to lighten the mood and show her I'm not judging her. "So complicated and frustrating. You think when you grow up, something will change. You'll get along better and finally act like adults. But then you're still dealing with their stuff and your stuff. Nothing ever really changes, we simply get older."

"Exactly! Are you close to your sister?" Dalice asks.

"It's complicated."

—*To say the least*, I add in my mind before the other thoughts push through.

*Change the subject. Don't talk about yourself.*

*Ask more about her life.*

I blink hard to shut off the noise in my mind.

"Are you all right? Do you have something in your eyes?" she asks.

"No, it's a tic. I've had it since I was little. Gets worse when I'm nervous."

*You're such a liar.*

"*Liars will find their place in the fiery lake of burning sulfur.*"

I turn my back to blink away the thoughts so Dalice doesn't see. Make like I'm looking for a tissue. The blinking *is* a tic. That part is true, but it's only been around for a few months. Just since I've noticed how much everything I've learned in the meetings consumes my mind. I find a tissue and blow my nose. I must calm these thoughts down. Ideally, get rid of them completely.

The meetings. I could bring Dalice, and Cash would be healed. But I walked out of Pig Out Place certain I'd get to know Dalice, become a friend and keep her separate from everything else. *Not* introduce her to my problematic group of friends—"family," as Reva calls us. But what kind of person would I be to keep healing from Dalice and Cash? I glance at her again. That soft skin, nut-brown eyes, brows arched, like she's asking me for something. Fact is, I want to help her. But I'm afraid of what it will cost.

"I haven't seen you at Pig Out Place before," I say. "We go there a lot because my friends like the unlimited fries, as I'm sure you could tell."

Dalice slips the muffin back into the paper bag and sets it down on the empty chair beside her. She breathes a soft laugh again.

"Yeah, my coworker warned me about you guys. Totally predicted that would happen. It's my second job, so I'm not there often. I work as a house cleaner most of the time, even though that's not my dream job either."

"What's your dream job?"

"I wanted to be a marine biologist. At least, that's what I was in school for before he came along." She nods toward the baby.

"So, his heart condition isn't the first curveball life has thrown you?"

"Definitely not."

"This might sound strange because we just met, but I can tell you're strong. Hard times strengthen us, make us compassionate. You've been through a lot, huh?"

Dalice sucks her lips in, almost like she's trying not to laugh, but a tear rolls down her high cheekbone. "Sorry, I think I'm just exhausted," she says.

That was probably too much, too fast on my part.

I sit down next to her, and I want to put my arm around her because the longer I'm here, the more drawn to her I am. It's odd even to me. But that would definitely be way too much, even if I'm right and there's something between us. I fold my hands in my lap instead. "Crying is one of our best ways to relieve stress. You're carrying a lot. I'd be concerned if you *weren't* crying."

Her eyes find mine, and she gives a soft smile. I walk over to Cash's bedside.

"He's a trooper," I say. "Bit of a spitfire too, though, I bet."

"Oh definitely. He's a handful, even if he can't walk yet."

"He can't walk yet," I whisper. I didn't mean to say it out loud, but it's a gut punch. This boy is really sick.

The thoughts barge in.

*It's not your job to save people. It's her job.*

*"But if the watchman sees the sword coming and does not warn the people, and they die, I will hold the watchman accountable for their blood."*

I'm a watchman on the wall. I'm the Procurer, in her words. It's my job to warn the people, to help them before it's too late.

*You're her recruiter! That's all.*

It's true, but still so hard to shift my thinking after so many years.

"You don't have kids, I take it?" Dalice says, interrupting my thoughts. "They should walk by eighteen months old, but Dr. Sonora—that's his cardiologist—says he may experience some delays because of the minutes he spent deprived of oxygen as a baby. Both during surgery and before I knew he was sick."

Dalice wipes a tear from under her eye, so I give her the box of tissues. I know Dr. Sonora, and she's a good one.

If there are any good ones. According to *her*, there aren't.

"I should have noticed that something was off when he was first born," Dalice goes on, "but I assumed he was just an easy baby who slept a lot. Thought the Universe was blessing me since I was on my own. I still don't know for sure how his heart got so shitty. But I didn't realize I was pregnant for the first several weeks, and I drank a lot during the time when he was forming."

"It's not your fault. Plenty of women drink before they find out they're pregnant and plenty of those babies don't have heart conditions, right? It's obvious that you're a good mom doing the best you can for him."

She clears her throat repeatedly, as if she's done crying against the will of her tears. "Thank you for saying that."

*Ask her out on a date.*

*No, invite her to a meeting.*

*How can you keep this boy from all the good that she can do for him?*

I blink hard again and say, "I should go. Thanks for letting me stop by. Is it alright if I text you in a few days to see how you guys are doing?"

She nods and goes for the door like she's seeing me out of her own home, and for a minute, I get a flash of a vision. Us in a house that's ours. Cash is there, but he's older, and there's another child too. A little girl. It's Christmastime and we're decorating a tree.

My stomach sinks because this is the sort of future I long for, even if it's not possible.

# DALICE

**THE NEXT DAY,** reality feels like a bad drug trip thanks to sleep dep. I call Brandy from the hospital after my meeting with Cash's cardiologist.

"Dr. Sonora wants to run more tests, but..." I pause and take a deep breath to stop the sob that wants to push out. Tears drench the phone, making it wet against my cheek—warm at first, but then cold. No use wiping it away. The tears aren't stopping. "...She's putting him on the transplant list. Low priority, but still."

"Oh Dal, I'm so sorry," Brandy whispers and sniffs like she's crying too. "But that's good, right? That he'll get a heart?"

I want to get off the phone, to not have to explain to Brandy why a heart transplant isn't ideal right now. I want to crawl into bed, pretend Cash is healthy, and snuggle him until we both fall asleep. But this is part of the deal. Keeping people updated.

"It's not great. We hoped his heart would last a lot longer. And there has to be a matching donor, so we're waiting for another family to experience a tragedy. Plus, even if he gets a new heart, transplants aren't like a heart you're born with. They rarely last as long, assuming the procedure even takes, but the doctor wants him on the list before it becomes...dire."

Silence on the other end.

"Bran?"

"I'm here. God, I don't know what to say."

"There's nothing to say. We have to wait and see. I need to pack our bags and get everything ready to go to Seattle at a moment's notice in case they find him a match. Hey, I'm dead on my feet. Can you meet me at my place in an hour to sit with Cash while I nap for a hot minute?"

Brandy hesitates, and it makes me want to scream.

"What's going on? Why can't you help me?" The words come out like I'm a bratty child.

"I had plans today. I'm not at your disposal twenty-four seven."

I swallow down fury and force my voice to be soft. Again, she's right. "Okay, I'm sorry. I know you have a life outside of my drama."

She sighs and says, "It's okay. I'll cancel. Sleep would be good for you and Cash."

I wish I could switch from angry to overly grateful, but the shift is too monumental right now. I'm bleary with exhaustion, so I say thanks and end the call, drop the phone into my lap, and run a hand through my grimy hair.

Dr. Sonora wants to keep Cash overnight again, but I refused. Brandy said she'd pay for the stay at St. James, but no way I'm letting her pay for two nights, especially since the doctor said it wasn't absolutely necessary. Now that Cash is on the list, I must save every penny possible.

Before we leave, the nurses get us squared away with Cash's new medications, the oxygen machine for "just in case," instructions for caregivers, all the things. At least he's awake now. But his lips are still bluer than normal. Dr. Sonora said that's to be expected and likely won't go away until after the transplant.

In the car, I glance at him in the mirror obsessively, as if he might go into cardiac arrest right on the spot, even though he should be stable for a while. Of course, the doctor wouldn't define how long "a while" was, but she said that a lot of people are waiting for hearts and have been waiting for a long time. It's still a race to get a heart before the one he was born with— the one I gave him—stops working.

*Don't think about that. If this is a race, then it's a marathon, not a sprint. Stay positive.*

At home, I get Cash out of the car and set him up in front of the TV. I refuse to feel guilty about it. If he doesn't want to crawl around and play with toys, then fine, screens it is.

Brandy arrives half an hour later, and she seems small, uncomfortable. Instead of picking Cash up like usual, she's distracted, hugging herself. She looks like a child waiting to be chosen for a sports team. Is she mad at me?

"He's not broken; you can touch him," I say.

"Sorry. I know." Brandy walks over and sits next to Cash on my secondhand brown couch.

"Well, I'm going to bed."

"Sounds good." Brandy doesn't look at me when she says it.

Sleeping is hard at first, and this shocks me. The more I lie awake and worry about not being able to fall asleep during this little window of time Brandy's here, the harder it is. My body melts into the mattress, screaming for oblivion, but my mind is a racehorse doing laps around the track of my problems. Heart transplant, hospital bills, debt, rent, leaving Cash with Brandy every single day. Not being there for him. It's a big carousel that winds and winds around my throat, tightening with each revolution.

**I MUST HAVE** fallen asleep, because when I open my eyes, it's dark outside.

Shit. How long was that nap? I claw at the nightstand for my phone and my eyes glom on to the time—5:15 p.m. I slept for four hours. But what really pulls my attention is a text from a number I don't recognize.

*Heyyy! It's Mickey. So crazy seeing you yesterday! Blast from the past! Wanted to invite you to a harvest party with me this Friday. Should be fun.*

What? I rub my eyes.

Michaela Jansbury, homecoming queen and cheerleader, is asking me to hang out? Weird.

I'm about to type a polite *No thanks*, but I think of Shane. Will he be at the harvest party? I can't exactly ask without being insanely obvious, and I still don't know what Mickey and Shane's status is. While I think I picked up that he's interested in me, I'm not sure. I need to analyze this, but not now.

I put the phone down and go out to see Cash. Brandy's in the kitchen, and, wow. The house is sparkling clean. It's a kindness from my sister that goes way further than watching Cash every day, because she gets something from that. This is so far beyond what I expect from her.

"Where's Cash?" I ask, walking over to the kitchen bar-slash-sink.

"Napping. We watched some TV, and when he started getting tired, I read a few books to him. He surprised me by staying awake for that. Hope it's okay that I put him down."

"Of course. Want some coffee?" I ask, fiddling with coffee pods.

"No, I need to jet."

I exhale. Of course she does. But really, I can't be bitchy about it. Brandy's done so much for me today. "Thanks for coming over. And for cleaning my place. Truly, I'm so grateful."

"No problem, I couldn't sit in this pigpen. It was sort of necessary for my sanity."

Right, she did it for herself. But God, who cares? I'm not tallying that one against her.

"Okay if I come a little early tomorrow to show you the ropes with all of Cash's fun new *accessories*?" I ask.

"Course. But please don't joke about his condition."

And now I'm tallying everything against her. Who the fuck does she think she is?

"Look, he's *my* kid. This is *my* problem. You're helping with his care during the day, but you're not his mom. You're certainly not my mom, so you don't get to tell me how to process this. Got it?"

It's harsh. So harsh, especially considering her infertility, but it comes out before I can filter it.

"Geez, bitchmode," Brandy says under her breath as she walks out the door.

And the moment's gone. We're back to our homeostasis as sisters.

I fix my thoughts on Mickey's text. What did she mean by *harvest party*? Do adults really go to those? And why does she want to hang out with me?

Then I think of Shane again. What I felt at Pig Out Place, and all the butterflies that dive-bombed my stomach when he came to the hospital. That tiny flash of a promise of friendship. Perhaps more. It's like I've known him for much longer than—*shit*, it's only been a little over twenty-four hours.

I really don't know this guy.

But I'm not going to the harvest party for him, right? I'm going because Mickey invited me.

Great, I'm talking to myself like I've already decided.

I'm so tired though. Tired of deciding, tired of disappointment, tired of being afraid. Tired of being alone, and yet, nothing will change unless I let it.

I'm typing to Mickey before I realize it. Some leftover robot-mode, I guess.

*What do you mean "harvest party"?*

I put the phone down. I can't turn it off, because I must answer if they find a match for Cash. But I can't deal with Mickey right now. I'll get a snack and bring Cash into my room where he can sleep in his crib right by me.

Fuck today.

# 1992

**IT'S THE MORNING** of Reva's first day of school. She hasn't told Mom about the gold hands, or *gold dust*, as she calls it in her mind. No reason to. It went away so fast. By the time Reva was back at the trailer after Shane took Fish into the woods, it was gone.

Plus, Reva doesn't want to upset her. Mom lost her job at Perkins Restaurant this summer, so she's been in bed or out drinking every day.

Reva finds a high curb at the trailer park's entrance, which is also her bus stop. She sits off to the side, away from the mess of kids, and finds a little hole in the knee of her dark pink stirrup pants. The pants were the nicest thing she could find to wear today. They're a bit too small and the stirrups make the waistband tug down. She could cut the stirrups, but that's the part she likes best, especially when she wears her rainbow socks. Feeling the pinprick of skin exposed by the hole, she imagines Mom quitting the booze, hugging her, even meeting her at the bus stop after school to walk home together like other moms do.

"Hi, what's your name?" A girl interrupts Reva's daydreaming. She didn't even notice anyone coming toward her. The girl has dark skin and a big scar going from lip to nose. Reva can't take her eyes off the scar even though somewhere in the back of her mind, something says it's rude to stare.

"Reva," she answers.

"I'm Kat." The girl reaches out her hand to shake, like an adult.

Reva squints a smile and takes Kat's hand slowly. Is this a joke? Why is this girl talking to Reva when there are so many other kids to talk to?

Kat's face glows like sunshine beaming out from behind her curly eyelashes and huge brown eyes. She's wearing a blue headband in her coily hair. She has dimples, and she's so pretty and friendly that she won't have any issues making friends. Why is she bothering with Reva? There must be a catch.

Reva surveys all around, like she can sniff out a prank. A pile of kids snickering behind a bush, watching Kat pretend to be her friend, only to pounce at the last minute and snatch Kat away. They'd all laugh at Reva for thinking someone might actually want to be her friend.

But nobody is paying attention to them.

"You don't talk much, do you?" Kat starts, but doesn't wait for Reva to answer. "I'm new here. Just moved in across the street." She points to the pretty neighborhood on the other side. It's like the one they used to live in when Dad was still here. The kind with a name—*Camelot*—carved into a wooden sign at the entrance. Reva imagines the sign with tulips and daffodils growing around it in the spring.

Nothing like Trailer Trash Town.

"What grade are you in?" Kat asks.

"Fourth."

"I'm in fifth. Mrs. Baker is my teacher, or at least that's what the paper taped to the school door said yesterday. Is she any good?"

"I think she's all right. My brother had her."

Kat sighs in relief and sags her shoulders as if she was so worried about her teacher. She plops down beside Reva.

*When is the bus coming?* Reva doesn't know what to say next, and if she says too much, Kat will discover what a weirdo she is. Being invisible is how she gets through the day without drawing attention. When you're invisible, they don't make fun of you, and Reva's pretty sure she wouldn't be able to face it if kids started making fun of her on the first day. But Kat makes being invisible very hard.

"Love your lunch box," Kat says. "*Teenage Mutant Ninja Turtles* are so cool. I like Michelangelo the best."

"I like Raphael," Reva says without thinking, and watches for Kat's reaction.

Kat smiles.

"It's old," Reva holds up the lunch box. "Used to be my brother's. He thinks it's too babyish for middle school."

"Well, his loss." Kat smiles and her teeth are straight, so white. Her lip scar sort of expands.

"How did you get that?" Reva asks, pointing to it, but when Kat's face falls, she immediately regrets it.

"I was born with a cleft lip. The scar is from the repair. Kids make fun of me for it."

"You have a pretty smile," Reva says.

Kat beams again. "Sit by me on the bus?"

Reva shrugs out a *sure* even though she wants to shout yes, but she can't get her hopes up that Kat is serious about being her friend. As soon as she meets some other girls, she'll move on. Reva can make friends but never keep them, since they always find someone more interesting than her. They've all been in school together since kindergarten, so now nobody really even tries to be her friend anymore.

The bus arrives, and Reva chooses a seat in the middle. It's away from the popular kids who always sit at the back, but not too far toward the front because that's where the nerds sit. Kat slides in next to her, and a rush of excitement goes through Reva.

Having someone by her side makes her feel strong, like she can do anything.

Then there's warmth in her hands. She opens them to peek before thinking about how close Kat is.

"Your hands are gold!" Kat shouts, like she's got a megaphone living in her throat.

"Shh!" Reva hisses, making fists in a too-late attempt to hide them.

Kids' heads pop up from the green vinyl seats, searching for the source of the commotion.

Everything slows down with Kat inhaling as if she's about to speak, and Reva lunging to cover the girl's mouth. The back of her pale hand is stark against Kat's brown skin, and the whites of Kat's eyes widen. Heat spreads from Reva's hand. Kat moans like she's trying to talk under the hand, but Reva can't let go because what if she yells about the gold dust again?

"Please don't," Reva pleads, tears springing to life in her eyes. "They'll make fun of me."

Kat gives a quick nod, so she lets go.

Reva surveys the bus again. Nobody is watching.

The school comes into view. A few more seconds and they'll be there.

When she finally turns back to Kat, the girl is running her fingers across her top lip, feeling up to her nostrils in silence.

She gasps, and Reva sees what the girl must have only felt with her fingers.

Kat's scar is completely gone.

# DALICE

**OH YOU KNOW,** *hayride, pumpkins, candy, fire pit, cider, the works.*

That was Mickey's answer to my text asking for clarification about the harvest party.

It's been a few days and I still haven't replied. The event sounds all right, but part of me has no desire to hang out with her. And sure, Shane might be there, but another part of me doesn't want to leave Cash. And a third part of me (is it possible to have so many parts of me?) is way too goddamn tired to think about being social and making small talk. Especially with someone from my past who I totally forgot existed, and who pretended throughout high school that I didn't exist.

I could text Shane and ask if he'll be there, let that decide for me. But we haven't spoken since the hospital, and I'm not sure I want to be the first one to reach out after that night.

I probably shouldn't be running around to parties, anyway. Plus, Cash and I have found a groove. Still no clue what weekends will look like when I'm on shift at Pig Out Place, but all things considered, this week has been normalish with Cash going to Brandy's while I clean two houses a day if I can, then pick him up. We grab McDonald's on the way home, and I read him a book and put him to bed.

It's not sustainable. Especially the McDonald's part, but I don't have any oomph left over to do things like shopping for groceries or cooking. I'm so beat. More so than what's normal for me, but I suppose it's also the stress of waiting. Killing time until some other poor family loses their child so Cash can have a heart.

That part shouldn't bother me as much as it does. It's out of my control whether another child dies tragically, but it's on my mind all the time. I can't help thinking about that family even before anything has happened. How they have no clue they're so close to losing their child.

Pulling up to my last house of the day, I turn the car off and sit for a second, take a deep breath. I should get moving. It's an easy house because it's on the smaller side, and my client, Julia, always cleans it before I arrive. She's one of those super clean people. So really, it's only bathrooms, dusting, and floors. Julia's is criminally easy, which is why I save it for last. Always do the hard things first while you have the most energy. Don't think, just work. Working is money, and money is food, shelter, safety, and freedom.

Except it's not freedom, not with the wage I pull. It's enough to keep us afloat, but no way I'd call it freedom.

The car engine ticks, cooling down, and here I stay, even though I don't have a minute to waste.

I exhale a sharp little cry, and it catches me by surprise. But I can't stop what's coming. Sobbing wracks my body, and then I scream. Anger fills the car and hurts my throat, and I'm sick of it. Tired of it all. Why is everything so hard?

Once I exhaust myself beyond the point of, well, exhaustion, I clench my jaw.

Stupid self-pity never got anyone anywhere.

I sniff, wipe my eyes, and try to breathe slowly again, but it's too soon for my body. Tears make rivers down my face, dripping off my chin. I don't stop them. I can't change any of this. Not for Cash, not for me. The only thing I can do is make sure we have money to pay the bills. Even if that's barely enough, like a nibble of dry toast when you're starving.

My phone vibrates on the passenger seat with a text message.
*Hey! What did you decide about tonight?*
Mickey again. God in heaven, I have to respond to her.
*Sorry, it's been a crazy week. Not sure I'm up for a party.*
*Oh, I hear you. Anything I can do to help?*
And then, I swear, because she isn't pressuring me at all, I do an on the spot one-eighty.
*Actually, I'll come. Where and what time?*
*Yay! I'll pick you up!*
Nope. That's too much.
*That's ok. Just text me the address*, I type.
I get out of the car and slip the phone into my back pocket. It vibrates again.
*Don't be silly. It's way off the beaten path. I got this!*
I growl out a little groan. I hate this stuff with women. It's so hard to tell if they're just being overly nice and offering to do something when they don't really want to, or if they're being aggressive and controlling. Like, is it a problem that I want to drive myself? Will she be offended if I insist? Or will she be relieved? There's no instruction booklet for female friendships, and I seem to have landed on earth inept.
Whatever. She can drive me. It's more gas money in my pocket.
*Ok. Let me see if my sister can watch my little guy and I'll get back to you*, I text.
I'll deal with Brandy's judgments about me leaving Cash and going to a party later.
*Bring him! It's a family event*, she replies.
I stare at the words and think about how much I'd love to bring him. It's not like I have a social life, but the few times I've done things with friends, it's always *no kids*.
Another text comes through while I'm deliberating.
*We do this every year and the kids love it. My daughter is four and she'll be there!*
Mickey has a daughter? Something about this makes me relax. Is it possible Mickey has changed since high school? Maybe life has squeezed the conceitedness out of her.

Bubbles of excitement rise inside of me. I should go. It'll be a little cold, but I can bundle Cash up.

I still hesitate. Is it safe for Cash to be outside in the cold? I'll check with Dr. Sonora first.

*Ok sounds good. What time?* I text.

*Pick you up at 5:15! Send your address. This will be fun!*

I type my address and return the phone to my back pocket. In the spirit of honesty, I admit to myself that, while I'm more open to spending time with Mickey than I was ten minutes ago, I just hope I get to see Shane again.

As if on cue, he texts me. The bubbles of excitement turn to fireworks in my gut when I see his name.

*Hey, just thinking about you. Wondering how Cash is doing and if you'd be up for dinner soon?*

Is he asking me out on a date? He hasn't texted, so I thought it meant he wasn't as interested as I am. Don't people usually text for a while before going on a real date? Then again, I guess we sort of already passed that part and had a hospital date. My mind goes into scheduling mode.

I'll see if Cash can hang with Brandy while I go to dinner with Shane, since I'm not using her for the harvest party tonight. It'll be a fight, but it feels a thousand percent worth it.

*It's a waiting game with Cash,* I text. *But he's doing all right. His lips are more blue than they were before, but the doctor says that's normal. I could do dinner tomorrow night?*

I'm starting another text about how I'll be at the harvest party tonight when his reply comes through.

*It's a date then.*

I can't help but smile. My day just got so much better. I text him back.

*Fun! Oh, hey, I'll be at the party tonight too.*

Text bubbles appear, disappear. They appear again. Disappear again.

I walk around my car so I can get my cleaning supplies out of the trunk, trying to ignore the uneasy pull inside my chest. Why is he typing and deleting so much?

His text comes through.
*See you there.*
That's all it says. Three words. No emoji. No exclamation point. No indication of his tone at all.
I scrunch up my nose because I can't tell if he's excited or not.

# 1992

**BY THE TIME** Reva walks home from the bus stop after school, what happened with Kat and the gold dust this morning feels a million miles away. It was weird, but like before, her hands turned normal again soon after.

The difference was how Kat's scar was gone. Reva can't make sense of that, so she pushes it deep down and decides not to think about it.

The trailer comes into view, and something else pushes into her mind.

Fish won't be at home to greet her after school anymore.

No brown stubby legs on the back of the orange-and-brown plaid couch until they paw at the glass like crazy. No speed-mode up and down the hall when Reva comes through the door. Fish was always so excited when she got home, and the dirty, still-smeared glass windows that remain are proof of her love. It needles a dull spot inside Reva's chest until the raw edges grow large, but it's somehow emptier than before. She's alone, and every step that takes her closer to home is no different from sitting in a class with kids who don't see you. Invisibility is good for staying safe, but it's tiring, too.

Walking closer, Reva dreads the moment her eyes latch on to that picture window in front, framing a whole lot of nothing.

Except, when it finally comes into view, it's not nothing.

It's Mom.

She sits on the couch sideways, arm stretched across the back like she's waiting for someone to arrive.

Reva climbs the metal stairs to the door, but stops before turning the handle to go in. Why in the world is Mom on the couch instead of in bed? She can't remember the last time this happened.

Mom tips her face up and waves her inside. There's no smile, but she notices Reva, and that's something new and different.

Did Mom get a job?

Do they have company today?

Then, the thing she doesn't want to hope for: Is Dad back?

She opens the door by slow inches, and Mom stands in the living room, hands folded in front of her, hair washed and styled, makeup on. She's in a white tee shirt with a peach-colored, sleeveless cardigan and jeans. It's the pair she only wears for nicer occasions, although those are nonexistent these days.

"How was your day?" Mom's voice is flat and there's still no smile.

Reva clears her throat. How long has it been since Mom was sober and awake? She doesn't want to ruin this by making Mom mad, but then again, why does Mom suddenly care about her day? Seconds ago, Reva didn't want to be invisible, but now she craves it because this is uncomfortable.

"Fine."

"Anything happen?"

Reva cocks her head to the side, and a teeny little voice says Mom knows about Kat's scar and the gold dust, even though that makes no sense. How would she have found out? And even if she did, would it turn her sober? The dots don't connect.

"Not really."

Reva goes through the small living room, past Mom, and toward the bedroom she shares with Shane.

The tiny attention Mom is giving her isn't worth how awkward it makes things. Mom noticing her isn't like she pictured it would be. Reva can't figure out the right thing to say to make her happy. Maybe if she slips away to her room, Mom will forget about it.

She has the room to herself right now because Shane's never home right after school. He plays with his friends until dinner time. Mom follows her and leans against the doorjamb casually, like she does this every day. She crosses one leg over the other. Reva thinks of the actor James Dean, like all Mom needs is a cigarette and a leather jacket to complete the look.

"Nothing you want to tell me about?" Mom presses. "For example, did you make a new friend?"

Reva doesn't make eye contact. She sets her bookbag down on the thin carpet and sits on her bed. Mom won't stop asking, and what if she gets really mad about Reva's unwillingness to answer?

"Her name is Kat. I met her at the bus stop."

Mom glides over and sits next to Reva. She's a foot away, not close enough to touch, but maybe Mom is trying.

"And what happened with Kat at the bus stop?"

"Nothing."

Mom pulls her lips in, rubs them together like you do when you put on ChapStick. She glances at the ceiling and sighs. "Okay, well, the school called. They said something happened."

"I didn't mean to. I don't even know—"

"You're not in trouble."

Reva inspects Mom's face because this isn't the reaction she expected, even if she didn't know what to expect.

Mom goes on, "The school didn't know how to handle it, and the principal was skeptical that the girl was telling the truth. But I know she was."

"What?"

"You have a gift. Now and then, the Lord blesses one of us with special gifts. He expects us to use them to the best of our abilities. To help others. You have the gift of healing."

"Is it real gold?"

Reva has so many questions, but this is the most important, because if it is, they could move out of Trailer Trash Town. Maybe Dad would come back if he knew Reva was special, and neither of her parents would have to work. Reva would be like the miller's daughter in Rumpelstiltskin, creating gold out of straw. Or would she actually be more like Rumpelstiltskin himself? Because the miller's daughter couldn't spin the straw into gold without him. Either way, she would make them rich and they would love her for it.

"No, I wish," Mom smirks. "It's not real. Just some unidentified compound. Totally worthless."

She might not know what *unidentified compound* means, but it's the other words that stand out.

*Totally worthless.*

Reva's insides deflate. But she still has questions. How does Mom know so much about the gold dust? She wants to ask, but Mom's legs flex like she's about to stand.

*No. Don't go.*

It's like breathing fresh air, this interaction with Mom. She wants to make it last.

"Why do my hands turn gold?"

"Why?" Mom scoffs. "*Why* isn't the point. Here, I'll show you."

She turns toward Reva. "Repeat after me: What would you ask of me?"

Reva squints. Is Mom asking her this question or does she really want her to repeat it? The hesitation is too long. Mom slaps her face.

Holding a hand to her hot cheek, Reva swallows, trying to keep tears back, but failing.

Her palm turns as warm as her cheek, so she pulls it away to look.

It's covered in gold.

Mom gives her a nod, like *Say it.*

"What would you ask of me?" Reva whispers.

"Heal my alcohol addiction."

Reva blinks but doesn't move. This whole thing is so confusing, and why is Mom asking her to do something that she can't know how to do?

Mom takes Reva's gold hands and places them on her own shoulders. "Think about what I asked for. About the booze."

Reva is too scared not to do this. Mom stares her down, so she closes her eyes and pictures Mom hating alcohol.

Mom pouring vodka down the sink.

Mom filling the trash up with every beer bottle that's in their fridge.

Mom smiling at Reva—sober, happy.

"There. You did it," Mom says.

Reva's eyes fly open. "How do you know?"

"I just do."

Mom stands. "Starting tonight, you'll minister to others in this way."

"Minister?"

It sounds like speaking in front of people, everyone staring at her, like an actual minister, like Dad was. Terrifying.

"I'll invite people over. The Lord will show His power. You'll see."

Mom leaves the room without thanking Reva for whatever that was, leaves no space for Reva to say what's simmering inside of her.

*No. I can't do this in front of people. I don't want to.*

Reva doesn't move from the spot on her bed. None of this makes sense, and her stomach folds itself into tight knots.

Then there's the sudden religious talk Mom has put on. How long has it been since they've gone to church? Not once since Dad left, and not for months before that. Really, they haven't been inside a church since Dad stopped being a pastor. But this won't be church, thank goodness. It's only some people in the living room. She can do that, right?

Reva lies down on her side and pulls her knees up to her chest even though she still has her shoes on. If she really healed Mom, that means she's sober now.

It's what Reva's wanted for months.

But all these good things cram to the back of her mind because of the worries expanding, taking up so much space. It's like shaking a can of Pepsi and cracking it open.

What if people laugh at her hands?

What if she doesn't know what to say or do? Or how about this one: What if she can't get the gold dust to show up? Mom will be angry and hit her again.

The worries fizz out all over until her pillowcase is wet beneath her cheek.

# DALICE

**I STAND WATCH** by my front window, because no way will I let Mickey come into my apartment. It's so messy.

Finally, raven-black hair emerges from a beat-up Camry in front of my unit, so I head out, carrying Cash.

"Hey!" Mickey says. "This apartment complex is nice. I'm so glad you could come tonight."

I smile and move Cash over to my other hip so I can manage Mickey's car door with my right hand. But as I bend over to put him in, I realize I forgot his car seat.

"Hi," a little girl says.

*Right.* Mickey mentioned she had a young daughter. The girl has pulled-back hair and crystal blue eyes. Different eye color, but I can see the resemblance between them. Dark hair, pointy chin.

"Hi there. What's your name?"

"Juniper."

"That's a cute name. I like your hair."

Cash leans into the car and I almost fumble him because I'm already bending over. "Just a sec, dude. I have to get your car seat."

"He can hang out in the back with Juny while you grab it. I'll keep an eye on him," Mickey says, now sitting in the driver's seat.

"You good here for a sec?" I ask Cash, as if he's a friend I'm about to ditch.

Cash seems fascinated with Juniper, even though she's not doing anything but sitting in her booster seat. He crawls into the car and reaches over to touch the book on her lap.

She smiles and hands it to him, and I already like her.

Once I return with Cash's seat and get him buckled in, Mickey takes off. We drive north on the highway for about half an hour, well beyond the turnoff to Brandy's house, discussing mundane things like what the people we went to school with are up to. Mickey does most of the talking. I don't stay in contact with anyone. And I really don't give a rat's ass about what the people I wasn't friends with are up to.

"How old is Cash?" she asks. She's wondering why he can't walk. That must be it.

"Two. But he has a severe heart condition, which caused a few delays. It's also why his lips are a little blue."

"I didn't want to ask. It's so hard to have a little one with issues. Juny used to be super ill." Then she whispers, "I had started to come to grips with the idea that I might outlive her."

What? The girl seems perfect, although I know better than most that looks can be deceiving. If not for the blue lips, Cash would seem perfect on the outside too.

"What was wrong with her?"

Mickey pulls up to a black wrought-iron gate. I didn't even realize we were getting close to anything. This is like a random gated estate in the middle of actual nowhere. Good thing we carpooled tonight, because I would have gotten lost for sure.

"Oh, I'll tell you about it sometime," Mickey says.

I want to press her, but she doesn't seem open to it, and I'm too distracted by this place to devise a way to subtly pull information out of her.

Behind the entrance gate is a bright house—but *house* is an understatement. This is a goddamn forest mansion. I can only see how big it is because every window is lit up, plus there are floodlights in the front, shining on a circular driveway that goes around a fountain.

Mickey punches in a code and the gate opens.

"Holy shit," I breathe, but regret it when Mickey stiffens like I slapped her with the cuss word. I turn back to face Juniper. "Sorry," I say, and she smiles. Mickey forces a weak smile.

I don't remember Mickey being so touchy about swearing in high school. In fact, she got into her fair share of popular-kid trouble. Underage drinking, for one, which I doubt she ever got caught for, sleeping around, cheating on math tests, and the like. Swearing was the least of it. But apparently this new Mickey is a bit more sensitive.

"This is incredible," I say, trying to smooth over my potty mouth mess-up.

"Isn't it?" Mickey's face lights up. "We're so lucky to meet here."

*Meet here*? Kind of a strange way to talk about a party, but I ignore it and turn to Cash while Mickey parks the car.

"Cashy, look at this big house," I say when I get out to unbuckle him. Then I hand him his pacifier, and he takes it, puts it in his mouth, and lays his head on my shoulder.

I can't stop staring. The construction is incredible, as if it was built by a craftsman, not a cheap contractor. As I get closer, I see how the base of the building is all stonework, like the pillars and columns of my old school, Shadle Park High. Nothing like the fake stone fronts they put on homes nowadays. The rocks are shades of gray and light brown, and they cover what must be the first floor, along with the turret on the right side, which is at least three stories high. The rest is natural wood, with overhanging eaves exposing rafters and beams, and an enormous wrap-around porch. Off to the side is another building. There's a set of three garages detached from the house but facing the driveway, so together with the house they make an L-shape. It reminds me of a huge carriage house for an old mansion. There must be a living space above, because of all the windows.

"Come on, I'll introduce you to everyone," Mickey says, and my heart surges because—Shane.

Mickey takes Juniper's hand, and they lead us between the main building and the garages along a lighted gravel footpath. We take concrete stairs that descend to a wide, open space. It's grassy, like a backyard. Pine trees surround this whole thing, so they must have had these couple of acres cleared, because the trees pick up further away from the house and go on and on.

From the backyard, a large moon illuminates a faraway mountain line and total wilderness. It smells like pine and campfire. There's a bonfire farther out by where the trees are thick, and I spy what appears to be a tractor pulling a cart full of people.

That must be the hayride.

I can't help but squint through the darkness for Shane. So far, no dice.

I turn around to survey the back of the house, and it's all windows. The whole thing glows like a jack-o'-lantern in the dark.

"This place is mind-blowing," I say, and vaguely realize I already said something like it. Mickey gives a soft laugh, like she's used to people falling all over themselves about the place.

"Hey, I want you to meet someone," she says.

We walk across the grass, and Cash is heavy, but awake. Good thing I bundled him in a snowsuit and beanie because it's not freezing, but it's certainly cold out here.

Juniper runs off to play with a small group of kids near a table of snacks and punch. Mickey weaves through clusters of people, showering greetings and toothy smiles on everyone.

Finally, I see what she's aiming for: a small group of girls who are probably a tad younger than us, but it's hard to tell in the dark.

Unfortunately, I still don't see any sign of Shane, and I'm starting to wonder if it was worth it to come out tonight.

# DALICE

"RENEE! HEY, THIS is Dalice," Mickey says.

Renee is short and quite pretty. Blonde hair swirling out of a gray beanie. She stands near the bonfire holding two paper cups of some steaming drink.

"Nice to meet you. I'm so glad you could come," she says, handing me a cup. "Cider. I just grabbed it."

It's hard to take the cup because of Cash, and I sort of shuffle him to the other hip slowly.

"Oh here, let me," Mickey says, and reaches for him.

I hesitate, but luckily recover before Mickey notices, and I hand him to her. He's groggy after the interaction with Juniper on the drive, and he lays his head on Mickey's shoulder.

"I miss this," she says in a little puckered-up whine that's probably supposed to be cute. She pets his head.

I smile and take the cider, thanking Renee. I really want to get serious about finding Shane, but it would be too obvious right now, so I channel all the self-control. Renee brings over a few more people, and I meet them too.

"Can your little guy have this?" some woman asks, holding out a huge caramel apple.

All I see is an atomic mess, but from his spot in Mickey's arms, Cash perks up and reaches for it, smiling. It's so good to see him happy. I don't even care if he licks it to death and I have to toss the apple afterward, so I nod.

"They're crazy messy, but kids love them," she says, handing it to him.

Mickey introduces us. "This is Carolyn."

Carolyn smiles and coos over Cash for a bit. The caramel apple teeters dangerously close to Mickey's gorgeous long hair, but if it bothers her, I can't tell.

"You don't have to hold him. He's going to get gross real fast," I say to her.

"It's totally fine!"

I borderline don't believe her, but I also don't push it.

Carolyn and Renee ask if I like to ride bikes or ski or hike. I tell them I love to hike and bike, but I'm not really a skier. We all exchange numbers and I try to tell them I don't have a lot of free time. They laugh and say they get it. What's free time when you're a mom? They suggest we all get together.

My brain tries to find fault with these people. They can't all really be this happy. It has to be fake. But how would all of them be faking it so well? I haven't met a single grump in the bunch. They all seem to love being together, and it reminds me of the group of friends I had in college. You don't even care what you're doing. It's being together that matters.

Those friendships are nearly impossible to find at my age, and I feel a tinge of jealousy that these people seem to have it.

Renee and Mickey ask me question after question. I tell them about how I couldn't finish my degree, so I moved back home because of finances and to be closer to Brandy. About how my mom died years ago, about how Brandy and I are always arguing. Then about Cash.

It's the whole goddamn Dalice sob story, and before I know it, Renee pulls me into an embrace. The hug is nice. Warm. A feeling I haven't had in a really long time.

"I'm parenting alone too," Mickey says.

My heart expands with affection for her once again. She really has changed.

Then Shane appears next to Mickey.

"Michaela, Renee," Shane says in greeting, but he stares at me. My insides curl up into a tight ball. Not sure if it's anxiety or a junior-high crush. It feels like both.

Mickey gives Shane a scolding face. "Shane's the only one who doesn't call me Mickey," she play-slaps his arm with the hand that's not holding Cash. Flirting? Ugh. She goes on, "You remember Dalice, right, Shane? We're catching up after a few years of not being in contact."

He nods. It's stoic, like some deep-thinking tenured professor. So quiet again, the same way he was at Pig Out Place.

Is he happy to see me? Annoyed that I'm here? I still can't tell.

What if Mickey and he are together? She's definitely gained weight, but she's gorgeous as ever and has never had trouble getting the guy.

"Just a *few* years, you know, like fifteen," I say. I want Shane to laugh or give me some sign that this attraction isn't all in my head. I get nothing but a non-committal smile.

Mickey laughs, though, and her gray eyes sparkle against the flame of the bonfire. They look like a moody ocean scene. The Oregon Coast on a rainy day.

Damn, she's so pretty.

Cash is sticky and wiggly, and it's painful to watch Mickey try to be nice about it, so I reach for him. She hands him over and still, no reaction from Shane. Not about what Mickey said, not about what I said. Nada.

Oh God, I can't read him. What's he thinking? The only shred of hope I have is that he hasn't looked away from me this entire time. He keeps holding my eyes when there are plenty of other people and things to look at.

"Don't talk to *me* about being old," some other guy pipes up out of nowhere, joining our conversation.

*Nobody was talking to you at all, dude.*

I hate it when men eavesdrop and push into conversations, but he goes on, "Wait until you trade diapers and tantrums for walls of silence punctuated by emotional drama. Also known as: The Teen Years." His voice drops an octave on the last three words, and he splays his fingers to make what seems like jazz hands.

I can't help but laugh a little. He's a parent too, and that softens me a bit toward him. I'm becoming a regular Squishmallow upon learning that these people I want to dislike are parents. And that they're all so kind.

"Stop, Colin, you're scaring her," Mickey says, laughing, and slaps his arm. Maybe she flirts with every guy, and Shane's not special to her. "I don't think it has to be that way. Surely not all teens are bratty. Hard to believe our babies could be that way, right?" She aims that pouty voice at Cash. He's not paying attention because he dropped the caramel apple on the ground, and he's pushing against me to get down. I don't really want him crawling around in the dark, though.

"I don't know. Mine's a firebrand," I say, holding him tighter and trying to find something else to distract him. "I don't have high hopes for a drama-free life with this one." I bite my lip to keep from crying, because it's way too true. And not for the reason they're talking about.

Mickey's mouth moves like she might make a comment, but Shane speaks. "Dalice, will you join me over here, closer to the fire?" It seems a little abrupt, and a lot formal, and Mickey sort of twitches in surprise. But she doesn't protest.

Next thing I know, Shane points to a spot on a huge log, which is stripped bare of bark so it makes a bench. Everyone else goes off to mingle with other people.

We're alone, and our jean-covered thighs touch on the sides because he's sitting so close. It zings my senses to life.

"It surprised me to hear you were coming tonight," he says.

"Mickey invited me?" It's supposed to be a statement, but it comes out like a question.

"I'm glad," he says, but it's flat. I don't believe him.

Cash moves around on my lap, and his hands are so sticky I try to dodge them but only succeed once or twice.

Renee notices and approaches. "Can I take him for you? Get him cleaned up? I'll bring him right back."

It's the perfect distraction for Cash.

"Are you sure? You don't have to do that."

She tips her head to the side a bit and smiles. "Course!"

Once she's out of earshot, I say, "Your friends are nice. Like, *really* nice."

"Too nice?" He winces in a joking way. There's the Shane I know from the hospital.

"No, but is it normal for people to give you their number when you've only just met them?"

Shane makes a *hmph* noise and says, "You should know. Isn't that how we met?"

Damn. Walked into that one.

"Yeah, but that's different."

He turns and our faces are inches apart. It's bold. Really forward, but I don't hate it. "Oh really? Why?"

"Because."

He stares at me, and his bright eyes hold an intensity I don't feel ready for but am still drawn to. The heat of his breath makes a white cloud in the cold. I hope he kisses me. It's way too soon for that, but I want it all the same.

I try to find words. "Well, because—"

He takes one of my hands and runs his thumb over the top. It's electric. He breaks eye contact to look around, as if he's trying to be sure nobody sees. There's something so innocent and schoolboyish about the whole thing, and it sends a wave of heat through my body.

We return to comfortable silence, staring at the fire. He hasn't let go of my hand. The warmth radiating from him is the only thing I can focus on. I try to lean into it without being too obvious. I have no idea how much time passes, because I'm a thousand percent in the moment.

"Here you go! All clean." Renee presents Cash to me, and Shane pulls his hands away, shoves them into his orange Cotopaxi jacket.

"Wow, thanks so much," I say.

"You bet."

After Renee goes, I turn my eyes back to Shane, but he's staring past me at something else. I trace his gaze over the top of my head and back toward the house to see what it is.

There, at the top row of windows, is a silhouette. A black shape haloed by light from behind.

Someone stands with their arms folded.

Shane reaches for Cash, seeming to shake himself out of whatever he was thinking about. "Let's go on a hayride. Can I carry him? Give your arms a break."

"Yes, please."

I follow him down another gravel path toward the tractor, where some guy is loading people up, and I can't help it—I look back at that window again.

Nobody is there.

# 1992

**THE PEOPLE IN** the living room tonight are Mom's friends from the various places she's worked. Not good enough friends to check on her when she loses a job and disappears for weeks at a time, but good enough friends to come over for beers and…this.

Whatever this is.

Mom is the life of the party. She attends to the small group of people like a hummingbird checking out the nectar in each flower, making sure everyone has enough to drink or has a small plate of Oreos and Chips Ahoy.

She hasn't said a word to Reva so far. Reva leans against the wall in the hallway, trying to stay out of sight, but she watches. Her head thrums in low pain and she has a carnival ride in her stomach.

Shane catches her eye from across the room. He looks at her, but his face is a big, open white space. Eyes wide, forehead a little crinkled. He's not mad—Reva is quite familiar with her brother's mad face—but what is he thinking?

Grownups take every seat. Two ladies sit in wooden kitchen chairs that Mom moved into the living room, and a big man straddles the arm of the couch. Mom would yell at her for that.

Reva digs toes into tufts of the avocado-colored carpet until they rub the rough backing below. Her palms are sweaty, but not the gold dust kind of warmth. Her left eye keeps spasming.

It won't stop, no matter what she does, so she smashes it with a finger, trying to get it to stop.

Shane keeps staring at her, but everyone else is distracted.

Reva raises her eyebrows at her brother, sticks her neck out a little, like *What are you staring at?*

He smashes his lips together so they make a flat line, and his eyes soften. Then he shakes his head.

He feels sorry for her, and that makes tears pinch at the back of her nose.

Before she can cry, Mom approaches and takes her arm, leading her to the center of the room.

"Thank you, everyone, for coming tonight. You're all here today to see God work a miracle." Mom clasps her hands together. She seems so nice. The smile is big. Too big, like it might crack.

Reva whispers, "Mom, it's not happening—"

Mom waves the words off, silently shushing her. People aren't totally quiet yet, so she clears her throat and puts the smile back on.

The room grows quiet. It's hot, and small, like the people are breathing up all the oxygen so she can't get any. Mom steps away, but Reva grabs her blouse and holds up a palm.

"It's not here," she whispers.

"Try harder." Mom pushes the whisper out through lips that barely move. "Your gift is powerful. You can do it." Then she smiles at the room and sits next to Shane.

How? How can she try harder? And try harder at what? How did it start in the first place? In a flurry of seconds, the room grows impatient. She closes her eyes and thinks about the times the gold dust came.

Shane taking Fish into the woods.

On the bus with Kat.

After Mom slapped her.

Reva opens her palms to check. Nothing shiny except sweat. She swallows down the worries.

Mom makes *C'mon, let's go* eyes at her, tiny nods with her head. The room shrinks, as if Reva's getting big. So big that she's ballooning out to fill every inch of space. Like she could suffocate everyone with her body.

*You came here for healing? Surprise, I killed you instead.*

She closes her eyes, hoping that will make her small again, but it doesn't work. Her breath comes fast.

"Maybe we should pray?" It's Shane.

Reva opens her eyes, and he gives her a half-smile. He's trying to help.

Reva nods, eyes pleading with Mom. But when she looks down at her hands to weave ten fingers together in prayer, she sees it.

The gold dust. It's here.

It could be the religious stuff, like prayer, that brings the gold dust. Either way, there's no need to pray, so she extends her hands toward Mom, who springs out of her seat.

"See? It's a miracle. You all saw her hands before, right? Nothing. And now? This!"

Why on earth did the gold dust show up this time? Reva wants to think about this, to figure it out, but she can't because a woman about Mom's age stands up with a bit of hesitation and approaches Reva.

"Will you pray for me? Have the cancer. It's in my lungs."

Reva blinks, trying to figure out how praying will help. She folds her hands and bows her head, anyway.

"No! Not like that!" Mom shouts, coming fast toward her. "Like I showed you." She grips Reva by the forearms and places small, gold hands on the woman's chest. The contact is rough, and the woman startles, but warmth arrives, and the woman shakes. It scares Reva, so she tries to pull her hands away. Mom clamps down harder, holding Reva's gold fingers captive just above the lady's huge breasts.

"Yes, Lord!" Mom yells. Reva flinches because she's never seen Mom like this.

Something goes out of Reva. It doesn't hurt, but it doesn't feel good either. She just knows that something has left her and gone into this woman. That didn't happen with Kat or Mom.

The woman cries and shouts, "It's warm. My lungs are warm, right where the cancer sits. I think she done it!"

The other adults swarm Reva. She repeats the question Mom taught her: *What would you ask of me?* And they respond.

Shane hangs back, the only one who doesn't get up from his seat. She watches him, but then has to turn away, because if she keeps studying his face—that look that says he feels bad for her—she'll cry, and Mom will get mad.

A tall man steps in the way so she can't see Shane anymore, and Mom moves Reva's hands to the next person, and the next. Placing them all over human bodies wherever the pain or disease is located. Reva doesn't want to touch all these people. They're too close, hovering. Rancid breath, the stink of skin, the rot of beer, it all surrounds her.

She steps back, but Mom jerks her wrist to bring her close again. Her black, hard eyes stare, and her mouth makes a grim line. Then it opens to speak. "This is your calling, your reason for living."

Reva draws closer to the adult bodies, not because she agrees with Mom, but because there is no choice. Mom is stronger than her and won't let go, plus now she's speaking in that gibberish that Reva remembers from Dad's church. The gift of tongues. Weird, because she doesn't remember Mom ever speaking in tongues before.

"Anyone here have a visible wound or a broken bone? Something we can tell is healed without a doctor's say-so? I believe the Lord wants to heal you right now," Mom shouts.

She's no longer trying to be prim and proper. Mom is impatient, fierce, and very scary.

Reva sees Shane's hand go up slowly behind the jumble of adults.

"Shane. What?" Mom's voice is harsh.

"I hurt my wrist." He tries to make a fist, but can't.

Shane sprained his wrist while playing keeper in a soccer game last weekend. He's tough, but the wrist has been bugging him. He can't move it all the way in a circle like it should go, but he wouldn't tell Mom because he didn't think they had the money for a doctor. Said he'd just play the field instead of in goal now. Don't need hands for that.

Mom scoffs. "No, we need to let our guests go first."

Shane slumps in his seat.

Reva rips her hands away from Mom, not even caring if it makes her mad. She gently pushes through the people and approaches Shane, reaching out a gold palm. Shane places his wrist in it.

There's that warmth again. The sense of something leaving her body, but this time, it's like being pushed over. She gasps.

Shane's face whips up. "Oh my God."

"Language, Shane!" Mom says.

Reva takes her hand away, and Shane makes a white-knuckled fist. He moves his wrist in a circle. Slowly at first, but then faster, with more aggression. He bends it backward.

"It's better. It's totally better."

Reva smiles. Up to this point, she's hated everything about this evening. About her newfound gift. But seeing how she helped her brother gives her a boost, like maybe she could be useful to people, and to the Lord. But then she's spinny. Her legs can't hold her weight anymore, and everything goes black.

# DALICE

**THE NEXT DAY,** all I can think about is Shane's hand, his fingers moving along the back of my mine. His perfect face, lit by the glow of fire. How natural it is to be with him, and how easy he is with Cash.

How is it I barely know him, yet I feel all of this?

When Shane arrives at Brandy's to pick me up for the dinner date we arranged yesterday, I introduce them. Confoundingly, she seems to take to him right away. Shane even makes her laugh, which is more than I can ever do. Then he says something about Cash and me at the harvest party last night, and it sends my sister right back to her favorite mode: cynicism with a dash of paranoia.

We say goodbye and Shane walks toward his car, but Brandy grabs my elbow.

"You hung out with him last night too? With Cash? In the cold?"

"Dr. Sonora said the social interaction would be good for him, and she told me what to watch for so I'd know if it became too much."

"I don't like it. Shane seems nice, but there's something that seems a little...off, too."

I groan, because what the hell? She sees the bad in everything. I sound like a child, but it's like she doesn't want me to have any fun or a life of my own.

I shake her arm off. "Bye, Bran."

The sun has set, but it's not dark yet. At the car, I realize this is a brand-new Rover. It's an insanely nice car, and it takes me a second to figure out where the handle is. I swear to God, there's no handle. Shane comes to my rescue, pushing a tiny button that makes the handle pop out. His hand brushes mine because I don't get out of the way fast enough, and again, a jolt of lightning at the touch. Same as last night, same as when our fingers brushed that first time at Pig Out Place.

There's something here between us, and I have to see what it is. It's so not the right time for me to be interested in someone, but how many people say they found love when they were least expecting it? It's like love's favorite thing to do. Spring up at the worst possible life moments.

*Heyo! Love's here. Never mind that you're in crisis. It's now or never, baby!*

Still, I need to play it cool. Somehow avoid jumping his bones.

Shane starts up the car, and a blast of music erupts. It's so loud that I let out a little startled scream. He rushes to turn it down.

"Rocking out to Radiohead, huh?" I say, even though I want to comment on the volume. I'd sound like an old lady if I did that, so I let it go.

"Sorry about that." Shane smiles and backs the car out. He turns left, taking us toward Spokane.

"A Rover. Nice. What do you do? I can't believe I haven't asked that yet."

Shane chuckles. "I work at the hospital. I know Dr. Sonora a bit, actually."

"Really?"

"Yeah, sorry I didn't mention it. We haven't really had the chance to talk on this level, and my knowing her didn't seem important considering your distress that first night. Then I was a little *distracted* at the harvest party." He lasers over a look that almost knocks the wind out of me.

It's me. I'm the distraction. God, my heart is beating so loud that I swear he can hear it.

Shane goes on, "Plus, I don't really *know her* know her. I've just had a few interactions with her while I was on shift at the hospital."

Is it a red flag that he didn't mention Dr. Sonora, or working at the hospital? I don't want it to be, so I shelve the thought.

"So, you're a doctor?"

"Oh no," he chuckles. "I work in patient transport, which means I push people in wheelchairs around. It's just a few hours a week. Very glamorous."

None of that explains the fancy car, though.

"So, how can I afford this car?" he asks like he can read my mind.

"Yeah, actually." I exhale what I hope sounds like a laugh.

"It's my sister's. Didn't want to lead with that, but it's the truth. Not something I like to admit. That I live with my sister. That I drive her car, you know. Sounds a little…"

He bounces his head back and forth like he wants me to finish his sentence, but I have no clue what to say, so I let the silence grow awkward.

"Under-achieving," he finally says. "Not how I thought my life would turn out."

"I hear you there," I say. Last thing I can judge is someone who isn't as far in life as they want to be.

"What's this?" I point to the big flat screen between us, because I can't think of anything else to say.

"Oh, just gadgets that are supposed to help me operate the car. Navigation, you can connect your phone, that sort of thing."

"Do you use it?"

"Nah, I like to feel like I'm actually driving, not like the vehicle is driving me. I don't need a camera to help me back up a car." He smiles and my stomach flips again. I like the way his eyes crinkle at the edges. I like how down-to-earth he is. Something about him is so real, so relatable. He's not trying to be something he's not.

I ask questions to try to learn more about Shane's life and his childhood, but he seems to only want to know about me.

Where I grew up, what my hobbies are when I'm not working or taking care of Cash (as if I have time for hobbies).

Whenever I try to reciprocate, he answers with one or two words and then turns it back to me. On one hand, it's annoying, because I really want to hear more about him. But on the other, it's nice. So rare to find anyone who is interested in someone other than themselves, and, it sounds sexist to say this, but men especially. Shane genuinely seems to want to know about me, and it only makes me like him more.

When we get to the Thai restaurant downtown, Shane orders five stars' worth of spice and then pretends like he's not in literal pain while he eats. He keeps saying "It's not that spicy" when he's not downing water and wiping his eyes and nose with a napkin. Why do people do that to themselves? It makes me laugh.

Afterward, we walk through Riverfront Park, which was the site of Expo '74. There's a huge clock tower and a river, and tons of grassy areas. When I was a kid, they had rides here, but those are gone now, and instead they use the big pavilion for concerts. It's a little cold outside, and the moon is a luminescent drop in the clear sky, reflecting on the wide river. I take his hand, and our fingers intertwine. I feel relaxed around him, like everything is going to work out.

I think about asking him back to my place. It'd be easy to shoot Brandy a text and see if Cash could stay the night. But is it too soon? I haven't done this dating thing in so long.

"I better get you home to Cash," Shane says once we've made our way through the park.

Well, that answers that. I smile and lay my head on his arm. "This was a lot of fun."

He kisses the top of my head. "I agree. Let's do it again soon."

# 1992

**SUNDAY COMES SOONER** than Reva wants it to. This evening, she sits in the car outside the church building where she will *minister* tonight, like the other day in the living room.

Mom took Shane inside with her, but made Reva wait in the car. At least an hour has passed, and a line of people keeps shuffling into the church. Reva can't believe how long it is—all the way out to the parking lot, where weeds push through cracks in the broken blacktop. There are a lot of wheelchairs and crutches, too.

The building is brick, and the roof grows moss in spots like it's very old. The windows are long and slim, dimpled orange. Poor man's stained glass.

How will all these people fit into the tiny church? The line barely inches along. Is it because there's no more room, and they're smashing bodies in there like brown sugar in a measuring cup? A flat hand pushing them to the back so more can fit.

*Cookies sound good right now.*

Dad's church used to have cookies after the service. It was mostly old people drinking coffee at round tables, but Reva and Shane would fill up on cookies until Dad finished making the rounds, chatting. Sometimes if she stopped when one of the old people tried to talk to her, they'd give her their cookies, too.

Maybe there will be cookies after the service tonight. It's a tiny hope, but it makes her body relax so that she can take in a big breath of air.

The line eventually shrinks until there's nobody else waiting to get in.

A side door opens—it's the kind with the bar you push to go outside at school. Mom's stern face emerges, and she waves Reva inside.

The metal door slams behind them, echoing through the tight hallway. Reva cringes, but Mom doesn't notice. She leads the way, already ten steps ahead and moving fast.

They walk through the foyer, past the closed doors of the sanctuary. Bright light shines from the slit underneath the double doors, and muffled conversation vibrates inside. The smell of coffee mixed with old wood is everywhere, sending her back to Dad's church and making her miss Dad. But it also reminds her of the cookies afterward.

The receptionist's desk is tidy, and on the wall behind it is a clock, along with a huge wooden cross and a framed print with a lot of words and a beach scene. Reva doesn't have to read it to know it's the "Footprints" poem. They have a copy in their bathroom at the trailer.

A small metal fan makes a scraping noise as it oscillates on the desk, and it's only then that Reva realizes how hot it is.

She runs to catch up with Mom, who turns down a dark hallway. With the wood paneling on the wall, it's scary-dark. The carpet is a big, orange blanket suffocating every inch of the floor. As they go further, a dusty smell replaces the fresh coffee scent from the entrance. It's hard to find anything good about this part of the church.

Mom and Reva arrive at a door at the end of the hallway, and Mom opens it without hesitation. The brightness hits Reva like a sudden spotlight, but when her eyes adjust, she realizes it's just a side entrance to the sanctuary.

She waits for Mom to walk in so she can follow, but Mom holds the door open for her. "Go on."

Does she want Reva to go in alone?

Reva shakes her head. Her hands are sweaty, and her throat is tight. She can't see how many people are in there because only the stage is visible. That, and the pastor at the pulpit. But she watched all those people stuff in, so she knows there are loads of them. No way she can make her feet go, especially by herself.

"Don't make Pastor wait," Mom whispers.

She scours Mom's face for something—anything that signals she could talk her out of this. But it's all ice, and there's no budge at all.

Reva touches her own cheek, remembering the sting of Mom's slap when she was too slow to obey last time.

She swallows back tears, then moves closer to the door's threshold. It's warm. Blazing hot, in fact. She feels like she's Gretel walking into the witch's oven. Ceiling fans whir so fast they rattle, but otherwise the room is silent. The pastor smiles at her from the stage, but it's not reassuring. It's the kind of smile grown-ups give kids when they want something from them. The smile Mom had the other night in the living room.

Reva finds Mom's face again, and upon seeing no understanding there, no way out at all, she steps into the sanctuary.

The first person she sees is Shane, right in the front row. His eyes are wide again. Something about it strengthens her, and a surge of bravery replaces the tightness in her throat. If anything, she can be strong to show him he doesn't need to worry.

The pastor reaches out for her, and she stands by his side. He walks her out in front of the pulpit and holds her shoulders in front of him.

It's quiet except for lots of coughing and wooden pews creaking under the weight of people shifting, trying to get comfortable while their shoulders smash the person next to them. People are even standing, lining the back.

"Everyone, please welcome our guest minister, Reva Prehner."

Loud clapping startles Reva.

"Let us say the invocation, and the praise band will lead us in a few songs until little Reva is ready."

The pastor gestures, and everyone recites: "We are hard-pressed on every side, but not crushed; perplexed, but not in despair; persecuted, but not abandoned; struck down, but not destroyed. And by His might, we will prevail."

The chorus of coughing seems louder, like a call and response across the sanctuary. Is everyone here sick? Are they all expecting her to heal them? What if the gold dust doesn't show up? Her breath comes fast until all she can hear is her own heartbeat.

The band starts up, and everyone closes their eyes and sings. They're not looking at her anymore, and she can finally relax a little. The pastor stays close by Reva, raising his hands and singing words to a song she doesn't recognize. Funny, because she knows a lot of hymns since her dad was a pastor. But this one is faster, like something she might hear on the radio.

Shane must not recognize the songs either, because his mouth stays closed and he keeps staring at her. If the gold dust cooperates, maybe she can do this. She'll show him.

She checks her hands.

Nothing but sweat.

"YOU READY?" THE pastor leans down and whispers. He smells like Old Spice and coffee breath.

Reva shows him her palms and shrugs because the gold dust isn't here. He lays a large hand on her head and prays in tongues.

Warmth blooms on her hands.

Praying worked this time. Reva taps the pastor's suit right where the buttons are and shows him her gold hands. He nods.

This is much better than it was with Mom. No way Reva wants to do this, but if she has to, at least this man is helpful, even kind.

The pastor invites anyone who wants a touch of healing from the Lord to the front of the sanctuary. The wheelchairs come up the aisle first and form a line at the base of the stairs to the stage. People trickle into the middle aisle until it's full all the way to the back.

Shane stays put.

Reva scans for Mom, but she can't find her, and the door she came through is shut now.

The closest person is at the bottom of the steps to the stage. It's a man in a wheelchair. He's about Mom's age. Reva steps down until she's in front of him.

"What would you ask of me?" she says.

"I want to walk again." Tears brim in his eyes.

Reva lays hands on the man's thighs and closes her eyes. Warmth goes out, so she pulls her hands away and glances up at the pastor.

He acknowledges her with a silent nod and asks the man to stand up.

She likes how they can communicate without words.

The man places his hands on the wheelchair's armrests and pushes his body up and out of the chair with some hesitation. The pastor asks everyone to back away, give the man some space. People part like the Red Sea, clearing the aisle by returning to the pews, even though a collective groan rumbles the room. They don't want to sit back down.

The man seems shaky at first, his arms holding most of his weight, hands gripping the wheelchair. But then he lets go and stands, still shaky. He takes a shuffling step forward. Then another. His legs straighten more every time, and he cries and hollers in celebration.

She smiles and glances at Shane. He still doesn't smile, but never mind. It feels good to help this man.

The man runs down the middle aisle. He jumps and whoops, and then everyone joins in the yelling. Some sing, some pray in tongues, and the pastor puts his hand on her shoulder. He smiles.

"You're a world changer," he says.

Reva smiles back even though pain sprouts from her skull, down into her neck, and then her arms.

# SHANE

**I GLANCE AT** the clock on my dashboard after I enter the gate code to the house. I'm about ten minutes late for the meeting, thanks to work. Reva will understand because the whole reason I have the job is to recruit. I'm not concerned about her getting upset. I am concerned, however, that I don't see Steve's car parked outside the house.

Steve wasn't at the harvest party on Saturday, and it bothers me because I keep thinking about what he blurted out during the meeting the week before. That and the way Reva glared at him when he did it.

He should be here by now. There's no way he'd miss the party *and* a meeting. You just don't do that. When she calls a meeting, you attend. You set your life up so it's adjustable to meetings. It's the first thing newbies learn—a flexible job is more important than a job you love. You need to keep your schedule open.

I grab my phone out of my coat pocket and call Steve. It rings a few times, then goes to voicemail: "Yo, it's Steve. Nobody answers phones anymore, so text, bruh. Read me?"

"Hi Steve, it's Shane again. Just...wondering if you're coming tonight. I don't see your car. Text when you get this."

At the top of the stone steps to the house, I reach for the doorknob, and a series of thoughts ambush me.

*What if Steve's out now, too? Like Joel and Carissa this summer.*

*"Bad company corrupts good character."*

*If Steve was leaning away from the truth, it's better for everyone if he's gone.*

I blink hard. It's been a few days since my brain has done this, and it was a nice break.

Who knew when I started reading the Bible all those years ago that the passages would burrow into my brain like this, informing everything I observe like a bully on my back?

When I open the door to the house, I can tell the meeting hasn't started yet. Everyone is still milling around, laughing, drinking coffee or sparkling water. The kids are already upstairs for their lesson, though, so it's almost time.

Reva stands at the edge of where the kitchen meets the large foyer. She angles her body to watch the front door. Lonny and Sheryl are talking to her, and Lonny's crying. He's such a crier. Their relationship is a role reversal—Sheryl is the stoic one, and Lonny's the feeler.

Reva glances over and her eyes widen when she sees me. I can tell she wants to talk to me, so I take off my coat, hang it up, and wait around in the foyer. She nods slowly at Lonny and Sheryl. This is what she does when she's trying to get compliance from them so she can escape the conversation.

*You know what I'm saying? You know what I mean?*

She just keeps repeating those words, smiling. It means you *should* know what she means, even if you don't. You nod along, because there's really nothing else to do. You think you don't understand because you're just being a little daft. It'll make more sense later, maybe when you're more spiritual, or when God's timing is right. Until then, you just need to trust Reva because it's too confrontational to say *No, sorry, can you explain it better?*

Plus, you never say no. It's yes. Yes to Reva is yes to God.

"There you are," she says, walking toward me.

"Hey, sorry I'm late. I was trying to get a hold of Steve before coming in."

Her brown eyes soften, and she cocks her head to the side so her long auburn braid, which is draped over one shoulder, dangles down the front of her fitted black cardigan sweater. She's wearing a black-and-white striped skirt and Doc Marten boots.

"New boots?"

"Old, actually. You don't remember when I got these in the nineties?" She lifts a foot and wiggles it to show it off.

I shake my head.

"You know, for all of your intuition, your memory really stinks."

"Thanks."

"Steve's not here, huh?"

"Nope."

Surely she's noticed his absence. Something like that wouldn't slip by her, but she shrugs one shoulder. It's flippant, and the concern on her face is gone. "Small is the gate and narrow is the road that leads to eternal life. Few find it."

I understand the verse and its application here because this was what she said repeatedly when Joel and Carissa left. She says it when anyone leaves. She thinks that I should put it out of my mind, that Steve has chosen to stray.

But it felt different with him. He was *in* in. Joel and Carissa were always on the outskirts because of Carissa's hesitation, but not Steve. He was family.

I rub one eye and realize what a long day it's been.

"Can you get everyone seated and ready?" she asks.

Great, she thinks I'm *under it*. That's her phrase for "distant," or even worse, "questioning."

*Anti.*

She always doles out insignificant jobs to people when she thinks they're *under it*. Her theory is that it helps them feel more a part of the family when they're struggling, and it gets their focus off of themselves and on to others.

She's not wrong.

If you don't realize she's doing it, this tactic works like mad. But not so much when you can see through it. Still, I let her think it works on me.

I let her think a lot of things, even though my throat goes dry at the possibility of her noticing something's up with me. If she only knew the boatload of *anti* thoughts I've been having lately.

"You bet," I say, and smile.

I go through the kitchen into the vast room on the left side of the house. It has cathedral ceilings and a massive fireplace. This room reminds me of a Victorian ballroom, the way it's flanked by tall windows along the front and back, with heavy teal velvet drapes that always stay open. The windows don't insulate well, so it's hot in the summer and cold in the winter. But she won't let anyone close the drapes, and she won't meet in another room either.

*This is the heart of the house. It's where the meetings should happen,* she says.

When she walks away, I get a flash of a vision: Dalice sitting in the chair next to mine during a meeting.

My heart beats a little faster at the thought of her. I wanted our time after dinner the other night to last longer, but I must be careful. Reva can't find out about my feelings for Dalice. I don't know what I'm doing, or where it could go, and I don't want to bring Dalice into this, but I can't walk away from the little spark between us either. I certainly can't leave the meetings.

It's a complete impasse.

I catch Colin's attention and he comes over. "Hey, can you start a fire? It's freezing in here," I say.

Colin is one of my friends, and he's been coming to the meetings for at least a decade.

"Yeah, sure. Sorry, I didn't think of it." He motions to his teen son, Jonah, to come and help.

The kids are all upstairs, but anyone fourteen or older gets to join the adults downstairs. They don't go through The Threshing Floor until they're eighteen, and they don't participate until then, but they still serve as silent witnesses.

Of course, Reva will heal the children by proxy if one of their blood relatives has gone through The Threshing Floor and gotten sealed to the group.

"Hey, where's Steve?" Colin asks, glancing around.

I shake my head slowly, and his features fall. He gives a hard shrug. "Many are called, but few are chosen."

I force my face to smile.

It's the phrase everyone uses to make sense of the people who leave. If you jump right to thinking *It's them, not the group*, you can avoid your own lingering doubts.

"Hey everyone! Last call for coffee or tea," I say. "Let's find our seats and get started. Grab a blanket if you're cold. Colin and Jonah are trying to get us some heat."

The hubbub dwindles, and people move into the big room. Some race into the kitchen to grab a last-minute refill, but most take their seats in the rows of soft-cushioned chairs. It's a pretty good turnout today, despite no Steve. Probably fifty people, not including the kids upstairs.

No new people today. Well, except Holly.

I met Holly at the hospital a few months ago when she was there for chemo treatment. She just went through The Threshing Floor last week and she looks nervous, so I smile, try to make her more comfortable. She smiles too. Her hair isn't growing back yet, so she's wearing one of her long-hair wigs, but she got the news just a day ago.

Cancer-free.

That feeling—helping people in such a big way—never gets old. It's one of the few silver linings of this choice I made so many years ago.

"Let's welcome Holly to her first official meeting as a sealed member," I say, and everyone claps.

Meetings aren't for casual seekers. People usually attend a few parties or social gatherings before they attend a meeting, and Reva won't choose someone for The Threshing Floor until she thinks they're ready.

After the clapping settles down, people naturally move into conversation with those around them. Reva appears and signals with a nod that she's ready.

"Okay, hopefully you have your coffee," I say. "We've got blankets, we've got a fire going. And now we get to hear from our leader, Reva, God's chosen, who will show the world what *healing* really means."

# SHANE

**REVA SMILES AND** takes my place in front of the fire, which is really rocking, thanks to Colin. I sit down in an empty chair by Michaela.

My eyes fix on Reva, but then travel above the fireplace behind her, where Dad's rifle sits, mounted to the wall.

His old .22, my reminder. It's a gut punch, as usual.

"Welcome, everyone," Reva says. "Look at your neighbor and say, 'It's a good day to do God's work.'"

I hate it when she makes us do this. It's so childish and stupid. But I face Michaela and do it anyway. Michaela is way too smiley, like this is the most fun she'll ever have.

"Tonight, I'm going to throw a bit of a curveball, but I know you can handle it," Reva starts. "Typically, we perform The Threshing Floor once a month, but I feel the Lord saying that it's just not enough. The days are growing evil, and we'll soon be under siege by the enemy. We must prepare ourselves now. And by now, I mean *yesterday*."

Excitement pulses through the small crowd. The Threshing Floor is what people love about the meetings, and normally she's stingy with the ritual. Especially since people have no control over when it might be their turn. She chooses, and she doesn't choose fairly—she chooses how she wants to.

"I know we just threshed Holly last week. Hi Holly, so good to see you here, now truly part of the family, healed and sealed."

Holly smiles again.

"But tonight, I want to offer another opportunity to someone who is hungry to obey the word of the Lord. You've all experienced some healing, but dig down deep and ask yourself if there might be another area where you're not totally giving yourself to the Lord. Most of you know how it works. After the threshing, we'll call upon the Lord to bring healing, and He'll move as He wills. So, who would like to go through The Threshing Floor tonight?"

Hands go up.

Every hand but mine.

This is the reason people are here, and why they stay. That, and Reva says they forfeit all healing if they leave.

The first threshing seals you to the group, like what Holly experienced, and then you can volunteer whenever you like after that.

I've never been through The Threshing Floor, but Reva doesn't push me on it, and nobody knows since I've been here longer than anyone else. As far as they're concerned, I'm sealed to the group. Every time she brings it up, I resist, and she gives up. It's the one instance where Reva seems to respect that I'm her older brother.

Or seems to respect me at all.

Reva cocks her head to the side. "Sweet Mickey. The Lord will bless your willing spirit." She points to the chair in the middle, instructing Mickey to take a seat.

A wave of disappointment ripples across the room as Michaela stands and everyone else deals with not being chosen. She brushes her hands against her dark jeans like she's trying to get rid of cookie crumbs. It must be a habit, because she does it a lot and there's never anything on her jeans.

Praying in tongues starts up, hushed, like always. I pray too, but my heart isn't in it. Why is Reva offering The Threshing Floor more often instead of less? It goes against the way she's done things for so many years.

"This isn't just for those new to the family," Reva starts as Mickey takes the hot seat. "Of course, it's for newbies. To bring about the healing they need to be sealed to us as one. But it's really for all of us. Anytime we run up against ourselves, against our dark tendencies to waver and doubt the absolute truth. Anytime we just can't rise above, can't shake the chaff away to be who we're called to be. That's when we need to be threshed and healed again. Over and over. In the Bible, The Threshing Floor was a symbol God used because people of those times understood it. Back before there was machinery to harvest crops, it was how they processed grain. The Threshing Floor itself was a flat, stone surface used to separate the wheat—or the valuable and pure, from the chaff—the excess and unusable. But the chaff would cling. It was stubborn, defiling the precious grain."

She smiles while giving this explanation. It's the same thing she says before every Threshing Floor session, and her voice is butter-smooth, like a lullaby. My whole body relaxes into the sound of it.

No matter my frustrations with my sister, the truth is that I could listen to her speak all day. It's really a gift she has.

"That's why the wheat had to be crushed. Either by animals treading it out, or by hand with a huge stick. But the Lord, in His mercy, has shown us how to make use of this practice today to winnow the grain of our spirits from the darkness of this world we live in."

A loud hum grows across the room as people softly pray in tongues. They raise their hands in the air as Reva's sermon wraps up.

"Now, let's say the invocation." She raises her hands and closes her eyes.

We speak as one: "We are hard-pressed on every side, but not crushed; perplexed, but not in despair; persecuted, but not abandoned; struck down, but not destroyed. And by His might, we will prevail."

Reva takes her seat next to the fireplace. It's just a black, crushed velvet armchair from some fancy furniture shop, but the way she holds herself makes it look like a throne.

"Your tone of voice is too harsh. You need to speak more gently," a woman says to Michaela.

With that, The Threshing Floor has begun.

Michaela doesn't flinch, because she knows what to expect. An onslaught of verbal abuse. Half of what's said during these sessions isn't even true, but it doesn't matter. You must participate if you want a chance at being selected the next time. Unfortunately for the person in the hot seat, everything feels true.

"Michaela, people can't tell if you're joking or serious, and you're really not that funny, so you should just keep it serious," someone else says—a man.

Eyes shift all around as people try to anticipate who will speak next in order to time their threshing.

"You cling to food for comfort. The Lord is displeased with how you treat your body."

"You're too concerned about your body. You need to focus on the Lord and not on your looks. Release your vain imaginations."

Both body comments are from women.

I stare at my feet. Not only have I never enjoyed this, but I don't know if I've ever even gotten used to it. The more my doubts grow, the harder it is to suffer through. This pit in my gut expands until I want to gag.

Joel and Carissa drift back into my thoughts while the harsh words fly in Michaela's direction. Carissa always resisted going through The Threshing Floor, even though Joel had been through many months prior. She kept putting it off, but he was devout and threatened to leave her if she didn't comply.

Now they are both gone.

The one time I asked about them, Reva said they left because they were offended. It proved they were wolves in sheep's clothing, only here to prey on our faith. Since they turned their backs on the Lord, we should let them go and instead focus on the ones who could be sealed to us.

"You smile too much, Mickey. People can tell it's not really in your heart. You're just performing."

Michaela stiffens just slightly, so I know that one got to her, but she plays it off. Still, a rush of heat warms my face. This is ridiculous. I know Michaela better than anyone. I brought her in, and this stuff isn't even close to true. It feels like everyone is being lazy, just grabbing for generic insults. Not that specific insults would be any better.

"The Lord disciplines those He loves, and He punishes everyone He accepts as a son."

"He was pierced for our transgressions, He was crushed for our iniquities."

Do you think Michaela should be treated differently than Christ Himself? He who was bloodied and battered but did no wrong?

I blink so the thoughts stop, and when I lift my face, Reva stares at me. She wants me to thresh Michaela. I give half a nod and rush to think of something. After someone brings up how flirtatious Michaela is, I jump in.

"Michaela, I think sometimes you're too nice. You give too much of yourself to others."

The room turns toward me, and Reva narrows her eyes. Michaela looks up, and I can see she's been crying.

I did the thing Reva hates: give a threshing that's actually a masked compliment. But I don't care.

Reva stands. "Mickey, let's go back to what someone said at the start. About your focus on your weight."

Her eyes don't leave my face, even though she's speaking to Michaela. Whatever comes next is my punishment for not participating correctly.

I clench my jaw. How much worse did I just make it for Michaela?

"I feel the Lord moving there," Reva goes on. "He wants you to know that you are so much more than your size or your body. His desire is for you to appreciate your body as a temple for the Holy Spirit. So, go ahead and stand up."

Michaela's eyes widen like she doesn't understand, but she does it.

"Take off your sweater."

My mind circles, wondering where in the world this is going. It's cold in here. Why is Reva asking her to take off her cardigan?

"Now your socks."

"Can I sit down to—"

"Oh yes, of course."

She sits and pulls off her socks, then stands back up.

"Now your pants."

What in the world is Reva doing? This has never happened before. Modesty is a big deal around here.

A light gasp comes from the rows of chairs, and it draws Reva's attention. "If anyone disagrees with the word of the Lord, you're free to go. You'll forfeit all your healing, though. If you stay, you participate fully."

"Sorry, what did you ask me to do?" Michaela asks, although I'm certain she heard Reva the first time. We all did.

"Remove your pants. The Lord wants to move in you tonight so you never think about your weight again. Trust me." Reva smiles.

Michaela doesn't even flinch toward obeying.

I alternate my gaze between Reva and Michaela, but my mind can't wrap around this. People shift in their seats, trying not to appear as uncomfortable as they are.

"Are you sure?" Michaela asks in a tiny voice.

"Yes."

Michaela unbuttons her jeans, and fresh tears streak her face.

I want to make this stop. But I don't move, because I'm afraid my fake threshing is what caused this in the first place.

When her jeans lie in a stiff pool on the floor, she stands there, shaking, crossing arms over her underwear, trying to hide.

Reva approaches and takes her wrist, moving it away. "Don't hide. That's the whole point of what the Lord is trying to teach you tonight. No more hiding. No more half-hearted participation. You must let go of everything but His will. Embrace His plan for your life."

My sister shoots a hard glare at me immediately after speaking. This whole charade is directed at me, just like I suspected. Michaela isn't the half-hearted participant, I am. But this is what Reva does. Why thresh only one person when you can thresh the entire room in the process?

"Now, take off your shirt," she says. "Dive headlong into this freedom."

Michaela's movements are mechanical as she reaches for the bottom of her tee. I can't watch. She's my friend, and I don't want to see this.

*"For my thoughts are not your thoughts, neither are your ways my ways."*

*"As the heavens are higher than the earth, so are my ways above yours."*

*Maybe, but do you really need to see this?*

"Shane," Reva says, interrupting the onslaught of intrusive thoughts. I glance up. "We're here to stand witness to Mickey's transformation in the name of love. Shame on you for looking away."

Michaela wears only her bra and underwear, and tears gather and drip from her chin. She stares forward, like she's not here. She's made herself disappear.

"The Lord is so proud of you," Reva says to Michaela, circling her. "Now the hardest but most crucial part. Your undergarments."

Michaela's eyes squeeze closed like she knew this was coming. Like she didn't even let herself hope Reva wouldn't go there.

I take slow breaths to calm myself down. I can't let Reva see how this is affecting me. How pissed I am.

When Michaela hesitates, Reva says, "Are you grateful for Juniper's healing? Are you thankful that she doesn't have cystic fibrosis anymore? That she'll live a long life, probably give you grandbabies?"

Michaela gives a sharp inhale, then nods wildly. Her energy feels different, and when her chin lifts, I can see her jaw ripple with determination.

"Then, let's go. Time to obey."

Michaela reaches behind her back to unclasp her bra, and it falls down her arms. She catches her large breasts, but Reva pulls her wrists away again. I don't want to see this, but Reva's watching me. It'll be worse for Michaela if I don't look, and while it doesn't seem like it could get worse, I can't put it past my sister. It can always get worse.

My body wakes up against my will when I finally look at her. It makes me want to cry that I could get turned on by this, my friend, a sister in Christ. Someone I don't even have any romantic feelings for. What a horrible person I am, such a dog at the core.

I survey the room carefully when Reva's not watching me. The women stare at Michaela, vacant and glassy-eyed. The men do too, but it's a pattern of staring, then realizing they're staring and trying to act like they're not without turning away. There's a lot of shifting eyes with unmoving faces. They don't want to get the same rebuke I just received. Yet, I read in them the same shame I feel. Shame for the physical response they can't help.

When Michaela loops her fingers into the waistband of her underwear, I move my eyes just centimeters to the side and make her blurry in my vision until she's just a fleshy, vertical shape. I zero in on one of the blue curtains across the room. I just can't do this.

Dalice has been below the surface of my thoughts ever since I met her, and it's the happy thing my mind dredges up right now. What right do I have to explore a future with her when I'm involved in this? The only option is to leave the meetings first. It's the only way that I can protect Dalice. But how would I do it? How would I leave?

"*Corrama shabadoama garramo geydo vaysa!*" Michaela shouts in tongues, pulling me back to the moment.

Her hands are in the air, and she leans forward slightly, shaking. Her dark hair, pulled up and held in a loose bun with a ballpoint pen, falls down with the movement. Everyone stands, raises their hands, and their bodies begin jerking in tight motions, forward and back, like Michaela.

This is normal, signaling the end of The Threshing Floor, but today seems different. More intense. For one, nobody has ever had to strip before. Threshings are always verbal only. Why is Reva upping the ante?

It wouldn't be the first time her gift has shifted, though. She used to heal people without conditions. But then the Lord led her to do The Threshing Floor, and it's been this way ever since. What if this is another shift?

"Yes, Lord, we receive your gifts gratefully!" Reva shouts.

When she brings her hands down, they're covered in gold. She lays them on Michaela's body—the pooch of her stomach, then her hips, thighs, rear end, triceps. All the areas where women can grow soft with weight gain.

"Everyone, close your eyes and pray in the spirit. I'm going to heal Mickey's self-image tonight."

Minutes pass, and the room roars as people pray in tongues.

We open our eyes and Michaela stands in front of us, but she doesn't look like Michaela. More like some Victoria's Secret model walked off the pages of a magazine.

Her body is perfect. She was beautiful before, but she would need to spend all day at the gym to achieve this. She has muscle definition in her legs and—holy crap, her abs.

Reva wraps a blanket around Michaela, whose tear-streaked cheeks lift in a smile. Her face is slim, no more double chin, and no evidence at all that she was carrying those few extra pounds. She laughs with joy.

It's over.

Michaela leaves the room with her pile of discarded clothes, and everyone gets up and starts chatting about mundane things. What they're planning to eat for dinner, or how early they have to be at work tomorrow. Like nothing strange happened here at all.

My thoughts are so all over the place that I don't even try to blink them away. I'm in free fall for the first time since everything started happening with Reva. I fold my hands and stay in my seat, trying to reconcile the horror of what just happened with how happy Michaela seemed afterward.

"Hi Shane." Michaela sits in the seat next to me. She's dressed, but her clothes are too loose. They hang off of her like her bones are a plastic hanger. Her face glows with an energy that's magnetic.

"How *are* you?" I whisper, not able to keep the concern out of my voice.

Her face pinches like I just asked if vampires were real. "I'm incredible. Never better. I've wanted to lose that weight for years. I feel amazing."

"Sure, yeah, you look great. But that was—"

"—That was Reva's will for me," she interrupts. "I recommend you don't talk about it if you can't be full of faith."

"Right, no, totally. I'm happy for you."

She smiles that huge smile again, stands, and goes upstairs, probably to retrieve Juniper.

I wasn't really planning to invite Dalice to a meeting, although I did waver at the hospital because of Cash's heart condition. But no way on earth I'm doing that now. Reva is a loose cannon, and I don't trust her.

No way I'm subjecting Dalice to this, and I have to find a way to leave.

# DALICE

**IT'S BEEN AN** entire week of hanging out with Shane, texting, and chatting on the phone.

I'm on shift at Pig Out Place and we're not supposed to check our phones, but I get a pass because I'm waiting for the transplant call.

A text from Shane is waiting for me. *When can I see you again?*

Butterflies in my stomach go ballistic.

*How about tonight?* I type.

I don't even care if I sound eager now. I am.

I shove the phone back in the pocket of my hoodie, which hangs on a hook in the back, but it vibrates right away.

The text says *Can't do tonight. I have a thing.*

*No problem. I'm at Pig Out Place tomorrow and Sunday. How about Monday night?*

*That works. Can't wait!*

I sigh like some Disney character in love and head back out to the floor, where I think I see Mickey in my section. But is that Mickey? She's so…thin. Much thinner than a week ago when I last saw her. Juniper leans into view, so I know for sure it's her.

"Mickey?" I ask, approaching the table.

"Hey! Yeah, course it's me." As if I'm silly for thinking otherwise.

Mickey gives Juniper an instructing look, and the girl sets her crayon down and smiles. Her hair hangs in loose curls today. "Hi Miss Dalice."

"Hi sweetie. I'll grab you guys some fries while you peek at the menu."

I start to go, but Mickey touches my arm. "You haven't texted me back. Is everything all right?"

*Shit.* I can't admit to Mickey that I always have my phone on me because of Cash, and that I've been texting with Shane like it's my full-time job, but I somehow don't have time to shoot her a one-line reply.

God, I'm the worst.

"Yes. Sorry about that. I must have done the thing where you reply in your head and forget to type."

"No worries! I was just checking in on you. Wanted to see how you and Cash are doing."

"Oh thank you. We're good. I'll be right back."

Back in the kitchen, I scoop fries and glance around for Kelly. I don't see her.

I slide into the booth across from Mickey and set down the fries. As long as my manager doesn't catch me, I'm fine.

I can't pass up this chance to pry into what used to be wrong with Juniper. I get that other people's success stories mean nothing at all regarding Cash's chances, but I still can't help being drawn to them and the hope they offer. And I have to find out how Mickey lost so much weight in only a week. What if she's anorexic?

But nope, she digs right into the fries.

Bulimic, then? None of my business, but I hope she's healthy.

She looks amazing. She was gorgeous before, but now the girl is dark-haired-Margot-Robbie levels of hot.

A flash of jealousy slaps me when I think of her being so close to Shane. Not only that, but it's like all the insecurity from high school rushes back in. As if her being overweight was some sort of equalizer between us, and now it's back to how it used to be. She's the popular girl who has become a real, live woman. Next to her, I'm a stupid, pink-haired kid posing as a woman.

What if Shane falls for her? My stomach sinks, but I shake the thought off. Truth is, if it happened, it would mean he wasn't worth shit to begin with. What, is he going to suddenly like a girl he's known for a long time just because she lost a bunch of weight?

Actually, yeah.

That's par for the dude-course. But Shane's not your average shallow guy. At least, that's what I hope. I want to believe he's not fueled by this superficial stuff, but my experience has proven otherwise when it comes to men. Plus, Mickey is sweet and genuinely seems like a good person. It's not just that she's hot.

But she is hot.

I can't stop staring at her.

Jesus, am *I* attracted to her?

Here I am getting all pre-pissed at Shane for pretend-choosing her over me when I can't stop checking her out.

"So…you look incredible," I say. "Different than a week ago."

I can't outright say *How the hell did you drop a small-child's weight in extra flab?* even though I want to.

"Skinnier, right?" She smiles and dips a fry in ketchup, then pops it into her mouth.

"Yeah, what's your secret?"

Mickey watches Juniper, who is coloring quietly again.

"I got healed."

"Of being overweight?"

I didn't realize it was a sickness.

"No, my self-esteem. The way I view myself. Healing starts as a truth in the heart, and then the body manifests it. The truth is that I'm beautiful, and once I could see it, accept it, my body had to obey. It made the truth come forward into the visible realm."

I squint, trying to make sense of that.

"But you were always *actually truly* beautiful, even before."

She laughs. "Aww, you're so sweet, but the issue was that I didn't believe it. Now I do."

She doesn't get what I mean, but it feels pushy to try harder to explain, and honestly, I can't wait any longer. I have to know about Juniper, even if I come off as some investigative reporter.

"Before the party, you said your daughter was sick. She's obviously not anymore. Do you mind me asking what she used to have?"

Mickey smiles again, like she was waiting for this question. "Course not. She was born with cystic fibrosis."

"Is that the lung thing? Sorry, I'm an expert at heart conditions, but that's about where my medical knowledge ends."

"Yeah. It's a disease that makes the mucus so thick, people have difficulty breathing. Juniper used to cough constantly, getting every sickness that came down the pipe. It always went straight to her lungs. She even had to wear this appliance that—well, it was awful."

I look at the girl and remember her running around at the harvest party. No issues at all. I'm happy for them, but I'm also jealous because I want it for Cash. It feels like I've never wanted anything in my life the way I want that for my Cashy.

"How's Cash's heart?" she asks, like she can read my motives.

"Oh, same old, same old. Waiting on a call for a heart transplant."

Mickey leans over and whispers, "She can heal him."

"Who?"

"Reva. She can do healing miracles. She's the one who healed my body, and she healed Juniper. You've got to meet her. There's absolutely nobody like her in the whole world. You're going to love her. Come to a meeting! There's one tonight."

Miracles.

Meetings.

God, it's more church talk. I keep forgetting they're religious, because Shane doesn't talk like that, and he seems so normal.

But wait. A meeting *tonight*? Shane said he had "a thing." Is it this? And if so, why wouldn't he invite me? Especially if they pray for healing. He's aware of Cash's heart.

It seems weird, but I set it aside for now, and ask, "Is it a church meeting?"

"No." Mickey laughs and leans back. "It's not organized religion. I wouldn't be involved if it were. Been there, done that!"

I relax a little.

"But I will say, it requires some faith in God. And we read the Bible. So, if you're anti all that, you might not like it."

I'm not *anti*. Not at all. I've just never been super interested in it, even though I'm a spiritual person. I believe in God and went to Vacation Bible School in the summer and Young Life camp as a high schooler. It's all the other stuff that usually tags along with religion—that's the yuck stuff. But she said it's not a church. And I'd probably get to see Shane. If I were to pro and con this thing out, that's a huge pro. Might even be worth three or four cons. But of course, the biggest pro is the possibility of Cash being healed. That's the entire pro column. Not sure there's a con in the world that can compare.

"I can handle that," I say.

"Well, then. You should come."

"What time?"

"Seven."

"Can I bring Cash along?"

It's a dumb question, because obviously he needs to be there to get healed.

"Definitely. Even if Reva doesn't pray over him tonight, that's okay. We have a nursery, and the lady who runs it is a retired RN. Not only that, but the kids are right upstairs, so if he needs you, you're right there."

I can't help wondering why this lady wouldn't heal him tonight, but I don't ask. Instead, I say, "I rarely leave him with anyone but my sister."

"Trust me, I understand! I was the same way with Juny. But Gina—that's the retired RN—knows so much, and the nursery has every first aid thing you can imagine, even a defibrillator."

Why would they need a defibrillator if this Reva lady can heal people?

My brain stalls on this question, but I don't want to do anything to make Mickey change her mind about inviting me to the meeting. I have the urge to say yes, but am I really going to do this? The pros are ginormous. But I don't really like the idea of "meetings," whatever they are. It sounds religious and boring, although it doesn't sound like *churchy* church. What if it's worse, though, like some fringe thing? But then again, what if I don't go? I'd be doing this, just sitting around and waiting for a heart transplant. At least If I go, I'm doing *something* while I wait. Even if nothing comes of it.

Yep, the pros have it.

I would do absolutely anything for Cash to have a chance at a normal life. Attending a weird meeting seems like a no-brainer. I can always leave if I'm uncomfortable. Plus, I'll get to see Shane. Maybe I'll even surprise him.

"We're in."

"**DID YOU SEE** this?" Ryan appears next to me in the kitchen at the end of my shift. Mickey is long gone.

I pull my hoodie on while Ryan reads out loud from his phone. "Huge storm. They're saying it might be like the ice storm Spokane had decades ago, but worse." He looks up. "Not that I remember way back then. I wasn't born yet. But my dad still has a mug that says *I survived Ice Storm 1996.*"

*Way back then*, I scoff to myself. I remember Ice Storm. I was eight or nine, I think. They canceled school. The power was out because ice had accumulated on the lines, and it was so heavy it pulled some down. A couple people even died.

I reach for his phone to read the article.

"Ryan, really? This isn't a news channel. It's some random dude making predictions. And some of them are questionable. Check it out: *EMP Attack on the U.S. Imminent. North Korea Buys Bitcoin.* Come on, this is garbage."

"Oh whoops, I should have checked into it more. My friend told me, and she was so freaked out that I just believed her."

"Is anyone else talking about it? You know, legit sites."

Ryan looks down to search on his phone. "Not that I can tell."

"I wouldn't worry about it, then."

# 1992

**THE NEXT MORNING,** Reva wakes up late and Mom comes in with some aspirin. She sits on the bed and places a warm hand on Reva's back. It's the first time in years Mom has shown her affection.

Maybe this is Reva's chance to find out more about the gold dust.

"Can I ask you a question?" Reva starts, as if asking a shark to open its mouth so she can check to see how sharp its teeth are today.

"Of course."

"How do you know about the gold dust?"

Mom stiffens but doesn't move away.

"My brother had it."

Reva can't help the sharp inhale that follows. So many more questions bang around in her brain, but first she wants to see if Mom will tell her more.

"Well, sort of," Mom adds. "For Rich, the gold dust showed up for days at a time, weeks if we were lucky, and then it'd be gone for years. When it was here, well, those were the best days." Mom sighs, tucks a strand of her hair behind one ear. "Dad would take time off work and load all four of us kids up in the Oldsmobile. He said Rich's healing gift was the family's calling. We'd take the road south to California, along the Oregon coast, looking for people to bless with his healing power." Mom pauses and her face turns up in a smile. She doesn't make eye contact with Reva, so it feels safe for Reva to smile too. "I remember Dad and Mom laughing in the front seat, my siblings and I playing road trip games in the back, while the baby sat on Mom's lap. The only time we all got along. Seeing Rich heal people was so…"

She stops and looks over like she forgot Reva was there. Her eyes are wet, and she wipes them fast, clears her throat, but doesn't finish her thought.

"I never knew you had a brother," Reva whispers. She knew about the others, all sisters, but not the brother.

Mom's chin lifts, and she stands. "Never mind that. The point is your uncle had it. That's how I know what it is."

"His gold dust came for a long time all at once?"

"Yes. And he couldn't turn it on and off like you can."

"I can't turn it on and off."

"What?" Mom crosses her arms.

Reva shakes her head, trying not to get emotional, because that will only make things worse. "It's true."

Mom softens unexpectedly and says, "That's strange. I thought for sure you were guiding it. You turned it on to heal that girl at school. You had no problem healing my alcohol addiction. You ministered at church. And unlike Rich, you're not very sick or tired afterward."

*But I am.* Reva wants to cry because the dull ache at the base of her skull still hasn't gone away even though she slept all night. She knows better than to argue.

"Did he get headaches?" Reva asks.

"Yes. And he would sleep for most of the day after ministering. Recovery was long, and he was very weak during that time. When the gold dust finally left, he'd sleep for days in a row."

Mom stands abruptly and strides into the kitchen, leaving Reva with more questions than answers.

So, what *is* the gold dust? Something passed down in families? And why her? Why did she get it?

Mom screams from the kitchen, so Reva rushes in there.

"I burned myself," Mom says, showing her palm. She's not crying. Doesn't seem upset at all. Just matter-of-factly burned herself when she's not even cooking anything. A single burner is on high, its coiled red glow mirrored on Mom's palm.

Reva opens her hands, and there's the gold dust. "What would you ask of me?"

Mom extends her wounded hand and smiles. "Good girl."

Reva touches her warm, golden palm to Mom's burn. When she pulls back, the red marks are gone.

**SINCE SHE MISSED** the bus, Reva walks to school along the narrow dirt road until she gets to the Newport Highway, which she must cross. Most parents wouldn't want their child crossing a busy five-lane highway, but of course Mom doesn't care.

Reva's head bangs like an old car engine, and it hurts to blink. Not even the aspirin Mom gave her helps. Her body slogs down the dusty road, and every step makes the ache grow. Tears blur her vision, but instead of giving in to them, she stuffs them down and lifts her chin.

*I'm a world changer. I'm helping people.*

Reva's shoe snags on an exposed rock and she trips. Dirt kicks up into a dust cloud, but she catches herself before going splat on the ground. Her head thrums harder, and she stands still, trying to get it to slow down. When it does, she brushes off her stained jeans and striped tee shirt and pushes her thick bangs out of her face.

Something is on the road ahead.

She can't make it out, but it looks like an animal. It's a gray lump. Roadkill, maybe?

No, it's moving a little. Reva runs to see even though her head jackhammers with every step.

It's a raccoon. A baby raccoon, by the look of it.

It's wounded, trying to move off the road but unable to. She can't tell how it's hurt, or where. It hisses at her when she tries to get close. It doesn't want her help, but she notices the gold dust on her hands.

Her headache tells her she shouldn't try to heal anything right now. But there's the raccoon, and since she may be able to help it, she really wants to.

The raccoon can't seem to move fast enough to hurt her, so she squats and touches its body with both hands, feeling for a wound until she finds a gash around the midsection. Its fur is soft; she's never pet a raccoon before. Her gold hands make a belt around its little waist. The gash disappears, replaced by more soft fur. She did it. She healed the raccoon!

But now that it's strong again, it's furious.

It hisses and whips its head back to bite her. If she lets go, it might be able to. She hangs on to it, trying to come up with a plan or some way to let it go and get away fast enough that it can't hurt her. The heat in her hands melts away until there's no heat at all.

Is the gold dust gone? She can't let go to look until she knows she's safe.

But she can't do this forever, either. At some point, she'll have to let it go and jump back.

Her hands tingle cold.

So cold, like grabbing handfuls of snow in winter with no gloves on. The raccoon calms down like it's falling asleep. This is her chance. She lets go and moves back fast. The animal doesn't move, but Reva's palms are still golden.

Did she make it fall asleep?

When it doesn't move for a few seconds, she gets close again to see. Nudges it gently with her foot to wake it up. But the only movement is the force of her foot pushing. She does it again, a little harder this time.

*C'mon buddy, you're all better now. Go find your family.*

When it still doesn't move, she gets on her knees on the rocky dirt road to see up close.

The raccoon's eyes are a milky white color. A little tongue lolls out of a gaping, baby-toothed mouth.

It's dead.

She gasps, and tears come.

Reva picks the baby raccoon up, cradles it, moves it off the road, as if this kindness will somehow make up for killing it.

But how did that happen? She had healed it. For sure, the animal was up on all fours, strong as can be.

When Reva returns to the dirt road, the aspirin must have finally kicked in, because her headache is gone. She feels so good that she sprints the rest of the way to school, her bookbag bouncing on her back.

# DALICE

**I PULL UP** to the closed gate at the big house in the woods, only to realize I don't have the code to get in. I shoot Mickey a text, half-expecting her to come out and open it for me, but she texts back the code. Guess now I know how to get in whenever I want? Doesn't seem totally secure, but then again, it'd be a tough place to rob with all those flood lights torching up the area like a prison yard.

Cash must have woken up at some point. He looks out the window, blue mouth a little O, binky in his fist.

"Remember this big house, Cashy? The harvest party?"

"Sticky appoh."

I exhale a little laugh. "Yep, you had a sticky apple here. Today, you're going to meet some new friends. Sound good?"

I watch him in the rearview mirror and wonder if staring at your child ever gets old. He doesn't even look that much like me, but I can never fill my eyes up to the brim. I always need more of him.

He slams the binky into his mouth and nods. Good, at least one of us is ready for this.

Mickey stands on the porch in her socks and without a coat, waiting for me to park. She folds her arms and does what resembles a potty dance, but I think it's probably an "I'm freezing cold" dance. I hurry to get Cash and save her from hypothermia.

"Heyyy! I'm so glad you made it!" she sings as I climb the stone steps.

"God, it's so pretty out here," I say as if the dozens of times I've already said it to her aren't enough.

"Oh! Take off your shoes," Mickey says.

When I sit down to do that, I try to take in as many details as possible without coming off like a tourist. It's this huge, open space, and there's a staircase on the right. The wood floors are honey-colored and polished. Floor-to-ceiling wallpaper covers the whole entryway—a charcoal gray, gold, and teal print. Not quite flowers, but also not totally geometric. It seems expensive, like a work of art.

That's as far as I get ogling because I can't help it, I only want to find Shane now. He appears in the kitchen at the end of the wide, wallpapered hall, and when he sees me, his mouth opens.

I can't say it's an excited-to-see-me face. Not at all.

What does that mean?

I give him a wincey smile, like "Surprise?" and he walks toward me.

Mickey's there helping me get Cash out of his puffer coat, and by the time Shane reaches us, she has Cash in her arms. She steps aside as if she's giving Shane and me privacy.

"Hey!" Shane says with a smile, and then he pulls closer to whisper, "What are you doing here?"

Oh God, I was right. He's not happy to see me. I've invaded. I'm an alien oozing into every corner of his life when he thought I was just a nice girl he could hold hands with and take out to dinner.

"Mickey invited me. Is that okay?" As if I'm genuinely asking for permission when obviously the deed is done.

Shane glances over at Mickey and she smiles. But it's not her usual huge grin. It's more like the one you'd give your brother if you just got him in trouble.

Only half a second passes, even though it feels like an hour, and Shane says, "Just a sec."

He goes to Mickey. His back is to me, so I can't hear what they're talking about, but it seems heated. I sneak up to Mickey and reach for Cash, mostly to get him away from whatever's happening. When I do that, they stop talking until I'm out of earshot again. They don't want me to hear what they're saying. That can't be good.

# SHANE

"**WHY IS SHE** here?" is all I can manage. I'm so pissed that it's hard to be nice.

"What do you mean?" Michaela says, with the most innocent look I have ever seen in my life.

"What do you mean, 'what do I mean?' Why'd you invite her?"

She squints at this, and I realize I'm coming across too anti. I dip my chin and try again with a softer tone. "How did this come about? Have you guys been in touch this week?"

Dang it, I still sound mad.

"Yes. In case you haven't noticed, she has a son who might die. Thought she was a perfect candidate. Plus, everyone knows you're off the deep end over her. You can't keep your eyes off her!"

*None of their business.*

"God is light; in Him, there is no darkness at all. If we claim to have fellowship with Him and yet walk in the darkness, we lie and do not live out the truth."

*You think they wouldn't find out that you're hiding little corners of darkness?*

I blink hard and try to focus on this conversation.

"Plus, it's all her doing," Michaela adds.

"Dalice's?"

"No. *Her.* Capital H. Maybe she doesn't trust you to procure anymore, so she's enlisted me."

Anger flares inside me, but I stay steady. What an idiot I was to think nobody would notice. I should have worked harder to keep my attraction a secret.

But also, why would Reva ask Michaela to procure? It's my job to bring newbies in. It makes no sense. Does she know I'm having doubts?

This is all my fault. Did I expect to be able to leave The Threshing Floor so Dalice and I could have some happily ever after?

I know that's not in the cards for me.

But why not? Why shouldn't I have some happiness?

I can't tell if I'm angrier at myself or Reva right now. Then a new thought makes my stomach drop: Reva must know about my feelings for Dalice too.

*Stupid. Stupid!*

I run a hand through my hair.

"You're stressed. You always do that with your hair when you're stressed," Michaela says. "Look, I don't know what's going on with you, but you can't listen to the enemy. The days are evil. There's a fight for our souls, and it's not the time to hold secrets from the family. All will come to light eventually, anyway."

"I know. I was going to invite her, but I was waiting for the timing to be right," I lie.

"Welp, newsflash, Reva thinks the timing's right, so it doesn't really matter what you think. And come on, she's doing you a favor. Either Dalice jumps right in and gets sealed to us, or she runs for the hills. Either way, don't you want to know whether she'll stick around before you completely lose your mind over her?"

"Way too late for that," I whisper, mostly to myself, but Michaela smiles, puts her hand on my shoulder, and leans in. "You know, Reva only wants you to be happy. She wants that for all of us, but not at the expense of our souls."

If Michaela only knew. The last thing Reva wants is for me to find the kind of happiness that might lead me away. Still, I can't do anything about Dalice now. She's here.

I must focus on what's bound to come next: Dalice going all in and getting sealed to the group. A son on the transplant list is motivation enough. Maybe I can persuade her not to volunteer.

Who am I kidding? That's not an actual plan. Dalice wants her son healed. I need a better idea.

# DALICE

**WHILE MICKEY AND** Shane are—fighting? Flirting? I don't know which—Renee approaches me.

"Hi, do you remember me? Renee from the harvest party."

"Yes, of course!" I try to focus on her, act like I don't care about whatever Shane and Mickey are discussing.

"I'm so glad you're here! Have you already met Reva?"

"Not yet, no." Cash squirms in my arms, silently asking to get down. I keep peeking over at Shane and Mickey, waiting for them to be done.

"She's Shane's sister," Renee whispers.

"Mickey?"

"What? No, Reva." Renee glances around. "But you can't tell anyone I told you. It took me forever to figure it out when I first started coming, and still, not everyone knows. Considering you and Shane are close"—she winks—oh God, she actually winks—"I thought you should know right away."

Why is this important information right now? Along with everything else that's happening, it's overwhelming. I know I need to respond to Renee, thank her or something, but I don't have time because Mickey pulls away from Shane and extends her arm out like she wants to lead me somewhere.

"Let's go upstairs and I'll introduce you to Gina and the nursery staff," she says. Shane's eyes find me, but his arms hang limp by his sides, and he doesn't move toward me.

God, they were practically hugging. Whispering. It was so intimate. Was it about me? Or was it about them, and they didn't want me to hear? I don't want to think about Shane having a thing for Mickey, but the thought floats to the top of the brain pile again. He wasn't very excited to see me today.

I get an urge to grab Cash's coat and leave, to escape this whole awkward scene, but I've missed my chance. Mickey turns at the top of the grand staircase, and I'd have to go up there to tell her I'm leaving, or yell it at her. Neither will make this less awkward.

I look at Shane again, trying to read something in his face, but he has a huge deer-stuck-in-headlights expression.

I take the few steps over to him and whisper, "Are you okay?"

"Yeah, totally. I'm great." His mouth turns up in a smile, but I don't trust it. The switch is too fast. "I'll save you a seat. We can sit with Michaela, too."

"Sounds good."

I want to press the issue, but this really isn't the time.

**GINA, THE RN** in the nursery, seems knowledgeable, and when I tell her about Cash's heart condition and the transplant list, she smiles and says she worked with a pediatric cardiologist for a few years.

Her warmth puts me at ease, and I'll be right down the stairs, so I reason that it's safe to leave Cash here.

For his part, Cash seems thrilled. He finds the wooden train set immediately, which is his current obsession. Brandy has one. In seconds, he no longer knows I'm alive, and it feels weird to stick around, like I'm some overbearing helicopter mom forcing organic snacks on everyone.

"Please get me for any reason. I'm nervous about leaving him."

"I got this, honey. And yes, I'll certainly find you if he needs anything."

Halfway down the steps, I see people are still wandering around, and there's a low level of chatter. I scan for Shane, but I only see Renee and some other girls I probably met at the harvest party, but don't remember. They wave to me, and I lift my hand in a tiny wave back.

Mickey stands with some redhead in the foyer, smiling at me.

"Dalice!" the redhead says, reaching for my hand. How does she know my name already? She has dimples and smiling eyes. She's shorter than me, and really nailing her look: high-waisted mom jeans paired with a thin cream-colored sweater that's snug, and brown ankle boots. Funny that she gets to wear shoes when Mickey was so adamant I take mine off. "I've heard so much about you. I'm glad you're here."

"Oh, thank you."

I haven't heard anything about her.

"This is Reva. She leads the meetings," Mickey adds.

Wait, what?

This is the Reva that Renee just told me about? The one who's also Shane's sister?

Has to be, because Reva is such an uncommon name, but this lady looks more like she could be his daughter. I want to ask about it, but I don't. I'm not supposed to know Reva is Shane's sister. But now that seems even weirder. Why is it a secret?

"Oh!" I finally recover from the split seconds of gawking. "So, this is your place? It's absolutely stunning."

"Thank you," she purrs, like I gave her the best compliment she's ever had. She tilts her head to the side and smiles. "I'm about to start the meeting, but I'd love to catch up soon and get to know you better."

"Yeah, sure. Sounds great."

Mickey pulls me away and my brain slows down to one-quarter speed, making the room move in slow-mo. I have to wait for everything to pick back up before I can speak, before I can find some appropriate words to say. Once Reva is out of earshot, a question surfaces.

"How old is she?" I ask Mickey.

"I don't know. In her twenties?"

Wait, but then how old is Shane? Is he that much younger than me? How? He's got a couple of silver strands in his hair. I want to escape to the bathroom to think and make all these connections. I can't do it here in front of them because I must keep my face smiley. But that doesn't stop my brain from trying.

"How old is Shane?" I ask, and immediately I know my tone is too eager, almost frantic.

Mickey raises her eyebrows and smiles like she knows a secret. *Shit.* I thought I'd done such a good job of hiding my interest, but I guess not.

"Forty-two. His birthday is in March." She turns to talk to someone else and Renee returns, so I can't sneak away to think this through. It's like they don't want to leave me alone or something, and I really want to be alone for a minute.

"She's half his age. A stepsister?" I whisper to Renee.

"No, uh-uh." Renee shakes her head. "His actual sister."

"But…how? Was their mom ancient when Reva was born?"

Renee gives an exaggerated shrug. "No idea."

But there's another thing. They look almost nothing alike. Shane's coloring is fair, and his hair is dark with some curl. Blue eyes. Reva has that auburn hair and big brown eyes. There are the freckles, though. They both have those, although Reva has way more.

Mickey turns her attention back to me, and Renee stands behind her, pursing her lips and shaking her head.

A reminder I'm not supposed to be talking about this. Or even know about it. I wonder if Mickey knows.

"Let's sit down," Mickey says, again taking my arm and pulling me along toward Shane, who sits in one of the chairs.

Shane watches me approach. I would think it's cute except that I'm so confused right now. Slightly pissed, too. Why didn't he tell me on the night of the harvest party that his sister lives here?

Wait, that means *he* lives here too, because he said he lives with his sister. Is this a big deal? We've hung out enough for him to tell me these things, and I've definitely asked him about his life. He changed the subject every time.

Doubts about Shane swirl in my gut, making me more irritated because I'm here for Cash. Now I have what feels like seventh-grade drama on steroids.

*Just get through this*, I tell myself.

# DALICE

**AS SOON AS** I get settled into my armless maroon conference chair, my shoulder grazes Shane's bicep and a rush of warmth courses through me. Great, just what I need right now.

*Focus. You're overreacting. Is he required to tell you everything in the first few weeks?*

No. We aren't even officially a thing. It feels like a big omission, yes, but what if he has a reason for it? I should give him the benefit of the doubt.

"All right everyone, let's take our seats and get started," Reva says, and people trickle in from the kitchen and foyer.

I take a deep breath and remind myself I'm here to find out about the healing thing. Need to keep my mind on that. I'll deal with the Shane thing later.

But he leans over and whispers, "Why didn't you tell me you were coming tonight?"

I can feel my eyes widen as all the Zen I just conjured flies out of me. He doesn't get to be confused about what I'm doing. Only *I* get to be confused right now.

"Do you not want me here?" I ask.

"It's not that. It's more—"

Reva stands in front of this massive fireplace, looking at us. I wait for Shane to finish his thought, but he looks at his folded hands instead.

"Okay, everyone turn to your neighbor and say 'Jesus is King.'"

Shane whispers again, while the room hums with the phrase. "This isn't for everyone. It's okay if it's not for you."

Before I can reply, a hush falls over everyone again.

He obviously doesn't want me here, but the bottom line is I'm here for Cash. If what Mickey said is real, and people can truly get healed, I'll do whatever it takes for my boy.

Doesn't Shane want Cash healed too?

I feel emotional because it seems like he doesn't. And I care way too much, because who am I kidding? I'm totally falling for him.

Next, the group chants something in unison. Reva calls it an "invocation."

That's when I notice all the chairs are situated around a single chair in the middle of the room. That chair is empty.

"Many of you know my history, but some of you don't," Reva says. "Before The Threshing Floor begins today, I want to share a bit about myself. I've always been a seeker, unsatisfied with what I knew. Craving more. My dad left when I was eight, and my mom was an alcoholic. Kids made fun of me because I was different, and so I was alone all the time. Loneliness is a disease, and if left untreated, it will destroy you. That's why we need each other."

It seems like she really cares about these people. I can feel it. There's this warmth coming from her.

"Many of you share some of that background, that history of being alone. Some of you, like me, even experienced abuse and neglect. The people who were supposed to care for us and be there for us, well, they weren't. They left us to figure everything out on our own and, as a result, life kicked us around and filled us with trauma. These circumstances don't define us. We can't let them. If you're sitting in this room, you're not alone. Period. Maybe you've been with us for years, or maybe this is your first time."

She looks at me and her mouth tugs up in a smile, then she returns to surveying the rest of the room.

"It doesn't matter, because you're here, and there's a reason. God brought you to this oasis in the desert. This refuge in the storm. This place where we can have genuine relationships instead of the kind most of the world experiences—people pretending to care only as far as it benefits them. We are a refuge for each other, exactly how God designed it."

Her tone. It's almost hypnotic. Slow, but smooth. Each word seems so heartfelt. I find it's easy to agree with whatever comes out of her mouth. God, who cares how old she is or isn't? She has something that I want, and it's not just the healing. She's magnetic.

I look around, and everyone else is as enraptured as me. Nobody fidgets. There's no whispering. Nobody even seems to be zoned out. They're here for it.

"So, we can trust each other," she continues. "We're all family here. Intertwined by the love of God and His promise of healing."

Next, she goes into this Threshing Floor thing. Something about harvest and chaff and crushing the wheat. Or maybe it was crushing the chaff? I'm not sure, but I don't have time to figure it out, because next she's asking for a volunteer.

Hands shoot into the air throughout the room. Every hand but mine and Shane's, actually. I turn to Mickey, trying to ask her with my eyes if this is the healing time. Turns out she's not raising her hand either, but she nods to answer my silent question.

Shane notices our telepathic conversation.

"Don't volunteer," he whispers.

"Why?" I whisper back, irritation flaring again.

"You're not ready."

Now I want to do it just to prove that I can. But I'm too slow. Reva chooses an older woman. This lady stands. The neckline of her yellow tee shirt stretches and dips below her collarbone, and there's a stain along the bottom that she tries to hide with her folded arms as she sits down in the empty chair. Her long hair is half up, but gray roots expand across her crown as if she hasn't colored it in many months.

"What's happening? Is Reva going to heal her?" I whisper to Shane.

Shane puts a finger to his lips, shushing me as if I'm a child and it's all right for him to whisper, but not for me. Renee stares at me from across the room, her eyes wide, and there's a warning inside there somewhere, but I don't know what. She might be telling me to shut the fuck up, but in nice, Renee-style eyeball words.

"Lorraine. Thank you for volunteering," Reva says. "The Lord has something special for you today." And then, to the group: "All right, who wants to start us off?"

There's not even a breath of hesitation. Some guy on Mickey's side of the room speaks up. "You're controlling, Lorraine. It's disgusting to the Lord."

I startle and whip my face toward Shane. I want to ask him if that really happened. But before I can, Mickey speaks. "You're annoying. The way you always walk up to people in conversation and say 'What are you guys talking about?' in the middle of a story is self-centered, very un-Christlike."

Mickey's face. It's so hard. Not like her at all, but she doesn't seem mad, not exactly. More like she's detached.

What is going on right now? That poor lady, Lorraine. She's not crying. She just sits there, taking it.

"Sometimes it seems like you enjoy conflict, Lorraine. You can't let things go. You keep bringing up an issue until the other person has had it. You force people into impatience, causing them to sin," someone says.

"Your poverty mentality dictates your decisions in life. The core belief that you're white trash keeps you from being useful to the Lord," another person says.

"You can't even pick out clothes that match," a woman says.

Shane's head hangs down, his hands folded, elbows on his knees. Is he praying? This is so fucked up, and I can't even get past that one thought to determine what the point of it all is. It goes on and on. They tell her she's naïve, she's not very bright. They say awful, terrible things, sometimes even contradictory things. Like how can you be naïve but also scheming? How can you be a loudmouth but also keep to yourself too much? It's beyond me.

I need to get out of here because this is super creepy. My eyes follow a pathway through the chairs to the foyer where I can get Cash and leave. But it would cause a huge disruption, and what if they get mad and put me in that seat?

I try to catch Shane's attention, but he's watching Lorraine now.

How can he be a part of this? I thought he was kind. This doesn't seem like him at all.

The strangest part—well, beside the fact that they're roasting this poor lady for no reason—is that none of them seem upset. They're like mean machines, no heart behind what they're saying. They seem blank, numb.

This drags on until, finally, Lorraine cries. And it's around this time that the room breaks out into a quiet gibberish-chant that grows in volume until everyone is yelling one word at Lorraine repeatedly: "Trash! Trash! Trash!"

The air grows thin, and I feel like I can't catch my breath. My heart is a thunderstorm inside my chest. Shane must be able to tell, because he puts his hand on my back, but no, I don't want him to touch me right now. I stiffen and lean forward, trying to send him the message to leave me alone. He removes it quickly. At least he can take a hint.

Reva breaks in, lowering her hands repeatedly to get the group to be quiet.

"That's what the world sees, isn't it, Lorraine? That you're trash. But that's not what I see. I see a vessel of love, useful in these evil days. What would you ask of me?"

Lorraine wipes tears from her face, clears her throat. "I brought my granddaughter. She fell on the playground and broke her arm. She's in a cast upstairs."

Reva smiles, and her eyes light up again. "Sweet Lorraine, always thinking of others. Go get her."

Lorraine barrels out of the seat and runs up the stairs, even though she's probably in her sixties.

So, Reva's going to heal the granddaughter? Or are they going to say horrible things to the girl? If they do that, I'm out. I don't even care.

The girl Lorraine returns with is probably about ten. A purple cast covers her entire arm, even over the elbow. The girl looks scared, but Lorraine leads her to the middle and points to the chair, then stands behind it with her hands on the girl's tiny shoulders.

"Hi honey, what's your name?" Reva asks, bending down in front of her.

"Nikki."

"Nikki. Such a cute name. I want you to close your eyes, okay, baby?"

Nikki nods and does it. Reva closes her eyes too, lifts her hands up until her arms fully extend, and when she brings them down, I blink to clear my vision.

Her palms are golden.

Like some bronze statue.

What the ever-living fuck?

She grips the cast with one hand and holds the girl's hand with the other. After a few seconds, she lets go and takes a step back.

A high-pitched whirring sound comes to life next to the girl. It's some guy with what looks like a cast saw. Holy cow, they own one of those?

The cast comes off.

Nikki seems tentative at first, but at Reva's instruction, she extends her arm and then brings her fist back up to her shoulder. She whips her face up to meet her grandma's smile. "It's better," she says.

No way this is staged. It's not staged, right? Because if it is, this girl is Millie Bobby Brown circa 2016 levels of acting. She should be in Hollywood receiving Academy Awards, not in Spokane, Washington.

Grandma Lorraine leans down to hug the girl. Everyone speaks all at once, but it's not English. It's that gibberish from before. I don't know what language it is, but some people are sort of singing. Shane does it too, but more quietly.

Mickey stands with arms raised, crying. The rest of them follow, arms straight up, and they bow fast, almost compulsive.

Standing ab crunches—something you'd see on a wall Pilates app. Shane doesn't get up, so I don't either.

That was weird, not gonna lie. But the fact is, she did it. Reva healed that girl.

Then it's over. Reva dismisses everyone for coffee and cookies in the kitchen, like we just finished a book club meeting. I stay still next to Shane.

I make a conscious choice to swallow down everything else that I thought was fucked up about the meeting. None of that matters, because it's true. Reva can heal people.

*Cash.*

My boy comes to mind, and I feel like I'm crawling out of my skin with hope and excitement.

"She did it. She healed that girl," I say, turning to Shane.

"Yeah." He refuses eye contact. "Reva's record is a hundred percent."

He's not excited about it. What's his deal?

"Can she heal anything?"

He nods.

"Like terminal stuff, too?"

"Terminal stuff, too."

"I'm asking her to heal Cash." I stand up.

"Right now?"

"Why not?"

"She only heals after a threshing."

I sit back down. "But Cash. He could—" I don't finish my sentence. I don't want to say the word *die*, so I swallow it down and lift my chin. "Well, next time I'm volunteering. For Cash."

"It's not that simple," he says, defensive.

"Seems that simple!"

Shane sighs. "Trust me, it's not. She decides when you're ready."

"But Lorraine volunteered."

"Everyone always volunteers. You can volunteer until you're blue in the face, but if she doesn't think you're ready, she won't choose you."

It's like Shane is hoping that will happen. That I won't be chosen. I clench my jaw, and an overwhelming rush of disappointment and anxiety hits me so hard that I'm shaking. I want to cry, but I can't do that here, and I can't stop it from coming, so I stand up. If Cash isn't getting healed, then why the hell am I still here?

# DALICE

"WAIT UP," SHANE shouts behind me. I'm almost to my car and it's dark outside, but the lights inside the house provide enough for me to see by. Cash lays his head on my shoulder. If he can tell I'm stressed, he doesn't care. He's too tired.

Shane followed me upstairs to the nursery, but I ignored him. I got Cash and left before anyone else could catch me on the way out.

It's not that I don't want to talk to Shane. I have ten million questions. It's more like my body is shouting that it's had enough for one day, and I'm afraid I'll really lose my shit if I stay for one more moment, or if I even utter a single word. I need to be home. Get into comfy clothes, put Cash to bed. Process this in silence.

"Please, wait." Shane puts a hand on my car door like he's going to prevent me from opening it.

I move to the back door and work on buckling Cash in. What if this was too much stimulation for him too? What if they did weird shit up there, same as downstairs? But Shane would have told me if Cash were in danger. Right?

Maybe. Maybe not.

I don't know.

I want to feel justified in not trusting him, I really do. I want this to be black and white, but it's not. I've seen Shane with Cash. I honestly don't think he'd endanger my son. But still.

"Let me explain," he says as I close Cash's door. He's still leaning against mine.

"May I have your permission to get into my car?" I fold my arms.

Shane moves back and I slide into the driver's seat, pull the door shut, and start the car like he's not even there.

He shoves his hands into his pockets, giving up.

Thoughts battle with each other in my mind.

*That was beyond fucked up.*

*But the girl got healed.*

*But what the hell? This is what Shane's involved in?*

*Cash could get healed, too. You just have to be ready, whatever that means.*

Next time. Next time I'll be ready.

I pull out and leave Shane standing there in the cold, watching me go.

I can't believe I'm considering going back. I shouldn't. But I'm afraid that the possibility of Cash being healed is like elastic tying me to this place, and no matter how hard I try to leave, it'll snap me back.

**I TUCK CASH** into bed. So far, I've successfully not replied to three of Shane's texts. It's pushing ten at night, and his messages are pulling me, demanding a reply. Especially since he keeps offering to explain, and I really want an explanation.

Another text comes through.

*Sorry I keep bugging you. Last one. There's another meeting on Tuesday, Halloween. There will be candy and games for the kids upstairs. If you want to come over early, I can make you dinner and explain everything.*

What the hell? After acting like he didn't want me there tonight, then practically chasing me down when I left, he's inviting me to another meeting? I want to scream. This is so confusing.

*Make me dinner at YOUR SISTER'S house, you mean???*

I type and send, but I instantly regret it. Should have stayed strong in the ghosting stance.

*No, my place. I have an apartment above the garage.*

I type and delete a million times until I've muddled out a decent response.

*I want Cash's healing, but I need a few days to decide for sure if I'll come back. Not sure I can after what I saw tonight.*

I groan. It's not a total lie. I *should* take my time because it was so messed up, but there's no way I won't be going back. Not when there's a chance Cash could get healed. I'm still mad about all of Shane's withholding, though, so I don't want him to know that I've decided to go back yet.

*Don't come to the meeting then! We can go do something else.*

Nope.

More confusion.

I cannot with Shane right now. He's wavering like a daisy in a hurricane. I set the phone down.

My bedroom is dark because Cash is asleep in the crib next to my bed. I check my phone settings, make it so Shane's notifications are silenced, but Seattle's wouldn't be, then set the phone on my nightstand. Climbing across the bed, I grab the edge of my duvet cover that was tossed aside, pooling on the floor, and get in, pulling the blanket over my head.

I can't process this now. I just want to go to sleep and forget about it.

# 1999

**SHANE'S EIGHTEENTH BIRTHDAY** is today, and Mom made him a small cake.

At sixteen, Reva has been ministering publicly for years. She accepts the gold dust as a part of her life, a special gift from the Lord. Healing people is very rewarding, and it brings something to life inside of her.

If only it didn't make her so sick.

Mom moved them out of Trailer Trash Town and into a nicer neighborhood than Reva's ever lived in. She also bought a new blue minivan.

Now Reva ministers alone on the stage while Pastor sits in the first row. She understands a lot more about her gift, her calling, but she still worries before each session that the gold dust won't show up. After all these years, she still doesn't know exactly what triggers it, but praying always helps. She wishes it was a knob she could turn on and off.

Mom keeps Reva at home when she's not ministering, and she spends most of her time in her room. Mom doesn't want Reva infected by the outside world. It's not like Mom locks her in, although that has happened before when Reva made her mad. Mom left her there for days.

Since she and Shane have their own rooms now, it didn't really affect him, although he sneaked her candy and notes when he could. CDs, too. Reva decided that would never happen again. She would stay in her room willingly from now on. It's not like she has friends, anyway.

She's used to being alone, but it would be better if she had at least one friend. She wonders if Shane could be that person for her. They've grown closer, but he's still so preoccupied with his own friends. There are some evenings when he's home, and the music plays loudly in his room. Reva raps gently on the door, and Shane lets her come in and sit on a beanbag and listen to music with him. She lets him talk about the bands and the lyrics. His whole face lights up, and she wishes she could make someone's face light up like that. It won't be Shane, because he's moving out in a few months when he graduates.

Mom hasn't gone to the bars since that day Reva healed her. All she does is read her Bible and make phone calls to set up healing meetings. Sometimes they drive to different churches, and they've gone as far as the Seattle area. Whenever they're home together, Mom treats Reva like a ghost—something she doesn't really believe exists unless she needs healing. Which she often does.

Reva's bedroom has become her sanctuary. She checks books out from the school library and hides them from Mom because Mom says she can only read other books in equal proportion to how much she reads the Bible. That's impossible. How would she ever read a whole novel? She can't read the Bible that long without getting bored.

Right now, she's reading *How to Win Friends and Influence People*. It could help her social life, and maybe that's a childish thing to care about, but she can't be alone forever. If she could figure out how to relate to people better, she could be normal, because she's not ugly anymore. Her thick hair has strands of sparkly dark auburn mixed in with the red, and she likes to braid two tiny pieces to frame her face. Not only that, but she finally talked Mom into paying for braces, and although metal still covers her teeth, they're already much straighter. Her face is clear, and with a little makeup, she is pretty.

Shane doesn't want to be here tonight even though they're celebrating him. He keeps eyeing his watch, and whenever

Reva tries to talk to him, his answers are short. Mom doesn't know he invited Reva to hang out with him and his friends after this. The possibility of making Mom mad is real, and that makes Reva nervous. Shane said he'd take care of it. Shane's friends are good kids; they're into sports and have good grades. Mom likes them.

"Turn off the lights!" Mom calls from the kitchen.

Reva reaches over and switches off the light, putting the three of them in darkness except for the glow of a single candle. It illuminates Mom's smiling face as she wanders toward the table singing "Happy Birthday."

She's a different mother to Shane than she is to Reva. For one, she's never made Reva a birthday cake. Shane is the only one who remembers her birthday, and he brings home a cake from the bakery at the grocery store where he works. She should probably be mad at Mom about this, the unfairness of it. But Reva understands that she's different. Set apart. Mom sees her gifting, and that matters. She focuses on this any time the anger tries to push from inside.

The candle shine transfers to Shane's face when Mom sets the cake in front of him. He doesn't smile, but his eyebrows are up, so he's not mad either. He wants to make Mom happy like usual, but there's tension in the room too that Reva can't figure out. It's more than Shane being eager to go out with his friends tonight.

He blows out the candle and Reva turns on the light before anyone asks her to. Mom is right there with a knife, ready to cut the cake.

"It's warming up outside, Reva. I think we should go downtown and set up a prayer station when Shane leaves."

Reva looks over at Shane. Has he not told Mom yet?

"She's coming out with us. It's my birthday." Shane's voice is hard.

"Well, I know it's your birthday, but the Holy Spirit doesn't always fit into our schedule, and we can't only obey His promptings when it's convenient for us."

Reva can't go downtown and pray over people. They had a big meeting at the church only last night, and she's still recovering.

She hasn't ever tried to minister this soon afterward. Not only that, but it's not warm. The snow is melting, but it's still coat weather.

Shane exhales. "Well, I promised she'd be there tonight because...one girl is bringing a neighbor who...has cancer." He's a terrible liar, and the hesitation in his tone announces that he's feeling his way around a lie. "The Lord told me to have Reva pray over her."

"Really?" Mom says in a singsong tone, and her brows and mouth both lift as she smiles. She works the knife into the cake, cutting the first slice, and when she goes to wedge the knife underneath to move it to a plate, she slips and cuts herself. "Ouch!"

Reva is about to stand up to go heal her, but Shane extends his arm to tell her to stay put. He gives her a sideways glare. There's that anger again. But why is he mad?

"I'll get you a bandage, Mom," he says, putting his hand on Reva's shoulder as if telling her to stay.

When he leaves the room, Mom's icy glare shrinks Reva down, but she says nothing. Shane rummages around the bathroom nearby, but he keeps talking. "Mom, you're not the only one who sees Reva's gifts. Or the only one who hears from the Lord."

Mom's face softens. She likes it when Shane acknowledges Reva's gift.

He returns, and Mom seems fine with a bandage for her cut, so Reva relaxes.

"Okay, Shane. You take her, and if the Lord moves, head downtown. There are always so many lost people down there."

"Sure thing." But Shane doesn't sit back down. Instead, he grabs his coat.

"Already? You haven't even had a piece of cake." Mom's voice is full of disappointment.

"Yeah, sorry, it looks great. I'll have some when I get home." And then to Reva, "You ready?" He nods toward the door.

It's too early. His friends aren't expecting them for at least another hour, but Reva understands. He's trying to leave before Mom changes her mind, which is a definite possibility. Reva's not ready, and at least needs to change into the new Doc Martens she got last week. They're going out of style, but she's wanted a pair for years and they never had the money before.

"Just a sec," she says and runs into her room.

With her door open, she can hear them talking.

"You know, I better take her downtown instead," Mom starts. "I really feel the Lord telling me that Riverside Street is where she needs to be ministering."

Where are Reva's stupid boots? She's chucking everything out of her closet, searching for them.

"Reva, let's go!" Shane calls out.

She looks at her feet. Low-top Converse. Boring. But if she doesn't get going, she'll spend the night ministering outside with Mom, and then what? Sleep all day tomorrow? What sort of headache would two nights of ministering in a row create? She can't do it. Plus, she wanted to try out some tips from the *How to Win Friends* book on Shane's friends. The easiest seems like "Give honest and sincere appreciation." Compliments. She can do that. She observes plenty about people, she just needs to say it out loud.

But what if she can't find anything she likes about someone?

Well, then she'll make something up and turn it into the truth in her own mind. Easy.

Forget the Docs, even though her low-rider jeans and flannel would look so much better with them. At least her hair and makeup are done.

Reva rushes out of her room and finds Shane already outside, starting up his big green and white Bronco. It's old, but he bought it with money he made working at the grocery store.

Mom stands on the porch, arms folded, watching Shane while Reva slips on her jean jacket. When Reva walks by, Mom grabs her arm and holds her bandaged finger up. "Real quick."

"We gotta go!" Shane shouts from the car.

"Sorry, the gold dust isn't here," Reva says and pries Mom's fingers off her arm. She's still trying to avoid making Mom mad, even if it's probably too late.

Reva opens the Bronco door and steps up to the front seat, and Shane shoves a CD into the player. It has "Grunge Mix" written on it in black Sharpie—his handwriting.

He doesn't say anything, but seems back to his normal self now, excited to listen to music together. She still doesn't know what that was all about or why he wouldn't let her heal Mom's finger.

Reva glances out the window to see Mom holding her finger like it's precious, then she uses her good hand to make a circular motion with her fist, asking Reva to roll the window down.

Reva does it but watches Shane the whole time. The corners of his mouth turn up, then he winks. Shane can handle Mom, and once he decides to do something, he doesn't back down.

"Don't corrupt her with that nasty music you listen to!" Mom shouts at Shane.

He stalls before he drives off, then he cranks the music. It's "Disarm" by The Smashing Pumpkins, so Billy Corgan's voice is the only answer Mom gets. It's so loud that the Bronco is like a traveling concert.

"It's just Jars of Clay, Mom," he shouts.

Mom yells something else, but they don't hear it. Shane backs out of the driveway and Reva leaves her window open, as if that somehow signals neutrality.

He straightens out the Bronco, and it's pointed down the street, but he stops and leans over Reva's lap, so his face points at the open window. He shouts, "Sorry Mom, can't hear you over the music. See ya later!"

Then he peels out.

## 1999

SHANE GIVES REVA a devilish smile and turns the music down. Reva rolls the window up.

"This isn't Jars of Clay," she says.

"Duh."

"You lied to her."

"Who cares? She's such a control freak. You don't have to do what she says all the time, you know."

"I want to obey the Lord, and she helps me."

"Jesus, Reva, listen to yourself talk. You're sixteen, but you act like you're still nine."

"You think I act like a baby?" She can't keep the hurt feelings out of her voice. Is this true? It pricks at her, because Shane's the closest thing she has to someone who cares about her.

Shane groans, tucks long curls behind one ear. "I didn't mean it like that. I meant you're not a kid anymore and you can push back sometimes. Teenagers are supposed to rebel a little. It's what we do."

Reva can't figure out what to say, and when she doesn't answer, Shane keeps talking. "Can you control it?"

"Control what?"

"You know. Your powers. Do you get to decide when it comes and goes?"

"They're not powers, it's a gift from the Lord."

"Whatever. You should try to figure out how it works. Then you'd have more of a say in your life."

"How?"

"Really?" Shane glances at her, and then back at the road. "You're not dumb. Can't you see? Because then you would be in charge. Not Mom. *You.*"

"The Lord is in charge."

Shane rolls his eyes. "Okay, fine, the Lord is in charge. But you have this amazing ability, and you need to have your discovery sequence, like Superman. The pages of the comic book where he's learning how to harness his X-Ray Vision and his Super Strength so he can help people better. Trial and error. Best part? If you could control the gold dust, Mom wouldn't be able to take advantage of you."

"She's not taking advantage of me." The words come out tense, and it surprises her. She's never been truly angry with Shane before. And she's never really had to defend Mom, of all people. But this is too much. Mom is distant, and yes, Reva gets upset with her sometimes, but Mom is helping her fulfill her destiny.

"You really have your head in the sand," Shane says. "How do you think we could move out of the trailer park? Did Mom suddenly get a high-paying job? Did that brand-new minivan fall out of the sky and into our driveway? Do they give out free braces to teens because they're cute? How about those Doc Martens you got? They don't sell those at Kmart, you know."

His gaze alternates between her and the road, and when he looks at her, he narrows his eyes like when they did the birthday cake.

"No."

"No. Mom charges people to come to your meetings. She's been doing it since the very first one. How on earth have you never noticed this?"

It takes the wind out of her, but instead of gasping like she wants to, she stares straight ahead. She hasn't noticed because Mom keeps her in the car until the services start. Shane knows that. Mom doesn't want Reva to have any outside influence, especially right before she ministers. So, she never talks to anyone beforehand, and Mom shuttles her away immediately after.

"If you could discover the limits of your powers, what you can and can't do, you wouldn't be anyone's circus sideshow. Or meal ticket," Shane says.

Words still don't come to her because she's trying to make sense of everything he's already said, but also, it's easy to believe this is what Mom does.

"It's worse than that, too." Shane does a head check and changes lanes. He's so much better looking than she is. Like he could be famous. He got all the good genes, and she got the gold dust. "She hurts herself on purpose."

"What?"

"Yep," he dips his head once, slowly.

Reva's insides steel up. She flexes her stomach to hold a feeling in. It's dark. She can't let it out.

"But why?" she whispers.

Shane presses his lips together. "After you heal people…they feel…good."

"Good? Like…?"

"Good. Full of energy, like you can take on the world. Or as if your body is superhuman. That night when you healed my wrist years ago, I could barely fall asleep at bedtime. I wanted to go run the school track to see if I was faster than normal."

So, people feel good after she heals them, but she's in pain.

It's not fair, and this knowledge digs deep into her. How could Mom use her like this? Does Mom even believe she's special? Or is Reva a circus sideshow like Shane says, there to make Mom money, to make her feel *good*?

The song ends and "Jeremy" by Pearl Jam starts. She's familiar with it, but it seems darker than it has in the past. Like it's reaching into her and needling something that's been sleeping in a dark cave.

Mom says that can happen with music, that it can open the door to the devil.

*Why does what Mom thinks pop into my mind like that?*

The inky spot inside of her expands, and Reva's heart beats faster. She can't shake what Shane said, and the song calls to her, pulling, tugging at whatever angry thing lives inside. As if it's saying "I see you buried deep down there. Come out, come out, wherever you are."

She turns the knob, making the music as loud as it was earlier. It fills the space between her and Shane, and it gives her courage.

"Nice," he says, and then starts gently head banging. "Sounds like he's saying 'Jeremy *Spokane, Spo-kane*' at the end of this one, huh?"

He's taking it like she's trying out rebellion. And maybe she is, but she can't show him this black hole inside of her. The way everything he told her feeds it, stirs it awake.

*Figure out how to control the gold dust.*

That's what she needs to do, like Shane said. Then she'll take charge of her own life.

Having this little seed of a plan helps calm her enough to enjoy the rest of the evening.

Still, the thought lingers: *How could Mom do this to me?*

# DALICE

**I GAVE IT** a good college try. Really, I did. I considered not going back to the meetings and cutting it off with Shane, placing all my hope for Cash's future on the impending heart transplant.

I double-checked our hospital go bag. Made sure the duffel had anything we may need for a few weeks—or months—in Seattle, depending on how long Cash's recovery would be.

But then I broke down yesterday, the day before the Halloween meeting. I dumped everything out of the bag and kicked it. I have no clue when Cash will get a heart transplant. It's been crickets from Seattle. We're in this weird limbo land. Cash seems fine right now, but he's only ever fine until he's not, and that's a ticking time bomb. Yet he's still considered low priority. For that to change, for him to get bumped up on the list, he'd have to get even sicker, which I don't want. If that happened, we'd be living in the hospital (and the Ronald McDonald House for me, bless them).

Bottom line is he may not even receive a heart in time. There are no guarantees.

After I put the go bag—and myself—back together, my brain went right back to the meetings.

*What's the harm in hearing Shane out?*

He gave me the space I asked for. Didn't text me once even though I really missed hearing from him. It's just dinner at his place. And if I don't like what I hear, I can always leave before the meeting.

Why do I delude myself? After breaking down over the heart transplant and Cash's chances, I know I'm going to the meeting no matter what Shane says. I must try.

Now Cash and I are in front of Shane's garage door. I remembered the code to the gate even though it was super weird to enter it as if I live here. The garage door opens, and he waits at the inside door in a long-sleeve tee and jeans. His hair is a little rumpled.

"Hi," I say, walking into the garage, carrying Cash.

"Thanks for coming. I made spaghetti. Pretty basic," Shane says to me, but waves to Cash. Cash reaches for him, leaning hard away from me. Interesting how quickly Cash has taken to Shane. He typically lets anyone hold him, but he *reaches* for Shane.

I want to get right into it, grill him. But we haven't spoken for a few days and it's a little awkward. I follow him up the stairs to the apartment, and we say nothing else while we climb. Cash peeks over Shane's shoulder at me and smiles around his binky.

I fucking love this kid.

Once we're in the loft area, I glance around. It's sparse, without much in the way of decorations. God, Shane has a lot of records. And piles and piles of CDs. They're stacked up on the floor next to an overfull bookshelf. Records are vintage and cool, so I get why he'd have those, but does anyone even listen to CDs anymore? I observe the kitchen is clean, which is a relief. I may have loads of clutter at my place, but I scrub my sink, and my toilet is clean. I do have standards. Still, his place is much nicer than mine.

"Do you have peanut butter and bread?" I ask.

"Yeah, why?"

"Cash won't eat spaghetti, unfortunately."

"No worries." He gets the peanut butter out of the fridge and sets a loaf of bread on the counter. "Jam?"

"Yes, please." I work on the sandwich and steal more glances around. He sits Cash at the kitchen table. I better hurry, or that boy will be TP-ing Shane's bathroom.

"This place is nice," I say, whipping the knife across the bread while Shane dishes up spaghetti. "Looks like you got the shaft though, compared to the rest of the property."

"It works. I'm not very high maintenance."

"Not like your sister?" I shoot him a look when I set the plated sandwich down in front of Cash. "You know, the mansion, the Rover, the iron gate."

"Okay, I can explain."

"All ears."

He sets the two plates down on the table and motions for me to sit. "Do you want something to drink?"

"Bourbon, straight up. Three fingers, please."

"Hilarious."

"Worth a try. Water's fine."

He brings over a glass of ice water and sits down.

I clear my throat and glance at Cash, who picks at the sandwich I forgot to cut up. "I get to ask the questions," I say, reaching for a butter knife.

"Oh-kay?"

"Is that a question? Because I'm asking the questions."

"No. Sorry, go ahead."

I turn from Cash's sandwich to face him, then lower my voice. "What the fuck, Shane?"

"Is that your first question?"

"No. I mean yes. What was up with how they trash-talked that poor woman? And is your sister some witch? Gold hands—is that real? It feels like you hid the fact that she's your sister from me. I asked about your family, and you were dodgy. Also, how old is Reva? She looks way too young to be your sister. Your daughter? Okay, but not your sister. And to own all this property and this mansion in her twenties? How? Why are you involved in all of this?"

Shane's cheeks puff up with air, and then he releases it with a big exhale. He waits like he thinks I'm not done.

"Do you want me to pick any of the above questions to start?" he asks.

"No. Answer the one about why it's necessary to verbally abuse someone like that. I don't understand."

He nods like he's happy I chose an easy question. "Reva says that's how it works. For someone to have the capacity for healing, they must be cleared of anything that might stand in the way. The chaff."

"And you do that by saying mean things to each other?"

Cash reaches for my glass of water, and I lean over to help him take a drink.

"That's why I didn't invite you."

My frustration shifts, latches on to this.

"Why? Because I'm not good enough?"

"No!" He messes with his hair. "Not that. I—I just…"

"I'm a big girl. I could handle random strangers saying shitty things about me. I mean, people I actually care about say shitty things about me all the time. I don't need your protection. And if it's real—if your sister really can heal Cash, then I don't care about anything else. You must understand that."

Shane twirls noodles into a spoon, then takes a clean bite. It's the correct way to eat spaghetti, even though I never eat it like that. I pick up my spoon so I remember to do that when I go to take a bite. So far I haven't touched my food, but Cash is making quick work of his sandwich.

"Is Reva really your sister?"

"Yes."

"How many years apart are you?"

Shane closes his eyes and groans. This is the question he was apparently dreading. "Eighteen months."

"No," I say. "No fucking way she's in her forties. For real, is she some witch?"

Shane laughs softly. "No. I've never heard of a witch who could actually perform miracles. Have you?"

I shrug. I'm no witch expert. No miracles expert, either. "Why do her hands turn gold?"

"They just do. That's how she heals. She can't do it unless the gold dust appears."

"Does she make it appear?"

"No. She can't control it like that. The Threshing Floor makes it appear. Once the ritual is complete, and the chaff is gone, her hands turn gold. But..."

I wait. When Shane doesn't continue, I can't hide my frustration. "But what, Shane?"

"But she never used to need The Threshing Floor when we were young. She used to simply heal people. And I don't know what to make of that. It never bothered me before, but lately, everything about The Threshing Floor bothers me."

What am I supposed to do with this information? It seems really important to him, but I'm not up to speed enough to understand the significance or to ask him to explain it. There's really one thing I need to know, and I can't help my impatience.

"How do I get her to heal Cash?"

"You can't get her to do anything. It's like I said, she decides when you're ready, and she chooses you."

I hate that answer, but I realize it's the best I'm going to get, so I take a bite of food.

"So you think she doesn't need The Threshing Floor in order to heal?"

"No idea. But I know she won't do it. People have tried. She usually cuts them off when they push too hard. She's sensitive about being taken advantage of."

"How can she lollygag around when there's a little boy in her home with blue lips who clearly needs healing? It seems so—"

"Selfish," he completes the sentence.

"Exactly."

"I don't have the answer to that. If you want Cash to get healed, you have to do it the way she wants it done. And that's on her own timetable."

I sigh loudly. I hate dead ends that I have to accept, yet here we are.

On to the other items on my agenda.

"You knew about Cash," I say. "Why didn't you tell me about Reva's gift when we were in the hospital?"

Shane closes his eyes slowly. "Because, while I absolutely want Cash to get healed, I don't want you to go through The Threshing Floor."

I drop my fork on the plate and it clatters. "Why?"

"Something happens when she heals people. I've only felt it once when I was really young. But it makes people want more. Like they get addicted, and then they're easier to control."

"But I don't care about any of that if it means Cash can get healed."

"I understand. But I still worry about what might come *after* Cash's healing."

"He gets to live a long and happy life. Unless there's something else you're not telling me."

Shane doesn't respond, and fire rises inside me, but I fill my mouth with spaghetti to avoid letting it out.

"I don't know anything for sure," he says. "Just that things have been weird at times."

"Well, that's not enough reason for me to change my mind about Cash. So, let's switch to the other thing you're keeping from me. Why does Reva look young enough to be your daughter?"

"I think it has something to do with her gifting. She tells people she's twenty-one to hide it, and she doesn't want anyone to find out I'm her brother—again, to hide it. I've never asked, because I don't think she'll be honest with me. My relationship with her isn't like a normal brother-sister relationship."

"You're sleeping together."

"*What*? No!" He throws his hands up in disgust.

"Kidding—sort of. Just getting the worst-case scenario out of the way."

"Gosh, why would you even think that? Gross."

"She's not gross though, Shane." I say it firmly so he can tell I'm not kidding. "She's stunning. Has she always looked way too young for her age?"

"No."

"So, your sister is lying about her age, and totally passing, by the way. I'd put her at twenty-five tops by the way she looks. Her breasts are perky!"

He winces. "Please don't."

"It's not my fault she was nipping out in that freezing cold room."

"*Please.*"

"All right, we won't talk about your sister's hot bod. Let's talk about your parents."

He lowers his face like he's suddenly inspecting his food. "My dad left when I was ten, and after the gold dust came, my mom became obsessed with Reva's gift. I don't like to think about that time in my life."

"Fair," I say, but only because he's clearly not ready for that level of questioning, and he's played ball pretty well up to this point.

"How did Reva get all of her money? Does she work?"

"No. She barters."

What the hell does that mean? I stare at him when he doesn't explain. It feels like he should know by now that I'm going to want more details. I'm tired of asking.

"She trades with people," he goes on. "You know, *I'll heal your wife's cancer for a new Rover off your lot*, that sort of thing."

"And people do it?"

"Of course. I've seen people make huge sacrifices when the prospect of a loved one getting healed is on the line. You, of all people, should understand that."

His tone is a little tight, but I ignore it. He's free to get mad, and I'm free to keep asking questions anyway.

"Do those people have to go through The Threshing Floor?"

"No. And that's why I've become skeptical of the whole thing."

"So, someone gave her a mansion in the woods on trade?"

"No, she had it built. The trading was on a case-by-case basis. She had lots and lots of different contractors and offered each one healing for their labor, materials, whatever. Then she'd let them go when they started asking questions and move on to a new contractor."

"Like H. H. Holmes," I say.

"Sorry, who?"

"The serial killer. H. H. Holmes. Chicago World's Fair in the 1800s?"

He laughs. "Yeah, but she's not a serial killer."

"Course not, it's just what came to mind. So, why doesn't she charge people for healing? That'd be easier."

"Long story, and it dips into my childhood, which I'd rather not discuss tonight, if that's all right?"

It is.

With that, I'm at a standstill in my questioning. I want more information, but what did I expect? Completely reasonable answers to my questions? I'm glad I can ask, and he's trying to answer, but his answers are still weird. I feel like if I keep asking questions, I might find a red flag that's not here right now. Plus, red flags are supposed to fly in your face, not hide under rocks you can't stop overturning.

I can't understand Reva's gold dust, yet she heals with it.

I still don't understand why Shane is involved, but do I care if I'm planning to be involved too?

I'm stuck.

"Honestly, the more you tell me, the more questions I have," I say. "And I don't want to have any lingering questions, because I like you. And that little girl's arm—Reva healed it. Not to mention Mickey dropping a cool forty pounds in one week. And her daughter! If it's true that Juniper no longer has cystic fibrosis, well, then why can't Cash's heart be next? I'd do anything for that. I'd give my right arm for it. Hell, both arms! I don't even care. Just knowing that he gets to live his best life, even if I couldn't ever hug him or hold him again because I'm armless, that would be enough. And if all it requires is people talking shit about me for an hour? Awesome. In fact, I'd sell myself—"

His fingers are suddenly warm against my lips from across the table, so I stop motormouthing. Good thing, too, because I was going to dark places next.

"It'll be alright," he whispers. "Can we revisit the first thing you said for a minute? Something about you liking me?" He smiles, and when he removes his hand, he gives me *that look* that transforms my stomach into an Olympic gymnast.

"Yes, I like you. A lot, actually. And you don't even want me around your super screwed up meetings even though Cash could get healed." I give him a pouty face.

"That's not it. Not even close. It's more complicated."

"I can do complicated. Look at my life."

"To me, that says you don't need anything else to be complicated."

"But what if I want it? What if I want complicated if it comes with Cash being healed? Tell me you understand that."

He turns to Cash, who is trying to find a way off the chair with greasy peanut butter fingers.

"I do. I want that for him, too."

"Then why did it seem like you didn't want me at the last meeting?"

"Do you not remember your initial reaction to the meeting? All your f-bombs? Plus, I invited you back tonight."

"That's not an answer. Why the back and forth?"

"I guess I hoped…"

I stand up and get a hold of Cash before he varnishes Shane's hardwood floors with PB&J.

"Well, I'm not sure I want to stick around the meetings forever, and I was hoping not to get you involved. I might want to leave someday," he says.

Cash grumps while I wash him off at the sink. He wants down. "You want to leave?" I ask Shane. "Why don't you, then?"

"It's not that easy."

"*Can* you leave? You know, if you want to?"

Because this feels like a huge red flag if he can't. Then again, it's his sister, and maybe he doesn't want to leave her alone. Especially if they don't have other family.

"It's a really long story, which I hope to tell you someday, but can it wait?" He comes over and stands close to me at the sink. He seems completely unbothered by Cash's whining.

I guess it can wait. But it's not lost on me that the normal answer would be something like *Oh, I can absolutely leave whenever I want.*

"Please forgive me for not telling you this stuff," he says.

"Of course," I say, drying Cash's hands. "But you must know this about me: I make my own decisions."

Shane puts his hand on my head, runs it down my short hair, and holds the back of my neck tenderly. His hand is warm. I want to melt into his arms.

"I like that about you," he whispers and then kisses the top of my head.

I take a breath and say, "I'm planning to volunteer tonight."

"I know." Shane's voice is laced with defeat.

# DALICE

**THE SECOND MEETING** was as fucked up as the first—actually, worse. I immediately raised my hand to volunteer, and I was quicker than everyone else, but Reva didn't even look at me. I stretched my hand up, almost getting out of my seat, like a preschooler trying to be chosen as line leader.

Reva picked some older guy.

They said their little motto and then went to town on him. Reva even slapped the guy across the face right before she healed him.

Blood pressure problem, I guess. The guy found out this week. No idea why it required a slap. I looked over at Shane when it happened, and he put his hand on my leg. He didn't look at me, though.

Now it's over, and a low hum of conversation and laughter fills the place as if we just did the most normal thing in the world. When I approach the stairs to get Cash, Reva appears in front of me.

"What did you think?" she asks, like she made a cake and now she's watching me take a first bite.

I'm sorry, but there's no way this woman is in her forties. She has almost no lines on her face. Her skin is fresh and rosy. Her body is fabulous. Shane said she's not a witch, but that *would* explain her youth.

"Oh, uh, it was…good, yeah," I say, searching for something to say that's not *You just slapped a dude*. "The gold hands. How do you do that?"

"A gift from the Lord. Most people want a scientific explanation, but I don't have one. Miracles usually elude science, anyway."

Again, what was I expecting for an answer? A detailed spell, including all the ingredients? I want to think of another question to keep her talking. I like the sound of her voice. It's low, comforting like Mom's was. But the only thing I really care about is Cash getting healed. Her first response to my gold dust question was so quick, almost dismissive, that I feel like I should wait to press her.

People are leaving out the front door, trying to say goodbye, but her eyes hold me like I'm the only one here.

Shane steps in and says goodbye to the people leaving, presumably on her behalf.

"I need to go get my little guy…speaking of which, he has a severe heart condition. He's on the transplant list, but his heart is badly formed and will always cause him problems. Do you think you could heal him?"

I know Shane said she doesn't like to be asked, but worst-case scenario, she says no.

She smiles, and a surge of hope goes through me. "Why don't you get him, and then we can talk?"

"Sure, yeah."

Is she going to do it? Maybe Shane was wrong about not asking her. I try to keep the hope at bay, to stay calm.

I return with a sleepy Cash in my arms, trying to maneuver his coat on, but his arms are limp and I can't get them through the sleeves one-handed. Reva takes the coat and helps me.

"He's so precious," she says. "I love healing children."

This is a good sign, and God, she's charming. Feels like we could be good friends, and full transparency, I want her to like me. It's nothing like how I normally am. My usual mode would be to push back on any expectations. But with her, even though I've been around her for hardly any time at all, it's like I want to do whatever she suggests.

"I have a portable crib we can set up in the other room if he needs to sleep. I'm sure he's exhausted." She motions with her hand to Shane.

"Oh, I don't think I'll be staying that long."

Almost everyone is gone. The last one to leave is Gina, the nurse. She makes a point of coming over and stroking the top of Cash's head. "He's a darling. I can't wait to see him again."

It's a sweet thing for her to say, and once again, I can't help but notice how nice and open everyone is. They're not afraid to tell you they like you, to show that they want to be your friend. Gina closes the front door and Shane sets up the crib. Cash is dead weight in my arms, and while I'm not planning to stay, laying him down sounds nice.

"Just a place so you can let your arms rest while we talk. You're not committing to anything, don't worry," Reva says, laughing softly.

"He gets tired so easily because of his heart."

It's my not-so-subtle attempt to move the conversation back to healing Cash.

She smiles but doesn't take the bait.

Shane comes over and reaches for Cash, but I say I've got it and follow him into the fireplace room, laying Cash down on the purple sheet Shane tucked under the pad. He hands me a soft blanket.

"It's so cold in here," he adds, as if to explain the blanket. Cash already has his warm coat on.

Our eyes meet, and he smiles. He knows how to set up a portable crib, and he knows the importance of sheets on a shared sleeping space, *and* he recognizes that it's the Arctic tundra in here. That's all so hot.

The forward momentum that's building between us is hard to fight against. I can't swim against the Shane current. It's a riptide. If I'm completely honest with myself, I don't want to try. I want to let go and see where it takes me.

"Shane!" Reva calls from the kitchen. "Can you give Dalice and me a few minutes?"

He nods and leaves through the front door, probably back to his place, like a dismissed servant. I don't love that, but I give him a little finger wave before he goes.

"Mickey tells me you clean houses for a living," Reva says when I walk back into the kitchen. She hands me a cup of coffee with cream. I take a sip, and there's a faint sweetness. It's exactly how I like my drip coffee, but I've never told Shane or Mickey this.

"Yeah, the cleaning gig isn't my ideal career, but it's good money and right now, that's what matters." I sit across from her at a little breakfast nook. It's all windows from the back of the benches on up. Outside is pitch dark, but I bet this view is crazy cool during the day.

"It's not ideal, but you're prioritizing. You're a wonderful mom."

"I don't feel like one. I have to leave Cash with my sister almost every day. But getting insurance through my Pig Out Place job will help. At least it'll lessen the worry I have about medical bills. It's a start."

"So you work full time as a house cleaner, and you also work at Pig Out Place," she states, like there'll be a quiz afterward.

"I know, I know. It's too much."

"Actually, I was going to say that you might be the hardest-working mom I've ever met. It's impressive, your drive to provide for Cash and meet his physical needs that go so far beyond food and shelter. And at such a high cost to yourself. You don't have a lot of spare time, do you?"

I look down because her kindness hits like a wound to my stubborn nature. Makes me feel weak. I don't want her to see that I'm crying, so I look down at the warm cup I'm holding with both of my hands, gather my composure, and then look up.

"It's all good. Once you're a mom, everything becomes about the child. Isn't that what they say?"

"Well, I think you're in a good spot, and your strength and determination are astounding. I'm sure it's very hard."

"Thank you for saying that." And I mean it. I really do. It's something I wish Brandy would say.

"Insurance can be so expensive," she says, and then to herself, "and completely useless."

"Which is why your gift is so incredible," I say.

"Thank you." Her tone is flat now, like I'm treading the line of being pushy. Last thing I need is for her to ban me from the group or whatever. I thought maybe she was going to heal Cash, but now I think I need to play this out slowly.

"Well, I better get going. Thanks for the coffee."

I lift Cash out of the crib and walk toward the door. Then, because I'm me and I never know when to stop, I ask, "Why didn't you choose me tonight?"

Reva flinches slightly, then narrows her eyes. "The Threshing Floor isn't for everyone."

My heart sinks into my toes. "Oh. I thought—"

"But," she continues, "if you can come to a genuine belief in the vision, you'll be ready."

"How will I know?"

She smiles. "You'll know as soon as it's time to know."

# DALICE

I THANK REVA and walk out into the biting cold air. It's night, but the sky has that tint of pink, like it's blushing because it's about to bury us in endless snow.

I want to say goodnight to Shane before I drive home, so I text him, and the garage door opens.

"Hey, can you come up for a minute? Unless it's too late," he says.

Cash is still asleep, so yeah, I have a sec.

Inside the apartment, I ask, "Where can I lay him?"

Shane takes me into his bedroom. The bed is made and there are no dirty clothes on the floor. He's definitely closer to a domestic goddess than I am.

Despite how totally wiped out I am, my body still perks up at the sight of his bed. It's the first time I've seen it.

"Is this okay?" he asks.

"Perfect."

I lay Cash down and grab a soft Sherpa throw blanket from the bed. I spread it over my boy, then join Shane in the living room/kitchen area.

"Can I get you anything? Bourbon?" Shane's little half-smile appears.

"You have some?"

"No, just beating you to it."

"Very funny. Water's fine."

"How are you after that meeting tonight?" he asks, sitting on the couch next to me.

I chew the inside of my cheek. Of course, it was all levels of totally fucked. But what's even worse is that I'm not nearly as fazed as I probably should be. I've locked all my questions and anything that might be a red flag away into a trunk and tossed it into a black hole.

"It was weird, like usual. She hit the guy. Why?"

Shane sighs. "She says that the Lord shows her what each of us needs, and she's just the vessel for Him to use."

"You realize that's not really an answer, right?"

"A lot of stuff Reva says makes no sense, but she does so much good, and that's what I tell myself. That the good outweighs anything I can't make sense of."

So, he's doing the same thing as me. Rationalizing.

"Why does everyone volunteer? And why don't you?"

"I don't need healing."

He doesn't answer the first part of the question, but since I've set my mind to stay until Cash gets healed, I'm not sure I want to know more.

"I hope she chooses me soon. I asked her about it, but she said I wasn't ready."

Shane scoots closer to me on the couch like I just shared a juicy bit of gossip. "You asked her?"

"Of course I asked her!"

"And how did that go over?"

He obviously already knows it was a fail. He wants to hear that he was right, and it's cute how he's trying to hide a smile.

"She didn't really answer but said if I believed in the vision and became part of the group, it'd happen. I guess I'll have to leave it at that and do what I can to be chosen."

Shane puts his hand on my knee, and my body heats up.

I don't want to think about Reva anymore, so I move even closer on the couch, snuggling up to him until our lips are almost touching. He runs the back of a finger along my cheek. "Can I kiss you?"

Instead of answering, I press my mouth against his and run my hands through his curls, and he pulls me closer with one arm and it feels like an invitation, so I swing a knee across his lap, facing him, then I pull back and watch his face. His eyes are bright, and I swear I see longing in them.

I kiss him again, and he pulls my chunky sweater off in one motion and stares at my black bra like he wishes it were off. Good, I wish it were off too.

But then he pulls away.

Weird. I'm throwing myself at him and he's the one putting on the brakes?

"Are you…" I cringe because I don't want to voice this, especially not in this moment when all I want to do is keep straddling him. But I also kind of need to know. "…Waiting?"

"Waiting for what?"

"You know…the Bible, God…abstinence…marriage."

He laughs and seems more at ease. "Well if I was, I messed that up a long time ago. But the group looks down on sex before marriage. So, as long as nobody really knows…"

He kisses me again, and I lean into him, but then I pull back.

"Wait, nobody can know? That we like each other?"

"No, they can know that. But let's not tell anyone about this part."

My heart hammers, and I want him, but what if Reva finds out and it lowers my chances of Cash being healed? I should probably follow all the rules to make sure—

Shane pulls me into him again, and my mind turns to mush. Right now, this is what I want. He stares at my chest and reaches around the back for my bra clasp.

Cash cries out.

*No!*

Shane stops and watches to see what I want to do.

"It's fine. He can wait," I whisper.

But then, no. Cash can't wait. He screams "Mom-meee!"

"Next time," Shane says, and gives me a gentle kiss. I nod and pull on my sweater, smooth my ruffled hair.

Once I've retrieved Cash and I'm back in the living room, the windows catch my attention. I go over to the one in the middle and peer out toward the house while holding him.

Fat flakes catch the lights in the courtyard outside. There's a skiff of what looks like powdered sugar all over the ground, the trees, everything. The sky is bright with the reflection of snow.

"Look, Cashy, it's snowing."

Cash stares outside, sucking his binky. Shane comes up from behind, takes Cash from me, and holds him with one arm. He wraps the other around my waist, and I lean into him. In this moment, for a breath, it's like we're a little family. My heart gapes with longing.

"You better get this boy home for bed," he whispers. "Let's plan it out better next time."

I smile and give him another kiss, then leave with Cash.

Once outside, Cash and I trudge through the thin veil of snow to my car.

So that's it, then. Shane and I are a thing. This is happening.

# 1999

**IT TURNS OUT** that Reva can control the gold dust.

She's not perfect at it yet, but she's seen good progress in the weeks since Shane told her what Mom has been doing.

Making it show up is easy. She's got that down. The gold dust doesn't appear on its own out of nowhere. This is never the case, even if it seemed like it was in the beginning. And it doesn't appear because of praying, either.

It's connected to Reva on a deep level. Her passion, anger, desire, anxiety—some powerful emotion has to manifest it. That's what triggers it. Positive or negative, both work.

You'd think only good thoughts spark it to life, since it's a healing gift. But no, as long as the emotional tide inside of her rises to a certain threshold, the gold dust appears.

She needs to spend more time practicing to find the perfect point when the gold dust will show up or not. She hasn't figured that part out yet.

Stopping the gold dust when it wants to appear is much harder, however. She doesn't have a lot of positive results there. It's about fifty-fifty with the practice sessions she's done.

Reva hasn't told Shane or Mom about any of her experiments with controlling the gift.

She should tell Mom.

She *wants* to tell Shane and share this part of herself with him, especially since it was his suggestion. But something inside says to keep it silent, let it be her one secret. A form of teenage rebellion, like Shane said.

"Are you ready?" Mom stands in Reva's bedroom, all dolled up.

"Ready for what?"

"You need to stay in tune with what's happening around you, girl. You're ministering tonight."

"But I just ministered last night." She has the headache to prove it.

Mom's glares. Reva shouldn't have quipped back like that. Should have worded it more softly, like the book says to.

But did Dale Carnegie really have Reva's mom in mind when he wrote the chapter "A Drop of Honey"?

Yes, actually.

Carnegie would tell her to use his approach, especially with Mom. That's the whole point of the book. You're not winning people over if they already like you.

"You're doing four nights," Mom says. "It's a special event. Why are you acting like you didn't know this?"

Because she didn't. It's the first she's heard of it. No way she can do that many nights in a row. One service turns her into a jar of jelly with a splitting head for at least twenty-four hours.

"I can't do that many. I'll get sick."

"You'll be fine. Hurry."

"What if the gold dust doesn't show up?"

"It always does."

Mom is right. Reva hasn't actually worried about it not showing up in a long time. It was only a lame excuse.

She could resist. Really lean into rebellion and refuse to leave her room. But it's pointless, because even if she succeeds tonight, what about tomorrow? The next day? Mom makes money off her in these services. So doing more of them will make her more money. This is a slippery slope, and Reva's on it, wearing roller skates.

Resisting tonight won't do anything. She needs a bigger strategy because she still has another year of living at home with Mom. A year without Shane to act as a buffer.

"Be right there," Reva says, and when Mom leaves the room, she glances at her hands.

*I guess it's now or never.*

**THE SERVICE STARTS** out like usual. Reva in the car, then the worship service, then speaking in tongues. And then the altar call. Throngs of people fill the front of the sanctuary and the aisles. She goes for the children first, while she still has energy. Healing children makes Reva truly happy. Plus, it's not their fault their parents are taking advantage of her.

Growth problems, cured.

Earaches, cleared up.

Various arms and legs in casts—easy. Healed.

A baby with a heart condition, done. They won't know for sure until they get a scan, but it's a done deal. Reva felt it.

Stuttering, gone.

Infections, healed.

The common cold and seven bouts of the flu shriveled up right before her eyes.

She's pushing hard, racing against her body, against her head that's pounding so hard she can barely see through the dim vision of a migraine, moving her gold hands from one child to another, and when she thinks she's got them all, it's time.

Reva collapses on the stage.

She holds still and listens to the surrounding murmurs.

*Is she dead?*

*No, she's still breathing.*

*What happened?*

*Should we call a doctor?*

*Can't she heal herself?*

*No, she can't, actually,* Reva thinks to herself.

Of all the miracles this gift offers, there isn't a single one for her to access for herself. The reminder brings anger up inside, but if she lets it spread unchecked, the gold dust will stay and her plan won't work. She needs to find a neutral mind space to make it go away.

The pastor tries to rouse her, Mom tries to rouse her, but she ignores them, and minutes pass. She uses the time to calm her breath, find somewhere else to be.

A beach, yes, that's it. She's never been to the ocean, but she's seen it on TV. She's at the beach. Nothing matters because the sun warms her. She has everything she needs. She's in control of her life. Nobody will ever take advantage of her again. She cages the darkness inside of her, and there's no desire to heal. In fact, she doesn't care about anything at all. She's swallowed up by this numb indifference to everything, and when her hands aren't warm anymore, she sits up.

"I'm sorry, I don't know what came over me," she says, smiling and touching her forehead. Then she stands. "Where were we?"

"Are you sure you can continue?" the pastor asks.

"She can continue!" Mom shouts to the crowd. Rage rushes into Reva's heart, but she pictures herself stepping aside so it can't pummel her.

*No. Keep it contained. Stay neutral, or this won't work.*

Reva smiles. "I want to keep going."

The pastor nods and directs her to some older guy.

"What would you ask of me?" she asks.

*Numb. Neutral. At the beach. Nothing matters.*

"Arthritis in my hands. Can't work no more."

She can see it. His fingers are like knotty branches.

Reva puts her hands out, open palms up. They're still pale. A little clammy.

*Don't get excited. No emotion. Nothing matters. These people don't matter.*

She sighs and pretends to pray, then checks her palms again. No gold.

*It's working.*

"It's not working," she says to the pastor, who looks over at Mom with eyes like UFOs.

Mom comes to the stage and lays hands on her, prays in tongues.

Reva wants to laugh, but that brings a flash of heat in her palms. *No. Stop.*

She can't enjoy this. Can't let any emotion take over. She has to maintain this state of nothingness.

Her hands cool down, and there's still no gold.

She's doing it.

Mom whispers threats, her face scrunched up like she might cry. The people whisper too. Some are leaving. Mom takes the microphone and tells them to stay. She suggests spending more time in worship. The ones who don't leave file toward Mom, asking for their money back.

Mom pulls out a gray cash box and begins handing bills out. She's crying. She's actually crying. This is the first time Reva has seen the money, and she can't think of the last time she saw Mom cry.

Reva sits down on the top step leading up to the stage. Nobody notices her anymore. They don't care.

It's wonderful.

Heat flares in her palms, and when she opens her hands, they're gold.

# DALICE

**EVERYTHING HAS BEEN** going so well. It's been about a month of meetings, late nights talking to Shane, and staying over at Shane's house, picking up where we left off that night it snowed. He bought a crib for Cash to sleep in. Shane even came to Thanksgiving at Hank and Brandy's with me. Such an amazing month.

Even though Reva still hasn't chosen me to go through The Threshing Floor.

I pull off the highway and onto the road that leads to Reva's for a meeting tonight, and my phone pings. I know better than to check it while I'm driving, especially since there's snow on the ground, so as soon as I can, I pull over. Cash is asleep in his seat, so I have a hot second. It could be information about the heart transplant.

Nope. It's a text from Brandy.

And great, now she's all up in arms.

Apparently, she googled *Shane Prehner*, so she knows about his sister with the magic golden hands. She found something else, too: His mom died while the kids were still at home. I punch in the gate code and pull up close to the house to park. Then I google Shane's name because I have to fact-check her before I reply.

Nothing super interesting shows up for me.

Screenshot after screenshot comes over from Brandy, and the first is a page from a newspaper article dated 1999. Did she pay for some deep sleuthing subscription to access it? There's a mention of Reva's gift, how she was active in local churches in the community, but it's cryptic.

*The healing thing is weird, Dal. Can't be real*, Brandy texts.

I told her I've been going to the meetings in the hopes of a healing miracle. I pitched it to Brandy more like a faith healing church. She seemed to buy it, but I guess that's over now.

*But what if it is real?* I text back. *What if Cash could get healed?*

*What if it's not and they're just preying on you?*

I stare at the words and heat rises to my cheeks. I start typing, but another text from her comes through.

*You don't really know Shane. You met him last month. Have you even met her? What's she like?*

Now my sister wants me to spill the tea? What the hell. I'm not answering. Makes me tired to even think about crafting a reply. I get Cash out and head inside.

**WHEN REVA ASKS** for a volunteer, I don't hesitate, as usual. My hand goes right up.

Reva's eyes find me, and she cocks her head to the side. This is progress. Normally, she pretends like I don't exist, and then, after the meeting, comes up and asks what I thought. At first it seemed like she cared about my opinion. But now it's like she's daring me to find fault. I can't figure out if she wants to scare me away, or rub in that I didn't get chosen, or what.

I'm not going anywhere. If anything, I've dug in deeper.

Sure, there's the whole verbal beat-down to endure, but my mind is unchanged. I can take a little smack talk for Cash.

"Dalice." Reva says, smiling at me.

I scan around as if there's another Dalice in the room and I'm trying to figure out if she means me.

Next to me, I sense Shane's body deflate, but I ignore it. It's time for Cash's heart to be healed.

I sit in the special conference room chair in the middle and take a deep breath. My eyes find Shane. His eyebrows are up and his lips make a thin line.

Suddenly, it occurs to me that Shane may say something to thresh me. Why didn't I think of that? Can I handle whatever he says? I have to. It doesn't matter. I'm doing this for Cash. Need to focus on that.

"Since we don't know Dalice that well yet, I'd like to try something different today," Reva says.

Wait. What does she mean by *different*?

I watch Shane, but his attention is on Reva.

"We're going to ask her questions and she must answer honestly. If she doesn't, I'll know, and her threshing will not be complete. We won't seal her."

Not be complete? Like Cash won't get healed?

"I'll start," Reva says.

What the hell? She never participates.

"How many men have you slept with?"

I blink, look around. Everyone stares at me, waiting.

My hesitation must be too long, because Reva says, "A reminder. This is The Threshing Floor. The point is to separate the wheat—your pure intention, your ability to sacrifice, from the chaff—your drive to control your own life. Perhaps you're not ready?"

"I'm ready!" I say right away.

I expected they'd tell me I was rude, ugly, no fun to be around, that sort of thing, but this is different. It feels more personal.

"I don't keep a list," I say. "So I don't really know. Probably a dozen over the years."

"Is that including Shane?"

I can't help my sharp intake of breath. Is she really going there? I try to make eye contact with Shane, but he stares past me, out the window.

*Healing for Cash. Healing for Cash. Healing for Cash.*

"Yes," I whisper.

"Does Shane bring you to orgasm?" she asks.

"What?" I can't help my tone. This is insane, even for her, but I seem to be the only one who thinks so. Everyone else is acting like she's asking icebreaker questions.

*What's your favorite candy?*
*What's the first movie you ever saw in a theater?*
*What's the last emoji you sent?*

"Do you orgasm when you're with Shane?" Her voice is monotone.

"I understand the question. I'm just not sure why you're asking it."

Reva's eyebrows raise, and she says slowly, like English isn't my first language, "This is the Threshing Floor. The point is to—"

"Yes, I understand all of that too, but what does my sex life have to do with it?"

"You're not ready. Take your seat, please. Another volunteer?"

"No, I'm ready, I'm ready. Sorry."

*Healing for Cash, healing for Cash, healing for Cash, healing for Cash.*

I think about no heart transplant.

Cash living a long life.

I fold my hands as if in prayer, shove them between my knees, stare at the floor in front of me, and channel something like anger. A feeling that's hard and steely to give me courage. If that's the price, who cares if they know all my secrets?

"Yes," I say.

"Yes, what?"

I glare at her. If she's going to be this way, then fine, I will be too. "Yes, I have hot and very satisfying sex with Shane that also leads to multiple orgasms."

A bit of snickering, but it quickly dissipates.

Reva smirks like she's accomplished something. I have no clue what it is. She waves her hand and sits down.

Permission for other people to ask questions, I guess.

"How often do you masturbate?" Mickey asks.

What the fuck, Mickey? Are all the questions going to be about sex? I've never seen this happen before. It's usually childish insults and then healing. Perhaps a little physical pain. That's what I signed up for.

"A lot less now that I'm with Shane."

She just stares at me.

"A couple times a week, maybe?" I say.

"Maybe?"

"A few times a week on average. How's that?"

"Have you ever been with a woman?" Holly asks.

"Yes." I respond with no emotion, matching how they're asking the questions.

"How many?" Holly follows up.

"I don't know, seven? I'm not picky about gender. Do you want details about how that works?"

She stares at me but doesn't reply. A surge of satisfaction hits. *One point for Dalice.*

"Have you ever been sexually abused?" This one from Colin. A man is actually asking me this. My bravado wanes and I feel like a child being punished.

"Yes."

"How old were you?" Carolyn from the harvest party asks.

Why are all my friends jumping at the chance to humiliate me? They're not even hesitating to let other people who don't know me as well go first. If they're really my friends, shouldn't they be trying to run out the clock instead of plunging in?

Of course, Shane is the exception. He's still staring off into space like he's not even here. Renee is too, but she's looking at the floor.

"I was six."

They're going to ask for details this time. It's obvious in the split-second hesitation of the room. I don't want to go here. I've spent a lot of time in therapy moving past this ugly part of my childhood.

"Shane, why don't you ask the next question?" Reva says.

My stomach bottoms out.

His eyes find me, and they're a little vacant. I can't read him at all, and I'm completely unmoored. "What's your favorite memory of your mother?"

A sly smile curls up one corner of his mouth. Reva can't see it from where she's at.

Soft gasping courses through the room, as if he did something bad, but I jump to answer this one.

"Oh, one time she took me—"

"No," Reva interrupts. "Shane, you know better. Ask her a proper question. And a follow-up question too, because of that little stunt."

Tears gather in my eyes—I can't help it. I kept them away by being angry, but I can't be angry with Shane. His eyes dart around like he's searching for an exit, and his throat bobs with hard swallows.

*Do it. I'm ok. I can take it for Cash.*

I sniff and wipe tears from my cheeks. The Threshing Floor often ends when someone cries, so what if this is it? Reva's face is dark. Her eyes are set, and she doesn't seem like she'll be wrapping up soon.

Shane exhales loudly. "Who abused you?" His tone is apologetic, like he's trying to get it over with.

"A neighbor."

Shane looks at his clasped hands.

"Follow up, please," Reva says. "And if it's not a good question, you'll keep probing her until I'm satisfied."

Shane sends a glare to Reva. He's pushing back in his own way, but she smiles, and he turns to me.

"What happened?" The words come out with no inflection.

Because he doesn't want to take part.

Because he knew something like this would happen.

Because he told me not to volunteer, and I didn't fucking listen.

Reva smiles at Shane, and I steal another peek at him. His eyes are a little wet, and seeing him like that makes me cry harder.

"He made me look through porn magazines with him. Then he got naked and masturbated in front of me."

There was more to it than that. A whole hell of a lot more, but there's no way they're hearing it. I will invent things to avoid telling the truth.

"What else?" someone asks. I don't care who anymore. My eyes are on my trusty spot on the floor in front of my feet. Just need to get through this. Surely I'm almost there, almost to my little boy's healing.

"Nothing else."

Reva raises her hands and prays in tongues, so people do the shaking, bending over, and shouting thing.

It's over.

It was horrible, but it was short, and now it's done. I wipe tears with my sleeve and turn to see if Gina has brought down Cash for the healing part.

For the first time since he was born, I know everything is going to be alright. Cash is going to be fine. It was worth it. Totally worth it.

But where is Cash? Maybe I need to go get him.

Before I can stand to do that, Reva squats down in front of me, lining her face up with mine. She takes my right hand in hers and turns my palm up.

"Do you trust me?" she asks.

I nod, because what other option is there?

"Close your eyes."

I do.

Bright pain explodes at my wrist, so my eyes bug open.

A thin bracelet of blood starts, and then it gorges out, dripping from my wrist. The sight of it makes me woozy, but I can't pull away. Reva holds on, and in her other hand is a small knife, smeared red.

"No!" someone shouts at Reva. My head feels light at the sight of my blood. I've always hated blood.

Everything slows, and through the fuzzy veil of my vision, I can see it's Renee who yelled out.

Reva looks over at Renee so fast that her long hair whips, dangling into the blood on my arm. Red soaking into red. Soaking into my lap, saturating my jeans. Reva won't let my hand go. I can't think straight. Thoughts are too hard.

They're talking, but it sounds muffled. I'm dizzy. Where's Shane?

Reva turns to me again. Her smile is huge. Magnetic, but also wobbly because my vision is so off.

"Dalice, sweet girl, what would you ask of me?"

Her words are slow, but I grasp them.

My mouth opens to speak, but I feel detached. Outside of myself, watching like this is happening to someone else.

*Cash. Heal Cash.*

The words are there, but I can't tell if I'm saying them or thinking them.

Everything goes black.

# SHANE

**I COULDN'T WATCH** Reva shame Dalice like that, so I was staring out the window, trying to make myself disappear. But that made it so I didn't register what was going on until Renee shouted at Reva.

And now I see the blood.

I run over to Dalice, dodging the row of chairs in front of me. Her eyes are closing by the time I get there, her body leaning like she might fall out of her seat.

Reva drops her hand and takes a single step back, but she's not exactly out of the way.

Everyone in the room is quiet. I think they're too stunned to do anything.

"What the hell?" I shout at Reva.

She flinches. I don't know if she's surprised that I swore or surprised that I yelled at her. I haven't done either since we were teenagers.

Someone hands me a thin blanket from the basket by the fireplace. I wrap it tightly around Dalice's wrist. Then I scoop her up and cradle her in my arms. Her bloody arm hangs limp, outstretched toward Reva.

"Heal her!" I shout.

I don't know what's gotten into me. A dam breaks, and all this anger I've ignored bursts through the baseline numbness I've felt toward my sister for decades. No way I can hold it back.

"What about her son?" Reva asks, looking at her own nails.

She's playing her game, and an instinct to tear her apart roars to life inside of me. I'm fully aware now, and all I can think about—besides Dalice dying in my arms—is everything Reva has put me through. How could she? I followed along with whatever she asked. Supported her ministry, tried to make it my own. For over twenty years.

Two. Fucking. Decades.

Reva looks at the crowd, as if she's speaking to them and not me. "I had to do it this way. I can't heal by proxy until we seal her to us. She didn't need healing in her body, so I created a need." Then, to me: "I'm only trying to seal her, Shane. For you."

No. She's trying to drive Dalice away. Reva can't handle that I have someone else in my life.

Dalice's coloring fades to a scary pale. She's still breathing, but there's no time. I can't get her to the hospital fast enough. Blood throbs out of her, drenching the blanket, my arms. It's too much blood.

"Heal her now!" I shout louder, moving toward her with Dalice cradled in my arms. Everything narrows until it's like nobody else is in the room.

It's just my Dalice, me, and Reva.

"I can only heal one of them. Her or Cash. What choice do you think she would make?"

But she said she has to heal Dalice before she can heal Cash by proxy.

Is she making this all up? I've had that suspicion before, but I couldn't truly entertain it. Couldn't comprehend everything that it would mean.

But now, I can't deny the possibility.

"Well? Make the choice she would make," she says, completely relaxed. "What will it be? Control—heal Dalice, or sacrifice— heal Cash?"

Cash. Dalice would choose Cash. There's no question.

But if I don't choose Dalice, she'll die. That's not happening.

"I don't care about her choice. She's not awake to make it," I growl.

"Interesting."

Reva crosses her arms over her chest. "You're choosing control over sacrifice. I'm surprised."

What the hell? Why is she getting philosophical right now? Time is running out.

"I choose her. Fix this!"

Reva smiles like I'm doing exactly what she wants.

The thought that this was all orchestrated squirms around the back of my mind. That she wanted to do this to me. I can't figure out why right now. I just need Dalice back.

"She won't forgive you," Reva says. "You know she wants her boy healed."

"Let me deal with that."

Then Reva lifts her hands and brings them back down. Her palms are gold.

"Shane is making the wrong choice," she says to all the people I've forgotten exist. "Love is sacrifice. Control is not love."

*Shut up and put your gold hands on my girl.*

"He knows all about choosing sacrifice, too, which is why this is such a plot twist for me."

If I didn't have Dalice in my arms, I might hit Reva and break her smug face.

Just when I worry it's too late, that Dalice is already gone, Reva puts her hand directly on Dalice's wound. Blood squidges through her fingers.

Reva doesn't close her eyes. Instead, she holds my gaze, and I can't read anything in her eyes.

It's pure emptiness.

# DALICE

**I WAKE UP** in Shane's bed. It's dark. The clock says 1:03 a.m. He's not here.

When I swing my legs to the side to get up, I notice they're bare. I'm in one of his big tee shirts.

I remember my arm and turn on the lamp to examine it. There's no cut. No evidence of a cut. No evidence of the blood I remember covering my legs, either. What the fuck? Did I dream all of that?

But no, my jeans are in a pile on the floor, and the denim is ruined. Hardened in places where the blood dried. Somehow, I got clean, but I don't remember that either.

"Hey, how are you feeling?" Shane says, walking into the bedroom. "I took off your clothes and cleaned up the blood on your arm and legs. I hope that's all right."

"It's fine. Cash. Did she heal Cash?" But even as I ask, I know who Reva healed. Me. My wrist. There's no cut.

He sits down on the edge of the bed. "Cash is asleep in his crib."

"That's not what I asked."

Shane sighs but doesn't make eye contact. "You know she healed you instead."

"I didn't ask her to heal me. I asked her to heal Cash."

"You passed out before you could say anything. She put the choice on me."

I scoot away, smashing my back against the wooden headboard, knees bent.

"Why would you do that to me?" I whisper.

He looks at me. "There was no choice. She cut you so deeply that I couldn't get you to the hospital fast enough."

"But Cash…"

"I know." He moves closer to me, but I'm not ready for tenderness.

Confusion gives way to anger. I shove him. "You should have chosen Cash!"

"In that moment, you had way less time than Cash does. I don't regret my choice." He reaches out and puts a warm hand on the top of my foot. I don't fight him this time.

"Did he see me like that?" I point to the dried blood on my clothes.

"No. I brought you over here and then got him from the nursery. He's fine. He's totally fine."

"Why did Reva cut me?"

He hesitates. "She said it was because you needed to be sealed first."

My anger stalls while I process this. Of course. She can't heal by proxy until that happens. I'd hoped she'd make an exception for me, but I guess she didn't.

It's not over yet.

I exhale and say, "Okay, so next time I'll ask for Cash's healing."

"Next time? Dalice, you almost died."

"I don't need healing for myself. It makes sense that she had to create a wound to heal so I could be sealed to the group."

I'm rationalizing, and I know it. But I don't care. I'm so close to having my baby healed.

Then something happens that I absolutely cannot explain.

This wave of euphoria drowns me. Shane's hand on my foot sends warm streaks of pleasure up my leg, warming me deep inside. Each breath of air energizes and feeds my soul like I'm growing too full for my own skin, but at the same time, I feel good in my body. Perfectly comfortable, as if my soul is a hand and my body the glove and we are a perfect fit.

Golden light haloes Shane's face, and I swear I can see desire pulsing through him. I can feel his heart rate increasing. It's primal, but so vivid.

I once read somewhere that we don't use our entire brains. What if, right now, parts of my brain that were asleep are suddenly working?

I move toward him and touch his hair. Has it always been this soft? I rake both of my hands through it and close my eyes. It sounds dumb, but even touching his hair makes my body light up. Is it his hair that's softer, though? It looks the same. Maybe it's my skin sensing more. My nerve endings registering touch better.

Jesus, I need to stop thinking and just go with it before this all goes away.

"You're not tired?" he asks, and his voice sounds like a concerto. I want to close my eyes and get lost in the music.

"Opposite." I kiss him and he deepens the kiss, but then breaks away.

"Of course," he says in a flat voice. "Reva just healed you."

*People get addicted.*

*It makes them easier to control.*

Perhaps, but right now, I can't see why it's a bad thing. This feels too good.

*You're not thinking straight. And you sound like every addict ever.*

Whatever. For now, I want to dive into this, whatever it is, and not hold anything back. And anyway, it's just sex with my boyfriend. It's not like it's a hit of heroin.

How is it possible that Shane only let Reva heal him once in his life? I'm already looking forward to my next go-around.

I kiss him again, trying so hard to be tender, but I'm ravenous. He doesn't kiss me back this time.

He's worried about me getting addicted or something.

"Please?" I beg. The one word comes from such a deep and desperate part of me that I shock myself with how vulnerable I feel. Can he tell?

He sighs like it's a chore, but then smiles and tugs my shirt off.

My body is floaty, like when you can swim through the air in a dream. He reaches for my ribs, under the arms, like he's going to lift me, but he keeps his warm hands there while running his thumbs along the sides of my breasts. I can't help it, I moan. It's just a simple touch, but it lights me on fire and anchors me at the same time.

I move to my knees and wrap my arms around his neck to push my chest into his face. Every particle of me throbs with need, every inch screams *go, go, go*. But I don't want it to be over too fast, either.

I pull his shirt off, and Shane gets the hint and strips. I push his torso down so he's lying flat, then I climb on him, and it's like I'm levitating over him—weightless, but still sensing every bit of skin on skin. He's so hard, and it's pressing at the thin fabric of my underwear. He reaches up and strokes my face, my neck. I gasp so loud that a hint of embarrassment registers, but I don't care enough to do anything to stop myself.

Shane flips me over onto my back, walks his fingers slowly under the waistband of my underwear. He lies on his side, propped up on one elbow, kissing my mouth, then down my neck. I thrust my hips upward, signaling for more pressure. He obeys. I close my eyes, because everything is building, and then when I'm right there, when the pressure is at critical mass, he slows down.

"Don't stop," I plead.

"I'm in love with you, Dalice," he whispers. His face is inches from mine, his blue eyes deep, piercing. "I never want to be without you."

This is the first time he's said he loves me. Before I can find coherent words, his hand is working again and I'm right back at the peak. My body clenches, suspending me in a moment of release that I know I won't be able to hold on to. I cry out as I go over the edge. I actually cry. Shane holds eye contact with me the entire time and it's so hot that all I can do is breathe out "I love you too."

Wave after wave, the pleasure keeps rippling through me.

"You're the most beautiful thing I've ever seen," he says during my last and most intense orgasm. And the thing is, I feel beautiful. I feel like a fucking god.

When I'm totally spent, I push his shoulders back, forcing him to lie down again. "You're talking a lot. Do you want your turn, or what?" I don't let him reply before I move his hands up over his head, one by one. I hold them down, my small fingers really doing nothing to keep his muscular arms in place, but he lets me pin him all the same. My knees grip his hips and then he's deep inside of me, and it's right. It feels like forever.

He arches up to kiss me, but I want to watch him, so I refuse the kiss. Then I ride him so hard, he can't help but explode.

Afterward, I curl up next to him, and he wraps an arm around me. We're both sweaty even though it's not warm in here. I'm clearly high, if there was any question.

"I don't want to scare you because it's so soon, but I mean it," he says. "I can't live my life without you in it. And when I thought you were…"

I look up at his face and smile. "Shh. That doesn't scare me at all, and I'm not going anywhere. But…"

A flash of concern covers his face like I'm going to break up with him or something.

"…can we talk about those orgasms on Reva-drugs? Because, wow."

Shane laughs and kisses the top of my head. "Can we *not* talk about my sister right now?"

I nuzzle into him and say, "Fine. Have it your way."

# 1999

**REVA CAN'T LET** Shane leave for Seattle for college. She can't. Not when they've grown so close over the past couple of months. He cares about her, and with him by her side, she could be somebody, and maybe even have her own healing ministry.

There's still time. Graduation hasn't even happened yet.

Upstairs in her bedroom, Reva waits for Shane to get home from his job at the grocery store. Through the window, she watches her mom washing the Oldsmobile in the driveway. Now that they have a garage, the car never gets dirty, but she still tends to it like it's her little baby. Mom wears long jean shorts, a tee shirt rolled up at the sleeves with a picture of Donald Duck sunbathing that says "Sun Your Buns," and flip flops. Her hair is in a sloppy bun.

Shane will be home any minute.

Reva goes downstairs and into the kitchen. She grabs a steak knife.

Mom doesn't seem to hear the screen door slam when Reva comes out the front. It's like her mind is somewhere else.

Reva stands a few feet behind Mom, waiting for her to notice. She squeezes the knife handle behind her back to ground herself in the moment.

"Oh!" Mom startles and drops the wily hose on the ground so it does a flip, throwing a few drops of water against Reva's legs. "I didn't see you there. What do you need?"

Reva motions with her head for Mom to follow her into the garage where the Olds is normally parked. Mom gives a heavy sigh, but she follows.

They stand on the blue tarp.

Reva walks to the wall nearest them and hits a button, closing the garage door.

"I don't have time for this," Mom says.

"Trust me, you do." Reva takes Mom's left hand and, before she can change her mind, she slashes Mom's forearm.

"What the—?" Mom yells, covering the gash with her other hand to stop the bleeding. It's not a deep cut. Not at all. Just enough to get her attention.

Mom doesn't speak. She watches her daughter as if she can't figure out what's going on.

"What would you ask of me?" Reva says, her hands already warm.

Mom's face softens like she understands.

"Heal my arm."

Reva places her hands on the cut, and it shrivels right away. Mom moans. Pleasure?

*When you heal people, they feel good.*

It makes bile rise in Reva's throat.

The two of them stand across from each other, staring. Blood covers Mom's arm, but there's no trace of a wound, and when she tries to wipe it away, it only smears.

Reva waits for the crescendo of a headache. It should happen right now. But there's nothing. Nothing at all.

In fact, in its place is a rush of something else. It powers through her veins with such strength that it's like she just woke up from a really long sleep.

Shane's Bronco door slams loudly in the front yard.

Reva hands the knife to Mom.

Mom smiles and seems to survey her own arm for a spot, and then decides on her other arm this time. Mom presses the knife into her own flesh and it parts, like lips smiling. She cuts herself deeper than Reva did.

Mom extends the now-bloody arm, but Reva just stares at her.

The garage door goes up and Shane stands on the other side in his black pants and white short-sleeved button-up, holding a burgundy apron that says "Rosauers" in one hand.

"What the hell is going on?" His anger flashes from zero to sixty.

Mom drops the knife.

Shane's eyes travel along the dried blood on her one arm, and his knuckles turn white gripping the apron. Fresh blood drips down Mom's other arm and across her hand. It *tap-tap-taps* onto the blue tarp.

Shane rushes her.

"Wait," Reva says, putting out her hand to stop him. Then to Mom: "Tell me what happened to your brother."

"What brother?" Shane whispers. He didn't know either, apparently.

"Heal me first. I'm already so weak from the cut."

Shane growls, but Reva puts a hand out again, trying to silence him. She has to get answers.

"Tell me, and I will," Reva says to Mom.

"It was an accident. We didn't know it would happen," Mom starts. Reva can't tell if she's exaggerating her ragged breathing, or if she's really having a hard time because of this one cut.

"The gold dust came during the summer Rich was seventeen, and it stayed for a long time. We took the Olds down the coast like always, but one evening, after lots of days of ministry, Rich wasn't well. He told Dad he couldn't heal people, and Dad let him have the night off. Rich was in bed that whole next day, too. I was younger, and I remember visiting him, taking him tea. He looked bad, and I was worried. But then our sister, Janie, got sick in the middle of the night. She couldn't stop throwing up. They thought it was her appendix. Dad was loading her into the car when Rich appeared right beside him."

Mom takes another deep breath at this point. She folds her lips in like she's trying not to cry. "I watched from the motel window. Rich staggered out toward the Olds. He could barely walk. I didn't have to hear them talking to know that he wanted to heal Janie. That was how Rich was. Dad shook his head, but Rich reached out with his gold hands and touched Janie anyway. Then he collapsed. He never woke up. The doctors said it was a heart attack." Bulky tears roll down Mom's face and she looks away.

Reva doesn't have any words. Her uncle, who had her same gifting, died from...what? Healing people too much?

"That wasn't an accident. You guys killed him," Shane says. "Pushed him to minister day after day. And now you're doing the same thing to Reva."

Mom's mouth gapes open, but she doesn't have time to speak. Shane throws his apron on the ground and walks into Mom's personal bubble.

"No, no, I swear! *She* cut *me*!" Mom says.

Shane looks at Reva, then back to Mom. He's head and shoulders taller than Mom now. Taller than both of them. In this moment, it strikes Reva that Shane is a grown man. And Mom looks scared.

He takes one of Mom's wrists and looks over her forearm like he's searching for something. He drops it. Does the same with her wounded arm, but doesn't let go this time.

Instead, he inches even closer, gets right into Mom's face, and grabs her by the collar of her tee shirt. "You were holding the knife. You're the one who hurts yourself on purpose. How dare you blame her?"

He brings a fist up to her face and Reva holds her breath. She's never seen this side of Shane before. "If you ever use her again, I swear to God, you might not live to regret it."

Mom nods quickly.

Reva can't believe it. How small Mom seems. How vulnerable. It gives her a thrill.

Shane lets Mom go and brushes past Reva to storm inside without another word. She quickly heals Mom and then jogs to follow him.

"Can you believe she did that?" Reva says. His response to it was even better than she'd hoped for. "What am I going to do when you move out?"

"You'll have to figure something out." Shane's words are clipped. He doesn't stop, but keeps pacing toward his room. Is he mad at her too?

"I can't. She won't back down for me like she does for you."

He whirls around and steps toward her. "Welcome to your life, Reva Prehner. People are always going to use you because of your gift. Figure out how to deal with it. I won't always be here."

"Why? Why can't you be here?" Reva yells back, losing her cool.

No answer. Instead, he walks into his bedroom.

She follows, standing in the open doorway. With his back to her, he unbuttons his shirt and tosses it aside. His back makes a V from his shoulders down to his hips. She's never noticed it before.

"Have you been working out?" Reva asks.

"God, you're so creepy sometimes! Why are you still here?"

Reva doesn't answer because she gets distracted by a red mark on his ribs. There's some purple bruising too. "That looks like it hurts."

"I'm fine. Just got elbowed pretty hard during the last game."

Reva's hands are warm, and she moves closer to him, reaching for the wound. "Let me help."

"No!" Shane all but shouts, then dodges her touch. "No thanks. I'm good. It really doesn't hurt."

Shane turns his back again and rummages around in a laundry basket until he finds a towel. "Look, I can't be with you twenty-four seven for the rest of your life. You have to stand up for yourself."

"Mom hits me when you're not here."

It's sort of true, even if it hasn't happened in years. Mom used to hit her when she was young.

He turns around. "You should call the cops if it happens again."

"On Mom?" Reva can't believe he is suggesting this. "Why? So I can get sent to a foster home? You're eighteen. They won't bother you. But I'm still a minor. No way I'm calling the cops. I need you around."

Shane pushes past her and goes into the bathroom. "I'm sorry this is happening to you. I really am. But I'm leaving after graduation." He shuts the door in her face.

This might be the first time she has ever felt actual anger toward Shane. How could he be so selfish?

# DALICE

**WHEN I PULL** the car up to Brandy's house this morning, my mood is not good. It's full-on bad.

Ten days have passed since Reva sliced and then healed me. Ten days since Reva sealed me to the group. Ten days since extra-hot sex with Shane thanks to Reva-drugs. Fortunately, we've repeated it a couple times, but nothing like that night.

The worst part, though, is that it's been ten days since Reva has held a meeting at all. This has me all shades of anxious, considering there's no way she'll choose me for The Threshing Floor immediately after I already went. It could be weeks, months, longer. And what if she pulls some other strange stunt that delays things?

In the meantime, no word from Seattle. Which, of course, could also take a long time. Years, maybe!

I know I need to stop feeling sorry for myself and locate some patience to channel, but it's like trying to teach a squirrel ballet.

I look at myself in the car mirror.

One step at a time. First, I got sealed. Next, she'll heal Cash.

This little pep talk helps a bit, and I'm finally ready to face Brandy, whose concerns haven't gone away. Then there's Hank, who has done his own digging and is bothered by the secrecy of the group. But Hank thinks everything is a conspiracy, so I don't get what the big deal is with *my* fringe group.

By the time I get out of the car and open the back door to unbuckle Cash, he's already working on it.

"Oh, let Mommy."

"Cashy do it."

"Cashy can do lots of things, but Mommy does the belt." I ruffle his hair.

He waves aggressively at the house, so I turn my head, and Brandy's on the front step, waiting and hugging herself because it's snowing hard. Nobody is making her stand on the porch to meet us. Why is she doing that?

"Hey," I say when I get within earshot.

"Can you come in for a minute, Dal?"

"Sure."

I really can't. I'm already late for my first house, as per usual. When I get inside, Cash crawls up the stairs.

"Did you hear about the storm?" Brandy asks.

It's been over a month since Ryan showed me that article, and I haven't even thought about it again.

"Ice Storm two-point-oh? Yeah, it's not real."

"Like hell it's not real," Hank yells from upstairs. I can't see him, but it sounds like he's in the living room above the landing. I widen my eyes at Brandy, trying to ask what this is about and why Hank is out of his cave. She purses her lips and waves me on to follow her up the stairs.

Hank sits in a brown leather recliner. Brandy points to a chair, and I sit down in it.

"What's going on?" I ask.

"Hank and I are really worried about you."

"What? Why?"

"Just let me finish, please."

I bite back the protests I already have lined up in my mind.

"We don't think that group you're involved in is good for you. You're spending so much time with them. This focus on miracle healing isn't healthy for you or for Cash."

"Yeah, and we don't need you involved in any satanic voodoo shit, either," Hank adds.

I could have this conversation with Brandy. I'd entertain her concerns and then brush them off like I always do.

But with my brother-in-law? Nope.

"Why, Hank? Because you think they're part of some entity controlling the government?" I ask.

"Dalice, stop. That's not what he means." Brandy gives Hank a let-me-handle-this look.

"Why is he here?"

"Because he cares."

"No, it's because you're afraid to bring it up with me alone. You know I can destroy you in an argument. You need strength in numbers."

"No, you're wrong. I care about you, and I don't want to see you get caught up in something…weird. You need to stop going to those meetings."

I want to throw punches. I want to kick in drywall and flip end tables over. I want to take all the ceramic bric-a-brac that Brandy's got on glass shelves like she's some fucking old lady and hurl it against the fireplace.

Instead, I breathe deeply and close my eyes right there in front of them. Take four seconds to breathe in, four seconds to breathe out. I do this over and over until it's very awkward.

"What are you doing?" Brandy finally asks.

"Channeling Satan for help with all the voodoo shit I'm gonna do to you. Be quiet." I keep my eyes closed and continue breathing.

Amazingly, they obey.

Then I open my eyes and speak to Brandy like Hank's not in the room. I shock myself with how calm I am.

"You're my sister, and I love you. I thought once Mom passed away, we'd cling together, and all the ways we're different would melt away, and out of that would come something beautiful because all we have is each other." I pause because, of course, I'm crying. "Instead, you look down on me. You treat me like I'm less because of the hand life dealt me. And I'm aware I dealt some of that hand to myself. But it would be nice if just once you found it inside your icy heart to encourage me instead of dragging me down. Now I've found people who are encouraging. Who love me for who I am, mistakes and all. And you want me to stop hanging out with them? Why? So I can be lonely again? So I can remember every day that my only family—my sister—is emotionally unavailable and critical?"

"That's not fair," she whispers, but my irritation only grows.

"I have to go. I'm late for my first house."

"You don't have to believe us about the storm, but I'm sending some of my old wool army blankets and a few water bottles along with you. Put them in your car," Hank says. His tone isn't belligerent like usual. It's markedly softer.

"Fine."

Brandy comes downstairs with me and goes for a big Amazon box by the front door that I didn't notice when I came in. I can't tell exactly what's in it, but army green wool pokes out the top, so the blankets for sure. It's not light, so there must be more.

I squint my eyes at her. "You guys are serious about this storm?"

Brandy nods. "It's not only the obscure websites talking about it now. They think it'll be bad."

I turn to go and she puts her hand on my shoulder, so I spin around again.

"I'm sorry for how I am," she says. "But that doesn't change the fact that I'm worried about you."

I think she means it. But that only solidifies my initial reaction: It's too fucking late.

She had the only ticket to The Dalice Show for years, and she never cashed it in. Now she's mad because other people are finally paying attention to me? Sorry, that doesn't cut it.

I roll my eyes and walk out, slam the door so hard that snow from the porch overhang falls all over the cement porch that Brandy likely scooped to perfection ten minutes ago. It barely missed me.

Once the box is in my trunk, I grab the scraper and brush off the windshield, which has accumulated a layer of snow during that short amount of time I was inside the house. All I can think is *How dare she?* Where does she get off acting like she cares about what happens to me? Telling me who not to have in my life? Not to mention that she liked Shane. He's polite and kind to them. And I'm madly in love with him. Still, she judges.

As I drive away, I repeatedly hit the steering wheel with an open palm. She doesn't know what's best for me. What's best for Cash. I know what's best for us. I'm staying until Cash gets healed. Period.

Instead of making me feel better, the thought makes me cry. I swipe at the tears so I can see, like a toddler.

My phone vibrates with a text, and it banners across the top of my screen.

*Reva called a meeting tonight at 7. Be there?*

I pull the car over because I really can't afford a ticket for texting and driving, plus the road is pretty scary. Too slick for my *fuck all, go to hell* attitude right now. I'll be extra late for my first house, but whatever, I'll bust ass and catch up at the next one. This is important.

It's from Mickey.

*Absolutely!* I reply.

I let myself enjoy a sense of relief—*A meeting! Maybe Cash will get healed today*—when another text comes through. It's Shane.

*Hey, can I take you and Cash out tonight? Dinner?*

What the hell?

*There's a meeting. You must know that,* I type.

Text bubbles appear, disappear, reappear. I wait.

*Ok. Need to tell you something important, but not over text. I guess it can wait until after the meeting.*

# DALICE

**THE FIRST THING** I notice when we walk into Reva's house for the meeting is that the mood is a little somber.

Nobody hangs out in the kitchen, laughing and catching up like usual. Everyone sits in the fireplace room.

Shane takes Cash upstairs to the nursery, and Mickey comes right over to me.

"Hey! So glad to see you. Did you not get my texts after the last meeting?"

*Shit.* Poor Mickey.

"Oh sorry, I've been crazy busy."

"I see how it is." She smirks. "You reply immediately when I tell you there's a meeting, but ghost me otherwise."

A fancy pen holds her hair up in a bun, and it sends me right back to high school. She did that all the time, but with a pencil.

"Just kidding," she continues when I say nothing. "I mostly wanted to hear how you were doing after your threshing. That was amazing. You were so strong, and I hope you felt loved."

I felt…something. I certainly *loved* how I felt afterward. But I can't label it as *feeling loved*. Also, I can't think too hard about the level of sheer fuckery I've reached, because someone cut my wrist, yet here I am, running right back to her like a lost puppy.

"Yeah, it was great. I hope I can go through again. You know, for Cash. Maybe a little less slicing next time." I expect her to laugh at my joke, but she furrows her brows like I said something wrong—again.

My eyes wander around the room.

Someone is missing.

It's a weird feeling, like a little hole in the house. A black spot.

"Hey, where's Renee?" I ask.

Mickey gives me a plastic smile. "Not sure. She's not late... yet."

Yes, she is. I'm always late, and Renee is always here by the time I arrive.

Shane comes downstairs, and Reva is nowhere to be found.

We wait in our seats. People chat and whisper for about fifteen minutes, and right when Shane is about to go upstairs to search for Reva, she appears in the foyer behind us. She wears high-waisted, wide-leg jeans and low-top Vans. A blue cropped sweater brushes along the waistline, not showing any skin. Her hair hangs in long, beachy waves. She's absolutely radiant.

"Welcome, family. I have a special announcement," she says while striding to the front of the room. She pauses for effect.

Shane's thighs tense up against mine. I put my hand on his leg, trying to reassure him.

"There will be no threshing tonight. The Threshing Floor has ended."

Now my thighs tense up. What does she mean?

I play it cool. Don't want her to see me freak out about this, because something tells me she can't know how desperate I am for her healing.

I survey the room, and everyone else seems to be hiding surprise as well.

Reva continues. "There's a winter storm coming, and the Lord has shown me it's time. It's time for us to put into practice everything we've been preparing for. The world sees a natural storm, but there's something else behind this one. The destruction it'll cause goes beyond the natural realm. The Lord's people must be together for it. We must all be of a truly pure heart, of one mind." Reva looks at me and smiles. "I will also heal anyone who is in need tomorrow."

She's making me a promise. I squeeze Shane's arm, but he's still tense. Probably worried about the storm. I'm worried too. What if I lose cell service and Seattle calls? Then again, if Reva is going to heal Cash tomorrow, that's not a worry, right?

Right.

We just need to ride out the storm, and before I know it, Cash will be healed.

# DALICE

**THE MEETING IS** short. Reva disappears upstairs, not even mingling afterward. Shane and I retrieve Cash and walk across the snow to his apartment. The harsh wind blows snowflakes like icy bullets against my skin.

Once inside, I put Cash down, and he crawls toward the toy bin against the wall.

Shane and I haven't spoken about The Threshing Floor, and it seems like both of us are trying to process what it means in our own minds. I don't really care, as long as Reva keeps her promise about Cash.

Shane's place has become more and more like mine as time goes on—toys everywhere. Except Shane puts them away after we leave, and Cash has to get them all out again when he arrives. That's probably the kid's favorite part.

"Look what I got for us tonight." Shane's voice comes from the kitchen. He holds up a bottle of bourbon like it's some trophy.

"You don't drink?" It comes out like a question, even though I don't mean it to.

He shrugs. "I've actually never been drunk before."

"What? How is that possible?"

"I was always busy with sports and work. And later, helping Reva."

He works on removing the top, and I catch Cash out of the corner of my eye as he pulls himself up to standing.

"Oh, my God!" I gasp. "Shane, look! Cashy-boy, you're doing it!" I clap for him.

He bends his knees, gripping the edge of the toy box and doing this little bounce, and he smiles like he knows he's doing something enormous. I'm witnessing a milestone. He's never pulled himself up before.

My eyes threaten tears, but I ignore that and pull my phone out, fiddle with the screen, and hit *record* so I can send Brandy a video.

It's so amazing to see him growing stronger. For a second, I wonder if his heart is improving. But I shoo that thought away. Developmentally speaking, he's so far past the point where he should be able to pull himself up to standing that this shouldn't be extraordinary. Yet, it is.

"Yeah, buddy!" Shane says from the kitchen. It makes Cash bounce harder. He gives us an open-mouthed, toothy smile.

I stop recording when I realize this is Cash's new normal. He's comfortable holding himself up now. It's like now that he's done it, he will never stop doing it.

Shane holds up the open bottle of bourbon.

"You game?"

"Hell yeah. Let's celebrate. Cash is going to be healed tomorrow."

I turn to watch Cash, and when Shane comes to stand next to me, it's with two full, eight-ounce glasses of bourbon. He hands me one.

"That's way too much," I say, stifling a laugh.

He lines up three fingers against the glass, spreading them out. "I have big fingers, I guess."

I laugh and we clink glasses, then I take a sip. It's been a while since I've had a drink, and it's good. Smooth. I don't recognize the brand, and that means it must be expensive.

Shane takes big gulps like it's water, and I gasp. "No!"

He coughs, makes a face, and shakes his head, but shrugs and does it again.

"I honestly can't believe you've never been drunk. First lesson: You don't guzzle this stuff. Surely you've at least seen that in the movies, right?"

"Don't care. Hey, I heard this song on the radio today. Reminds me of us. It could be our anthem."

He taps his phone and then turns on a Bluetooth speaker. He's swaying a little. Tipsy already? Or is he pre-dancing before the music comes on?

Cash finds the big dump truck, and he's lost in play.

This is a side of Shane I've never seen. Party Shane. My first impression is that I like it. I like that he's as relaxed around me as I am around him.

The song comes on, and I know it—Rhianna, "We Found Love." He's got it on quiet, but this song isn't meant to be quiet. I reach over to the speaker and crank it up.

Shane's glass is already half gone. He throws back the rest of it and pours some more, takes another big swig. Does he know the world of hurt he'll be in tomorrow if he keeps that up? I sip mine and watch him move to the music. He's not a good dancer at all. He moves like a wiggly robot, and it makes me laugh so hard.

"I used to be obsessed with music. It was my one safe place," he says out of nowhere, sitting down and staring out the window.

"Used to be?" I smile and nod toward the wall stacked with vinyl albums and CDs.

He laughs. "Oh, that's nothing compared to the old collection."

"What happened?"

"Reva."

What does he mean? Before I can ask, Shane plays the song over again, and I finally consider the words.

"'We found love in a hopeless place'? Pig Out Place?" I ask. Isn't this the song he said was about us?

"No. There." He swings his glass of bourbon toward the front window. "Somehow, in the middle of my sister's shitstorm, we found love."

The booze is slowing my mind down, but did he just swear?

When his second glass is empty, he grabs the bottle and takes my hand. He turns the music down and pulls me close, his fingers on the small of my back, his other hand holding the bottle. I hold him with one arm, my other gripping my glass.

Cash crawls over to us like he can't be left out. Shane picks him up, and we all dance together. Again, I see us as a little unit. A family.

"I have to tell you something," Shane says, taking a drink right from the bottle.

I finally get it. Liquid courage.

My head is dizzy, but my gut twists in anxiety. Whatever he has to tell me won't be good. But I promised I'd listen, and it'll be better if Cash is tucked into bed.

I down my glass and get Cash, then turn the music down. Shane plops on the couch.

"Bedtime, little dude," I say to Cash. One thing that boy rarely fights me on is bedtime. He's always tired.

Once I help Cash brush his teeth, and he's wearing the jammies Shane keeps on hand, I dim the living room lights and lay him in the crib.

Shane hasn't moved from the couch. It's quiet, and he stares into nowhere.

My heart pulses because I'm afraid of whatever it is he wants to say, but I take his hand and lead him into the bedroom. Standing there, I nuzzle up under his chin and we move like we're slow dancing to a song that's not playing anymore.

He runs a large hand down the back of my head to my neck, like he always does. "I've never told anyone this before."

The wind picks up and howls so loud outside that it sounds like screaming.

"What is it?" I whisper.

"I killed my mom."

# 1999

**SHANE'S GRADUATION CEREMONY** is tonight. He plans to move to Seattle and attend the University of Washington in the fall.

Reva hasn't stopped crying all week.

These past months since Shane's birthday have been the best of her life. Shane is her best friend, and he accepts her for exactly who she is. He believes the best about her. Most importantly, he stands up to Mom on her behalf.

When he moves out, she'll be alone with Mom.

It seems like Shane hates Mom now. He barely speaks to her, and when he does, they fight. He tells Reva that she needs to get away from here as soon as possible, and she knows, but she still has another year of school.

Mom begs Reva for healing whenever Shane isn't home.

She's traded her alcoholism for Reva's healing, but the addict is still there. Mom almost seems ashamed of what she's doing, but is powerless to stop.

Reva gets whatever she wants in return for healing. Mom never turns her down. This gives Reva more chances to experiment with her gifting. It started by accident one day when, before Reva healed her, she gazed into Mom's eyes and said, "I hate you."

A moment of bravery Reva had never known before. She felt so strong. Mom closed her eyes slowly, as if Reva's opinion actually mattered to her. And afterward, Reva had no headache.

She waited for a moment, for the spark of one starting up, but it didn't. An hour went by, and nothing. There was no rush of pleasure either, not like when she cut Mom and then healed her. But no headache was almost as exciting.

The next time, Reva thought of something else to say to Mom before she healed her: "You're a terrible mom."

It worked again. The humiliation Mom must feel from these statements neutralizes Reva's adverse effects from healing her.

It's a way to heal without ending up in pain.

Reva's mind spun at the possibilities this discovery opened up, at the excitement that she could continue to help people without hurting herself. Turns out it doesn't even matter what Reva says. She could say "You're ugly," which isn't true of Mom. Even so, her headaches stay away. Truth doesn't matter. What matters is that the person feels that it's true.

Shane gets ready in his bedroom with Ben Harper blasting so loud that Mom has banged on the door at least twice, screaming at him to turn it down.

At least it's not The Prodigy, or Rage, or any number of bands in Shane's vast collection that would actually be offensive to Mom. That's so like Shane. Putting in some effort to be kind, even as he's reminding her she doesn't control him. Reminding her one last time before he leaves.

*Leaves me.*

Once Reva has gotten on her cotton pencil skirt and baby tee, she walks into the kitchen. She hears the washing machine crank on in the basement, followed by a rush of water. Mom is doing laundry.

Reva gets a small knife and walks down the stairs. She has another question for Mom. The most important one.

"I'M NOT TELLING you that," Mom says, holding her bleeding arm.

"You will if you want your hit of healing, you bitch."

Mom flinches but lifts her chin. "It's my money. I'm not giving you access to it."

*Actually, it's my money.*

Reva shrugs. "Fine. I'll get you a bandage for that wound."

"Wait," Mom says, and bites her lip. "Get me something to write on."

Reva goes upstairs for a pencil and paper. It's Dave Matthews Band from Shane's room now, and she can hear him singing along. Notebook and pencil in hand, she goes back down the wooden stairs to the basement.

Mom scrawls something down and hands Reva the paper. It's her bank account information, including the PIN for her ATM card. Reva lays hands on Mom's cut and stares at her face. Her weak, sorry face. Addicted to using her daughter. It's vile.

This time, when Reva's hands cool off, she doesn't remove them from Mom's arm.

She's done dealing with Mom. Done with Mom's dependency on her, done with Mom's abuse. Just done.

"Let go." Mom's eyes widen and her breathing hitches.

Reva's hands grow chilly and Mom tries to pull away, but she's already too weak. Her legs buckle beneath her, and she falls to her knees on the concrete floor.

Mom blinks, but says nothing else. It's like she's drugged.

Reva doesn't let go, even though her hands are numb with cold. Not until Mom's mouth gapes open, and her eyes stop blinking.

Immediately, something surges through Reva's body. This energy makes her mind clear, able to process thoughts at twice the normal speed. She feels like she could do anything she wants.

Maybe she can.

Shane's music turns off. Heavy footsteps thump above. He's in the kitchen, right above them. The door to the basement is wide open, and Mom is dead. Reva's certain.

The thought does nothing for her. It's no different from saying *Water is wet.* She looks up the stairs. The only thing she's really afraid of is what Shane will think when he finds out what she did. But an idea sparks.

Reva moves quickly. She grabs Mom's body by the arms and pulls it on top of herself as she lays down on her back on the floor. Once it's in place, Reva reaches for the knife Mom dropped on the cold concrete. It's still bloody, and she sets it carefully next to the body, so it'll be in plain view when Shane comes down the stairs.

Reva screams.

It's the most guttural, deafening scream she's ever released. The scream is real. Like everything Mom has done to her, pent up over the years, is finally gushing out.

She moves around underneath Mom's body like a puppet master.

Shane flies down the stairs, shouting her name.

"It's Mom! She's attacking me," Reva says.

"What the fuck?" Shane growls, grabs Mom by the shoulders, and throws her off Reva in one smooth motion.

Mom flies like a rag doll.

*Smack.*

She lands face up on the concrete floor, and there's a splotch of blood on the edge of the butter-colored washing machine. She must have hit it.

Shane steps over to her. "Mom," he says, rustling her gently. His voice quivers. "Are you okay? I didn't mean to push you that hard."

Blood seeps along the floor, pooling fast. Shane watches Reva, and she watches the guilt in his face, the fear, the regret. She can sense it.

In Reva's mind, everything slows down to a dreamscape. Shane bends over. He retches, but nothing comes up. He jostles Mom again. He stands and grips his curly hair.

It strikes her as funny, this scene. Shane ripping his own hair out of his head. It's not funny. She can see that he's yelling, crying, but she can't hear anything. He reminds her of a mime, acting out his devastation in silence.

"She's still alive. Heal her," Shane says, only inches from Reva's face, pulling her back into the moment. "Get your hands out and heal her!"

*No.*

Reva is so blank inside that she doesn't even have to fake that the gold dust isn't here. Even if it were, she'd seek the nothing-place in order to keep it away. Mom being out of the picture might solve everything.

"I can't," Reva replies, showing Shane her palms. No gold dust.

"You have to!" he yells.

"I can't control the gold dust. I'm sorry," she lies.

Shane returns to Mom's body, two fingers stabbing around the surface of her neck. "There's no pulse. Go call 911," he says.

But Reva doesn't move. She whispers, "She's gone, Shane."

"No, she can't be. I just need to—" His face whips back at Reva, and he screams, "GO! Do what I said!"

Reva startles enough to run up the stairs. But she can't call 911. She won't.

When Reva returns, it's with Dad's old rifle.

"What the hell?" Shane stands and then cries harder than ever before. His face is wet, puffy, red.

"Here's what we'll say happened when they ask: Someone broke in tonight. You and I weren't here. We were out celebrating your graduation. But someone shot Mom. That's how it went." She holds out the gun to Shane. "Do it in the head to cover up the wound."

He refuses it. "No. This was self-defense. I'll tell them she was hurting you."

"There's no proof. They'll expect to see bruises or cuts on me."

"So she *wasn't* hurting you?" Shane narrows his eyes.

"She was, but I don't have any marks to show for it. You know how she abused me by hurting herself. It'll look to them like you simply pushed her into the corner of the washing machine out of anger. It was an accident, but they won't see it that way. Especially with how much you and Mom fight."

Shane stares at Mom's body like he's trying to decide, but it takes too long.

"Fine, I'll do it then." Reva cocks the gun.

He yells, "You can't shoot her! She's our mom. It's wrong."

Reva lowers the gun. "She's already dead, Shane. Do you want to go to prison for the rest of your life?"

"Maybe it's what I deserve."

"No!" Reva says. "You can't. I'll be alone."

Shane pulls his eyes from Mom and glares at Reva. "You'll be alone? That's what matters to you right now?"

"You could get the death penalty," she blurts.

Shane shrinks to the floor, knees bent as if he hadn't considered that. He stares at Mom's body again.

"We have to call the cops and report an intruder. Are you going to do this, or am I?"

Shane doesn't acknowledge her. He seems to disappear into his own head.

It's clear he can't do what needs to be done. It's just not in him.

But it *is* in her.

This is an area where Shane is weak, and she is strong. They make a good team.

Reva lifts the gun, motioning for Shane to move away from Mom's body.

"This is so wrong," he whispers.

"It's the only way."

He slides out of range.

Reva moves closer, pulls the trigger, and lands a shot directly in Mom's temple.

# 1999

**THE COPS WHO** responded to Reva's call instructed her and Shane to stay upstairs. Detective Syl Dixon would want to interview them, but they can't be tromping around, contaminating the crime scene in the meantime.

*Crime scene.*

The words stick in Reva's mind. She sits on the couch next to Shane, like they're both in time-out. Now that she's had time to process some of this, she's nervous. Does Shane doubt at all that he was the one who killed Mom? She keeps stealing side glances at him, and it doesn't seem like he does.

When Detective Dixon arrives, the cops pull her aside to bring her up to speed. They point at the broken glass door at the back of the house, and then toward the basement, which pretty much sums it up.

Reva watches the detective to determine what the chances are that she'll see through their story. The woman is so short. Her brown hair is pulled back into a poofy French braid; it's probably really curly and hard to manage. She seems about Mom's age and has a serious face with smile lines that turn down, like she's a chronic frowner. Reva hasn't seen her smile even once. But then again, there's not much to smile about here tonight.

After spending a good amount of time in the basement, Detective Dixon approaches Shane and Reva, then introduces herself.

"Tell me what happened tonight," she says, getting right into it.

"We...uh..." Shane starts, but no, he can't be the one to answer. He fumbles words, and his eyes dart all over the room. Everything about him screams *guilty*.

"—Shane and I were out tonight, celebrating his graduation," Reva interrupts. "When we got home, we noticed the glass on the back door was broken. I called for our mom, but she didn't answer. Shane and I began looking around for her, because her car was still here. That's when we found her in the basement."

The detective scribbles a few things on her notepad.

"Where were you two celebrating?"

"Oh, driving around listening to music. We do that a lot. We love music."

It's not airtight because nobody can vouch for them, but it's better than nothing.

Dixon turns to Shane. "What sort of music do you like?"

*Why does that matter?*

Reva slows her breath, tries to keep her cool. She can't let this detective outsmart her.

"A lot of stuff. Anything they play on the radio, really."

"I like music too. Classic rock, mostly. Do you play an instrument?"

*What does this have to do with anything?* Reva keeps her breathing even, but it worries her that she can't tell what the detective is doing. The more Shane talks, the more nervous Reva gets.

"No, no. Nothing like that. I'm just a connoisseur of sorts. Or I like to think I am."

Shane folds his hands in front of him and looks at them again. At least he gave a coherent answer.

"Did you two stop anywhere while you were out tonight? A gas station, perhaps?"

"No," Reva says.

"Have you noticed anyone strange lurking around before tonight? Maybe staring at the house or parked on the street?"

Reva and Shane both shake their heads.

Amazing how little she actually has to lie, because so much of this is the truth. It makes her more confident in her answers.

Dixon sits down in a chair across from the couch and puts her notepad on the coffee table. "Look, I know about your gift, Reva. I also know how your mom was taking advantage of it."

Reva can't hide the surprise she feels. It's probably all over her face. Dixon reads it immediately. "I've seen some crazy shit in my life. When I heard about you, I went to one of your meetings. A long time ago. Wanted to see for myself."

"Did I heal you?"

"No. I only went to observe."

Reva didn't expect this and doesn't know how to respond. The silence is uncomfortable, but she offers nothing else. Shane seems to be zoning out.

"I feel for you," Dixon says, closing her notebook. "I'm sorry you're going through all of this. And I'm really sorry about your mom."

Reva resists the temptation to sigh in relief. Dixon doesn't suspect them.

**WHEN DETECTIVE DIXON** comes by the house days later, Shane's at work.

When Reva opens the door, there's that tiny woman. Dixon motions like she wants to come inside, so Reva opens the door wider.

"We got the results from your mom's autopsy," Dixon says, and hands a sealed envelope to Reva. "This is for your brother. The report. She died of a heart attack."

*Careful. Tread carefully here.*

"Okay, but why would the intruder shoot her if she was already dead?"

"That's what I've been asking myself. I don't have an answer, but ultimately her cause of death isn't considered foul play, and since nothing was stolen from your house, it's not really a robbery either. I have one question, though. Why didn't you heal your mom when you found her in the basement? You know, with your gift."

"She was dead. I can't raise the dead."

Another truth.

Dixon chews on the inside of her cheek, nods, and says, "Hmm. Has Shane begun the process of establishing guardianship over you?"

Shane doesn't want to stay in Spokane, or bring Reva to Seattle, or leave Reva alone here.

"We're still talking about it," Reva says. "How long do we have?"

"The sooner, the better. I think Shane could make a pretty good argument to the court as to why he should be your guardian. It's only about a year until you're eighteen, right?"

"My birthday is in October, so a year and a few months."

"You could also request emancipation."

"As in…be on my own, legally?"

"That's right."

No. Being alone is exactly what she doesn't want. Therefore, Shane can't know about this option.

After Detective Dixon leaves, Reva lights the gas burner and destroys the report.

# 1999

"I CAN'T STAY here, you know that," Shane says. He boxes up his room to the sound of Ben Folds Five on his stereo system. He doesn't even bother to turn around and say it to Reva's face.

"Shane, if you won't be my guardian, I'll have to go into foster care."

He's said over and over that all he's wanted for years was to get out of Spokane and live his life, but she knows he wouldn't want that for her. His shoulders slump.

It's like a little crack in the vessel. A crack Reva can work to expand until his resolve shatters.

"I can't give up my life for you," he says, tossing a shirt into a box.

"I'm your sister. How can you leave me alone here? Plus, you're not *giving up your life*. Don't be so dramatic. You'd be moving to Seattle a year later than planned. That's all."

"Everything doesn't revolve around you. I know you have it hard because of your gifting, but I can't put my life, this opportunity to go to school, on hold."

His voice. It's so harsh. So unlike him. Reva senses the anger seeping out of him. Like the anger he used to direct at Mom.

Rage erupts inside of her, and it's a surprise. The force of it. Her unwillingness to comply with Shane sentencing her to loneliness.

His back is still to her, like he's hoping she'll disappear. But she's not disappearing. Never. Reva walks up to him and shoves him from behind. It's not enough to push him to the ground, but it's enough to get his attention.

"What the hell?" Shane says, turning.

"You *will* stay in Spokane," Reva pushes the words out slowly. "Or I'll tell them you did it. That you planned it out and ruthlessly murdered our mother."

"It was an accident!" Shane yells. "Why would you do that?"

"Detective Dixon came by yesterday," Reva says, letting the words hang.

"So?"

"Mom died from the head injury. They know the gunshot wound happened after she was already dead. You killed her, Shane. *You.*"

Shane sits down on the edge of his bed and rakes a hand through his hair. "Do they know it was me?"

"No. To them, we're just two sad children who have lost their only parent. At least, that's what I gathered from the detective."

"They should suspect me. It's strange that they don't. I'm an adult. I've had conflicts with Mom over the years."

"I told Dixon you and Mom were fine. That you fought no more than anyone else fought with their mom."

Shane glances up. "You lied to her?"

"I had to. To save you."

"Save me," he scoffs.

"Yes. And if you stay, you'll never go to prison, but if you leave, I'll tell Dixon the whole thing and then some. I swear I'll do it, Shane."

He puts his face in his hands.

She has him. Reva has him for as long as she wants to keep him.

# DALICE

"IT WAS AN accident," Shane says. His eyes are full of tears, and despite being drunk as hell, he got the story out. "Our mom was hurting Reva. She'd been hurting Reva for years and years. I had to protect her."

"You pushed her off Reva, and she hit her head...and died?"

He nods. "And if I leave Reva's side, she'll tell the police I murdered her. Premeditated it and everything. I'll go to prison. Or worse."

"Hold on. Reva really said that? That she'd go to the cops and tell them you *murdered your mom* if you don't—what? Spend the rest of your life with her? That's crazy."

Reva is a manipulative psychopath, and I've decided I hate her. How could she do this to someone she claims to love? How could she do this to Shane?

"I know. And maybe I should have pushed back a little harder, but I'm afraid of going to prison."

"Shane, you've been *living* in a prison," I whisper.

The words linger in the air for a few minutes.

"True," Shane finally says. "I think I need to come clean. It's the only way to get out from under Reva."

*Cash, though. My baby has to stay to get healed.*

My thinking pivots to this, like I've forgotten he just told me he accidentally killed his mom and his sister has held him hostage because of it for most of his life. But I don't want him to face these inner demons until my child gets healed.

It's totally, one thousand percent self-centered, and I hate myself for it, but that doesn't stop me.

"Right now? Can it wait until after the meeting tomorrow?" I say carefully, but when he doesn't reply, I move closer and realize it's because he's asleep.

# SHANE

**I WAKE UP** in the middle of the night hot. So sweaty and whoa, so thirsty.

It's not light outside yet, although soft moonlight leaks through my window. I'm afraid to look at my phone because it's probably only about two a.m. Not time to get up yet. Dalice breathes softly on her side, facing away from me. I want to wrap my arms around her, to press my body against her back and never let go. But she needs her rest.

My head is killing me, so I go into the kitchen for a pain reliever, and holy cow, I'm a little off-balance. Am I still drunk?

On the way back to bed, I swing by the crib and check on Cash. I put my finger below his nose to make sure he's breathing. He's so quiet.

I'm worried about him. I don't see Reva healing anyone without The Threshing Floor. She hasn't done that since we were young, when Mom was in charge. After that, she said God told her this was required in exchange for healing.

I get into bed slowly, trying not to wake Dalice. I lie on my back and stare at the ceiling. Thoughts drift.

I can't believe I told Dalice about Mom. I can't believe she doesn't hate me for it. Maybe it hasn't sunk in yet. That she's in love with someone who killed their own mother. It feels good to have it off my chest, but the thought of calling up the police and turning myself in churns in my stomach. I wish there was another way. I'll wait until after the meeting. Who knows? What if I'm wrong, and Reva will heal Cash? I hope so.

Renee comes to mind—how she wasn't at the meeting tonight.

I know where she lives. I'll go by her house later and see if she's there. She wouldn't miss the meeting, but that's what I always think about anyone who misses a meeting and then disappears.

Just when I'm about to fall asleep, I see something in my mind's eye. It's Reva in a long dress. Her massive hair is a hovering backdrop of red. Fire blazes behind her, and she lifts her arms up high. What comes next is a flash, a blip on the screen of my mind.

Reva, covered in blood.

Her hands are red, and it drips down to her elbows. It's speckled all over her face, and crimson baptizes her white dress.

I sit up fast, drenched in sweat again.

It's light out, and the bed is empty beside me. I look at my phone. It's ten in the morning, and Dalice has already left for the day. I didn't even hear her go, and for a moment I worry that she's *gone* gone. But whatever her feelings might be about my secret, I know she wouldn't leave until Cash gets healed.

**I'VE LEFT MESSAGES** for Renee. I've texted her. No response.

It's exactly like it was with Steve.

Except for one thing: When I drive by Renee's small home in Hillyard, a lower-income part of Spokane, someone is there. Not only that, but Renee's car is parked out front.

The door is opened a crack, but I still knock.

"Hello? Anyone home?"

An older woman opens the door wide. She has blonde hair, but it's going gray. No makeup on, bags under her eyes.

"Can I help you?" she says.

"I'm trying to find Renee."

"Who are you?"

"Her friend, Shane."

"From that cult?"

"What?"

I can see inside the small home. It's decorated in grays and soft pinks. Very Renee.

"You're from that group she goes to. The one that's turned her against us, her real family."

"I'm sorry, I don't know what—"

"You're the one who sucked her in, too." Her face moves into recognition, as if she's seen me before, but surely she hasn't. "With your good looks and charm. She told me about you before she stopped taking my phone calls. I've only seen her in person a handful of times over the past year."

"It's not a cult. It's just a group of people who get together and encourage each other."

*And abuse each other verbally.*

*And force each other to strip naked.*

*And slash each other's wrists.*

Whoa, it's totally a cult. I guess I've never realized that until now.

"Seems like a cult to me. Renee changed completely after she started going there. Sure, her speech impediment was cured, and that's what she always brings it back around to. But if you ask me, the whole thing is wrong."

I can't address this. The fact that I may be in a cult is too new, and everything in me resists it, so I change the subject.

"When did you notice Renee was missing?"

"You here playing detective, like suddenly you care about my daughter?" But then she shakes her head, and her defenses seem to drop a bit. "Hell, the police won't listen to me. They say she's an adult, and maybe she just left for the weekend without telling me. But all her stuff's here. Why would she leave without packing a bag at all? Who does that?"

"That is weird. Hey, whatever you think about the group, I am Renee's friend. I want to help."

The woman's eyes fill with tears.

"Not quite twenty-four hours ago, to answer your question. That's when I noticed something was fishy. Even though she thinks being around us will pollute her—her words, not mine—she must have forgotten that I still have a key to her house. Her ignoring my calls is typical, but something about it this time made me want to come over and check on her. A mother's intuition, you know?"

"Where would she go without her car?"

"Your guess is as good as mine. Alls I can do is try to convince the police to get moving on finding her."

I wrap up the conversation and walk toward the Rover. I can't help but accept the truth. Renee is actually missing.

Nobody knows where she is, and her car is still here.

She didn't leave The Threshing Floor, and she didn't move away.

She's gone.

# SHANE

**I CAN'T BELIEVE** how hard it's started snowing just in the time it takes to drive from Renee's to the meeting. The sky darkens like a cloud going over the sun, and it feels much later in the day than it is.

Flakes sound like hail on my windshield, and they turn to ice when my wipers try to clear them. Heavy sleet is collecting like snow does, forming a thick layer of ice everywhere.

I open the door to Reva's house, and the first thing I see is Dalice.

Ice has covered her parked car, so I know she's been here a few minutes, but her boots are still on, as is her coat. She grips Cash in her arms even though he wiggles to get down. Her eyes are wide.

"Come here, I have to show you something," Dalice whispers and nods toward the front door.

I don't like the expression in her eyes, so I follow without question. At least we have some shelter underneath the porch overhang even though the wind is biting.

She hands me Cash, and I pull up his hood, tucking his blonde hair underneath it. Dalice stuffs a hand in her coat pocket and retrieves a piece of paper. She unfolds it.

"It was a heart attack, Shane. You didn't kill her. Not even by accident."

Cash leans for Dalice, so we swap. I take the paper; she takes Cash.

I scan it, trying to take the words in faster than reading it line by line.

My eyes stop when I see "Linda Prehner" and "Cause of Death." Then, "Acute Myocardial Infarction."

"How did you find this?" is all I can manage.

"Brandy."

Heat rises to my face despite the freezing cold. "You told her?"

"Of course not! I asked her to find out how your mom died. She was already digging around because she ran across a news article."

"Digging around? For what?"

"She doesn't trust you. And there's no depth of Google Brandy can't plumb."

No time to get into that.

"And this is a copy of the real thing? My mom's actual autopsy report?"

"Yes. You can leave Reva without being blamed for your mom's death. After Cash gets healed, we can go."

"But she was healthy," I say. "I saw her just minutes before it happened."

But what exactly did I see? Reva was on the ground with Mom on top of her. Was Mom moving at that point? I can't remember. Reva had screamed, and that's what brought me to the basement. Could Reva have done something to her?

My mind whirls at this new possibility, but it's unable to gain any traction. The result is a word salad: "A vision. My sister. She was covered in blood. Reva's hands. Renee is missing."

"Missing?"

"I went to her house. Spoke with her mom. She's gone, Dal." I don't know how all of this connects, but I'm certain that it does. And certain that we need to leave. Now.

Dalice closes her eyes and shakes her head slowly in disbelief, like she's trying to clear out whatever she thought before to make room for this new reality. "Wait, what?"

"Take Cash and ride the storm out at Brandy's before it gets too bad to drive."

She stands there like I didn't speak. "Shane, you know I can't leave yet."

No. Not this. Panic surges inside my chest. She can't be serious. Something like anger flares inside me. "You have to. You're in danger."

The last thing Reva wants is for me to leave and be happy with Dalice. She'll at least try to stop that from happening. Cash reaches for me, and I put a hand out to prevent him from flopping into my arms. "Stay with Mommy, bud."

"Why?" Dalice asks. "Why am I in danger?"

I lower my chin and stare right into her eyes. "Because I love you."

Dalice bites the inside of her cheek. Her eyes dart side to side like she's trying to decide. I'm about ready to pick them both up and carry them to the car myself when the front door opens behind her, and Reva stands in the doorway.

She's wearing a long, white dress.

I step aside to hide behind Dalice so Reva is out of my line of sight.

*Go now. Run*, I mouth, but Reva steps closer. An arm's length away from Dalice and in full view of me.

I look at her hands. Something about her gift makes her able to hurt people, too. That must be it.

Reva watches me and rubs those hands together as if to warm them. She doesn't have a coat on, and her hands are way too close to Dalice. "What's going on? Why are you guys out here?"

"Dalice forgot something at home. She needs to run back real quick," I say, staring at Dalice.

She holds my stare and shakes her head. "No, I'm good."

I feel my eyes flaring. Is she really this stubborn?

"Shane, can you please check Cash into the nursery?" Reva says. "Come with me, Dalice. Let's get you some coffee."

When Dalice moves closer to hand Cash to me, I whisper, "We need a plan. Meet me in the foyer. Don't let her touch you."

I don't know if she'll listen to me, but I hope to God she does, because there's no time to explain all of this to Dalice without my sister overhearing. One of my only advantages is that Reva doesn't know that I know she can hurt people.

Cash cries now. He's so ready to get down.

I could leave with just him. Turn around right now and go. At least get him to safety.

But I can't leave Dalice with Reva. That's a terrible plan.

Then something clasps around my mind as I hold Cash's warm head against my shoulder.

Maybe we're all in danger.

# DALICE

**INSIDE THE HOUSE,** I pull off my boots and hang my coat up.

Shane is scaring me. His face—it was like saw a ghost. He's never been that forceful with me before, either.

I can hear Brandy in my mind: *You never listen!*

But I can't listen this time. I trust Shane, but it's physically impossible for me to walk away right now when Cash is so close to being healed. I don't even know why he thinks Reva would suddenly want to hurt me.

*She already hurt you once before.*

But she was planning to heal me that time.

I let out a little whimper as I follow behind Reva toward the kitchen.

What if I'm wrong? What if I am in danger?

But Cash.

I hate that I can't let that go. If I were watching someone else in my situation, I'd be screaming *Get out of there, you idiot!*

The minute Cash gets healed, we'll run. I'll tell Shane as soon as I get back to the foyer to meet him.

But that doesn't happen.

Reva calls me back every time I step away, once even trying to take my elbow, but I dodged her touch. She keeps giving me things to do. All these stupid little tasks.

*Can you get some coffee for Holly? She likes it black.*

*Can you check the firewood to be sure there's enough?*
*Can you make sure these chairs are all straightened?*

Just as I finish with the chairs, she announces it's time to start, even though there are only about a dozen people here instead of the usual number.

Shane can't stand in the foyer anymore without drawing attention. He joins me in the same seats we always occupy.

"Sorry, I was trying to get away," I whisper.

"We need to leave," he snaps back, monotone.

"Definitely. As soon as Cash gets healed."

"She's never going to heal him," Shane says, tears gleaming in his eyes.

How does he know that? But I search his eyes and can tell that whatever he knows, he's certain of it.

"Dalice, we're starting," Reva says.

The small group of people watch me. I notice that it's all the core people in the group, the ones that seem the most committed.

"Sorry."

Reva talks about this storm and the evil it signifies. How the outside world is manifesting the disease of sin. How only she can heal it. How we'll only be safe if we stay here to ride it out. Her tone is hard, and that white gown she's got on has a real Manson feel to it. She suddenly sounds insane. How can a storm signify people's sin? Has she always sounded this crazy? What else have I been missing?

I put my hand on Shane's knee, and when he turns toward me, his blanched face makes the tiny hairs on my neck prickle.

For the first time, I'm scared to be here.

Shane's right. We have to leave. Whether Cash is healed or not.

Maybe he can keep Reva occupied while I run upstairs and get Cash. The storm isn't so bad that we couldn't drive out of here. What's she going to do? Lock us up?

I'm so deep into contingency planning that I don't notice Reva has wrapped the meeting up early again.

Like always, people stand and move toward the kitchen.

"I think you're right about her," I whisper. "I'm getting Cash. Meet you at the Rover?"

He sighs in relief and nods.

But Reva is close by again, this time with a little wire basket. "Phones here."

Why do we have to give up our phones? I'm not doing that.

"I need mine," I say. "Waiting on the call for Cash's heart transplant." I hold it close to my chest.

Reva cocks her head to the side, but it doesn't land as friendly as usual. "I'm going to heal Cash. You don't need the transplant."

Her tone is flat. It's as if she's shed the skin of kindness.

"When?" I ask.

"When it's time. Have faith."

A text from Brandy comes through.

*Where are you? Power's out here. Love you.*

The two tiny words at the end bring up tears. I don't know why it feels so meaningful, but it does. Maybe Brandy does care and just has a super-duper shitty way of showing it.

Can't think about that right now.

I go to reply, formulating some response like *We're stuck in the very last day of a cult. Might be a death cult. TBD*, but Reva reaches for me. Shane slaps her wrist before her fingers make contact. He rips my phone out of my hands and puts it in the basket.

"What was that for?" Reva snaps.

"We can put our own phones in the basket," Shane says.

Reva rolls her eyes, huffs a little disgusted noise, and takes the basket around the room, collecting phones.

"I almost had a text out to Bran."

Shane wraps an arm around me and kisses the top of my head. "It's okay. Just get Cash and meet me at the Rover."

I nod, and as I place a foot on the stairs to go retrieve him, the power goes out.

# DALICE

**WHEN I COME** down the stairs holding an already-asleep Cash in my arms, Reva stands in front of the entryway door, blocking it. A small group of people are gathered around her in the foyer. She holds a propane camping lantern in one hand, so there's some light. It's not pitch black, but darker than it should be for this time of day. The ice comes down at such a deep slant that it sounds like a machine gun as it pelts the windows.

I don't see Shane, so he must have made it to the Rover before she planted herself there. How will I get past her?

"Where's Shane?" she asks the group, but stares at me.

"He was just here..." I say, glancing around as if I genuinely don't know.

"How are we supposed to stay warm without power?" someone asks.

"I have a battery-operated space heater in every bedroom. Plenty of batteries. Let's get room assignments taken care of, and then you can all settle in," Reva says, but her eyes keep wandering around the place.

God, it's like she knew the power would go out. I mean, I guess it was a possibility because of the storm, but something about this feels so orchestrated.

I move toward the back of the group so I can go last. My anxiety is through the roof, and it's all I can do to keep from straining to see out the window for Shane. I don't want to expose his plan.

*Don't let her touch you.*

Shane's words echo in my mind, so I rule out pushing past Reva and running for it. I doubt I could beat her in a foot race carrying Cash, anyway. And in the snow? Forget it. Something tells me I shouldn't let her put me in a room either, though.

*Think. Think. Think.*

Gina comes up to me, and I can tell she wants to say something, but not in front of other people.

"What's going on?" I whisper.

"No idea." Her words are barely audible. "Something is off."

Goosebumps ripple across my skin. We aren't the only ones scared. How did I not see that Reva could be dangerous? I was so blind.

And if I couldn't see that, how can I trust anyone's intentions? What if I can't rely on my gut instincts anymore? Clearly I don't even know what's best for myself, let alone my son.

Anxiety pounds at my chest, gripping my throat and making it hard to swallow. Coming up with a plan feels impossible thanks to this new revelation.

Cash pushes against me, his universal signal for *Let me down.* He's been doing that most of the day, but it feels like a big ask from Cash right now. To require me to let him go. I cling to him.

Shane comes in the front door, bringing a violent blast of wind and ice along with him.

Reva steps aside. "Shane! Where were you?" She's obviously relieved.

*No.* Why is he back? We were supposed to meet at the Rover.

We make eye contact, but he answers her. "Just checking outside for any extra wood we may need." He comes toward me and takes Cash, then squeezes my arm gently, like *I'll explain later.*

Reva narrows her eyes, but goes into the kitchen, and everyone else tags along like little lost sheep.

"Let's go!" I whisper, stepping past him toward the front door.

He takes my arm. "She changed my garage code. I can't open it."

"Power's out. Can't you lift the garage door?"

His eyes square with mine. "Power's not out at my place."

"What?"

"Only here in this building."

What the fuck. She absolutely planned this. My stomach clenches like I might retch.

"What about the gate?" I push out in a whisper. If she changed his code so he couldn't get to his car, did she change the gate code too?

"I tried it. That code doesn't work anymore either, but I found an ax out by the woodpile. To take out the gate controls."

I furrow my brows at him. "It'll set off the alarm."

"Maybe not. Do you have a better idea? I'm open to anything."

I exhale and shake my head, then add, "We'll take my car."

He nods like he already thought of that. "It's covered in ice, but I guess it's all we have to work with. You have your keys?"

I pat my front jeans pocket to show him.

"Good."

"Oh! Hank gave me a box of survival-type things too. It's in my car. Might come in handy."

"What's in it?"

"Blankets and water were on the top. I'm not sure what else."

Shane's eyes shift over toward the kitchen where Reva went.

"Go see what's in there and bring back whatever you can hide."

**I OPEN THE** front door just enough to slip out and not create a scene, but outside, the wind is deafening. Slivers of ice fall from charcoal clouds and pepper the house, the ground, my skin. There wasn't time to grab a coat, so the freezing air cuts through my chunky sweater like I'm wearing nothing. I have regrets about that choice.

I pull the key out of my pocket, and it won't go into the trunk lock. It's frozen shut.

*Shit.* I bend down and breathe hard on it, trying to warm it up. I slip the key in, turn it, but now the trunk door won't lift. It's frozen shut too. I pull as hard as I can, my feet slipping on ice, threatening to take me down flat, but I don't give up.

Finally, the trunk cracks open, and there's the box. Way too big to bring the whole thing inside and still keep it hidden. I lift the wool blanket, toss it to the side, and paw around. My hand hits hard plastic, then something that feels like an antenna.

I pull out a walkie-talkie.

*Fuck yeah.*

When I switch it on, I get loud static. A piece of tape on the front says "Channel 5," so I turn the dial.

"Hello? Hank?" I say, hoping he's on the other side.

Garbled words come over the speaker, completely drowned out by the loud storm.

I climb onto the porch, where there's a break from the wind, and cup my hand over the speaker. "Hank, we're at Reva's. We're in trouble. Call the police."

"Dalice, where are you? Over." Hank's voice cuts through almost immediately after mine.

He didn't hear me.

"Hank! Are you there? We're at Reva's."

"The wind is too loud, I can't make out what you're saying. Over."

I groan and fight back tears. Sleet freezes into my hair. I'm right outside the house, so someone would only need to open the door and I'd be exposed, along with the walkie-talkie.

*Get inside the car.*

I work the driver's side door open as fast as I can, fighting again with the ice that's clamping it shut. Once it's open, I slip inside and press the call button. But nothing happens. I try again. Nothing. The damn thing is dead. I want to scream.

*Breathe. Think.*

I stare at the dead walkie in one hand, and my car keys in the other. Maybe I can find a battery. But I'm leaving the keys here in case something happens to me. I swallow hard at the thought of maybe not being the one to drive my car out of here and drop the keys on the passenger seat.

The house's front door opens and I duck down, trying to hide. When I finally get the courage to take a peek, I see it's Gina. And she's holding Cash.

# DALICE

**I SHOVE THE** walkie into the waistband of my jeans, pull my sweater over it, and rush into the house. Where is Shane? And why would he pawn Cash off to Gina right now?

I mean, I'm grateful she has him, but I'm not sure who I can trust, and I don't like that Shane handed my baby off at seemingly the first moment he could.

In the foyer, I take Cash from Gina. He's holding a wooden train in each hand—his two favorites from the nursery. Juniper sits by the fireplace, playing with a doll.

"Where's Shane?" I whisper.

Gina shrugs. "He handed me Cash and made me swear on my life to watch after him. Then he went out the side door while Reva was upstairs."

"There you are," Reva appears from the kitchen. A random thought hits my brain that she's been in the kitchen a lot today. More than normal. Why? She stares at me, and for the first time, I swear I see nothing behind her eyes. Whatever act she had going during The Threshing Floor is officially gone.

"Why are you out of your room?" she asks Gina, who doesn't reply. "Take Juniper up to Mickey's room and keep Cash with you for a bit longer. I need Dalice."

I look over at Gina and Cash. I can't leave him. But when nobody hops to obey Reva, she steps closer. Her presence is dark, like fury might bubble out. I pull back to stay away from her hands. Thankfully, Gina is still out of reach.

"Take off your boots and help me get more lanterns," Reva spits out the words and walks down the wallpapered hall toward the kitchen.

Gina hovers over me as I slip off my boots. "You can trust me." There are tears in her eyes. "Whatever comes next, he's safe with me. I swear."

I exhale a cry and hug her because I have to trust her. I don't have a choice.

"Here," I give her the walkie-talkie. "It's dead, but I don't know. Maybe we can find some batteries. If not, I left my keys in my car. Find Shane and get Cash out of here."

"We're not leaving you," she says, taking it from me.

"Dalice?" Reva calls out from the kitchen. Her tone makes me feel like a child in trouble.

"Please. You have to," I whisper.

I don't want them to go without me, but Cash cannot be here a minute longer either. I don't wait for Gina to argue again. Instead, I walk away to follow Reva. Except that once I'm in the kitchen, I don't see her.

My heart hammers in my ears.

*This is bad. Turn around.*

But it's too late.

Reva grips my wrist.

Fatigue hits me like a speeding truck. I try to pull away, but she yanks harder and spins me so my back is before an open door.

The basement.

My unreliable gut informs me that Reva is doing something to my body. I feel so tired.

Her hands are growing chilly, and her eyes are dead. She smirks. Something about this strikes up a hurricane of emotion in me.

No way this bitch is taking me down like this.

I can't scream. I can't cry. But I laser the strength I have, the determination to live, toward Reva, and with a big scream, I ram my entire body into her.

She stumbles backward and hits the ground with a loud *thunk*.

I land on top of her, and my wrist slips from her grasp.

She doesn't move.

But neither can I. My body feels so damn heavy, and my head—it's pounding.

*Go. Go. Go. Get off her!*

I slither myself off and slowly get on my hands and knees, and it's like trying to move with cinder blocks attached to my arms and legs. I pant and clench my jaw to channel that strength again.

Reva's eyes flutter.

She's not dead or unconscious.

*Move!*

I get to my feet, but she's blocking the way out of the kitchen. I can't get around her.

*Shit. Shit. Shit.*

My brain blinks to life again, and it's easier to move. My body isn't one hundred percent, but I'm not stuck anymore. I glance around.

That open door behind me. The basement.

But no! How stupid is that? I can't go into the basement.

I can hear everyone watching the movie say *Don't go into the basement, you idiot!*

But it's that or face off with her Medusa hands again.

Reva pulls her feet under her and touches her head. Squeezes her eyes shut and then opens them. I think she hit her head on the floor. She brings her hands out in front of her and glances down at her palms.

The huge kitchen windows send enough light through for me to see them gleaming gold.

The basement it is.

I slip down the dark stairs and pull the door shut. Lock it.

# DALICE

**BLOOD THRUMS LOUDLY** in my ears. My head hurts, but I have to keep going, keep pushing farther down this dark corridor. Turning back isn't an option.

It's cold blackness all around, like an abyss yawning to consume me whole. I blink a few times to confirm my eyes are open. There's no difference, but if I could see anything, it'd be the white fog of my own breath. I shiver and tuck my hands inside my oversized sweater to drum up some warmth.

I'd hoped this basement would have a window to climb out of. Maybe even a door to the outside. It's a fucking mansion, after all. But I've been moving down this pitch-dark hallway for what feels like hours, rushing as fast as I can. It has to lead somewhere. Preferably somewhere I can hide.

When the pressure in my skull becomes a vise grip, I slow down to walk, keeping a sweatered fist against the wall for support. With only socks on, the soles of my feet feel numb as I move across the polished concrete floor. It's like sneaking across a Home Depot. Or a prison.

Smooth drywall gives way to rough brick with sloppy seams of grout. It snags my sweater, so I push my sleeve back and feel as I go.

The concrete floor ends abruptly in a one-inch drop. It would be nothing in the light, but since I don't see it coming, my footing falters, and I hit…dirt?

What the hell?

It's like I've entered some part of the corridor where they gave up making it look nice. Probably assumed nobody would see it anyway.

A tentacle of fear snakes up my neck at that thought. What the fuck is this basement for?

I finally turn a corner to see something ahead.

A red light cuts through the darkness, radiating from a razor-thin gap below a door.

But the power is out in the whole building. How is it possible for one light to be on?

And why?

I pause to watch for shadows moving on the other side of the door. A brush of dark to punctuate the crimson line. Evidence that someone is inside.

There's nothing.

Somewhere behind me, footsteps thump down the stairs leading to the basement.

Leading toward me.

Panic flushes through my body. If someone comes down this corridor, they'll crash right into me. I need to find cover or I'll be pinned here, and that's not an option.

I reach the door, expecting it to be locked, but with hardly any force, it creaks open an inch.

My gut drops. Unlocked.

This is probably a trap, but I have no choice.

The red light goes off. Then it flashes in long strobes.

Red. Dark. Red. Dark.

The dark is so much longer than the flashes of red, and it messes with my eyes.

The door is heavy when I open it, like steel, and holy hell, it's got to be five inches thick. The smell of rot and shit assaults my nose, and I gag. I can't go in there. I can't.

Feet tap polished concrete behind me, and my pulse spikes again. Sure, they haven't reached the dirt yet, but they're close. Way too goddamn close.

I walk into the room. The putrid smell is *so* much stronger inside. I gag again and nearly vomit. I step toward the wall, trying to orient myself. I have to get as far away from the door as possible. Perhaps find an exit, or a closet to hide in.

Underfoot, I feel a squish and a crunch. I flinch back, and now my sock is wet.

*What the hell?*

My mind goes right to dead animals, which would explain the smell. That thing felt about the size of a squirrel. Or a rat? Could be a rat.

"Who's there?" A female voice cuts through from deeper inside the flashing red darkness. It sounds like she just woke up.

Chains jangle.

I freeze, breath hitching in my throat. Someone's down here? Chained up?

*What the actual fuck?*

"Help me." The voice is a breathy whisper.

I strain to see, but the strobe effect is aggravating my head, making it hurt worse than it already did. I have to help, but terror tightens around me like a straitjacket.

I don't want to go any further

I must go further.

*Move forward. Just take a step.*

I move, hugging the wall so I don't trip again.

"Where are you?" I whisper, raising one arm in front of my face, protecting it from whatever I can't see in the dark.

Another soft crunch underfoot.

*Shit.*

More icy wetness squidges through my sock and between my toes. The taste of bile rises, but I swallow it and keep moving.

"Toward the back," she says.

My hand collides with some sort of metal hanging along the wall. I finger it until I realize it's a chain attached to the ceiling. It doesn't sway easily, so I can tell there's something bulky at the bottom, but with the doses of red light so short, and my eyes so night-blind, I have no idea what it is.

When I go to grip the chain and move around it, something scrapes my hand. I gasp and bring my hand close to my eyes, straining to see during the blinks of red. But all I can make out is a substance, wet and warm.

My palm is covered in blood.

Then I see a meat hook. The kind in a butcher's shop. Or a horror movie.

But when I squint closer, it's not just one. It's dozens and dozens of hooks.

I seize up inside as my brain registers what's attached to the hooks.

Hands.

All these dismembered hands. A bouquet of them, speared through the wrists and dangling from the chain.

I stumble backward to get away, but I fall on my ass on the dirt floor.

"She keeps them," the woman whispers from across the dark room. "Her trophies."

Oh God, oh God. She said "trophies." As in *serial killer*.

"Who is that?" I breathe.

"It's me, Renee."

Oh God. Renee. That's why she wasn't at the meeting.

"Why...? What is this?" I ask.

Words are hard. I can't make them line up together correctly. On the back burner of my mind, I realize I'm probably in shock. It explains why I'm still sitting on the ground. Why I haven't stood up.

I plant a hand on the dirt to pull myself up, but it touches something smooth. Cold. I feel it and make out—a nail bed. A finger.

It's a hand. Another hand.

That crunch underfoot from before was bones. I stepped on and crushed human *hands*.

I whimper and make myself stand.

More chains jangle. Closer to me this time. A man groans.

"That's Colin. He just got here," Renee rasps. "It'll be a while before he's actually awake, though. She gets you good and high right off the bat. Less of a fight when she strings you up, I guess."

Good and high.

Like that night with Shane when I was invincible. The best sex of my life.

"Why does she have you down here?" I ask, trying to move toward her, toward the back, to find somewhere to hide while I conjure up a plan.

Renee coughs, rattling her chains louder. She's far from me, but now I can see her in the faint blinks of red light. She's chained by the wrists above her head. Her toes touch the ground, but they're not planted. I move closer so I can see, and her face sends a shock wave of fear through my body.

It's hollow. Dirty. Sunken cheeks. Smeared blood all over exposed skin.

This doesn't look like Renee at all.

"She uses us. It's how she stays young. She gets just enough from us to make herself feel good without killing us. Or without killing us right away, I guess." She pauses, listening. Then: "You should run."

Footsteps scuffle dirt on the other side of the metal door.

It's her. She's here, and I have nowhere to run.

# SHANE

**I HAD NO** choice. I had to give Cash to Gina so I could slip out the side door and take that ax to the gate control box.

After two swings, it powered down. No alarms, nothing. All this time, Reva hasn't had the damn gate hooked up to an alarm. It's all for show and no better than a locked door.

Whatever, that only makes it easier for me. Once I get to Dalice and Cash, we'll leave.

I turn the front doorknob with caution. I don't know where Reva is, and I need to sneak Dalice out.

We'll slip out, get into her car, and somehow drive through this storm.

Before I push the door open, a wave of doubt comes over me.

How the hell am I going to pull this off?

It doesn't matter. I have to.

I'm shocked when I walk into the foyer and nobody is there except Gina, Cash, and Juniper.

"Shane. Dalice said the keys are in her car. She wants us to go, but—"

"—I'm not leaving her," I say.

She nods fast. "I know. She gave me this. I was just about to look for batteries when you walked in. Had to wait until Reva was out of the kitchen."

Gina flashes a walkie-talkie.

Hank's survival box. My heart leaps. Not only that, but there's no way a guy like Hank would toss a walkie-talkie into a box and not include a backup battery. That's our best bet for finding the right kind.

"Where's Dalice?" I ask.

"I think she's in the basement. With Reva."

*No!*

My eyes land on the rifle. Dad's .22. There, mounted above the fireplace, is Reva's flex. The symbol of my imprisonment. A reminder of that night, the reason I thought I could never leave. The lie I've been living.

I climb on a chair and pull the gun down, then open the bolt to confirm it's loaded.

Cash is asleep on Gina's shoulder, and looking at him, my mind goes in two directions at the same time.

*Get him the hell out of here.*

*Find Dalice.*

I need to do both *right now.*

I pick Juniper up, and she wraps her arms around my neck.

"You have to get them out of here," I say to Gina. "In Dalice's car."

She nods. "But what about everyone else?"

"No time. Let's go."

We run out the front door, and Gina gets the kids into the car. I go straight for the box in the trunk, feeling around for something that could be a battery.

*Come on, Hank. Come on!*

I feel like fucking fist-pumping when I find it, but there's no time for that either. The kids are in the car, and I change out the battery and switch it on. The wind is too loud outside. I slip into the passenger's seat and close the door. "Hank? Are you there?"

**HANK ANSWERS IMMEDIATELY,** and we make a plan for Gina to get the kids to his and Brandy's place, where they can hunker down through the storm.

"Drive slow," I say.

Gina smiles. "I cut my teeth on Spokane winters. I'll be fine. And I'll call the police as soon as I can. I just worry about how long it might take them to get here in the storm."

I worry about that too.

In the back, Cash is asleep again, but Juniper stares at me. I smile and nod at her, trying to tell her it's going to be okay.

"I want my mom," she says.

"I'll find her. Don't worry."

The walkie-talkie comes to life. "Shane? You ready? Over."

"Yes. Gina is heading your way with Cash and another little one."

"I'll meet her at the Yoke's parking lot off the Newport Highway. Over."

Gina makes a confused face at me. I shrug and say, "He's ex-military."

She nods.

I watch the red taillights disappear into the sleet and put Cash out of my mind.

Now, where the hell is Dalice?

# DALICE

"YOU FOUND MY stash, I see," Reva hisses as she walks into the murder dungeon.

There's nowhere to hide, but I stand pressed against the wall on the far side of Renee anyway, buying time. I squeeze the metal in my hand—one of those massive meat hooks. It's on a chain that's attached to the wall behind me, so it's not useful unless she's close, which terrifies me. I'm still weak from whatever Reva did to me upstairs. I feel dizzy when I move too fast.

"Does Shane know about all this?" I ask. As the words come out, an idea lights up my mind.

Reva's feet drag a little as she walks. It's not extreme, more like a little shuffle, but it makes me think she's hurt. I must have wounded her when I launched her to the kitchen floor.

"What do you think?"

"Fuck no, obviously."

She moves slowly toward me.

"Doesn't matter. He'd stick around either way. He has to."

"Why? Because he thinks he killed your mom?"

She stops walking.

"How do you know about that?" She's unable to hide the surprise in her voice. She takes another step, and she's almost to Renee, who has agreed to be perfectly quiet and act like she's not here.

I can't move closer to Reva with my hook on this leash. I must wait for her to come to me.

But then Renee's cry cuts through the darkness, and I can see Reva's shadow on the other side of her, gripping her neck.

Renee.

Before I can react, she lets go, and Renee's head drops to her chest.

*Oh God, oh God. She killed Renee. Right here next to me.*

"I'm surprised he told you he killed Mom," Reva says, as if she didn't just pause the conversation to murder an innocent girl. "He's always been so terrified of prison. I suppose most men are. It's the only place where they might be victimized. Where they have to watch their backs because there's bound to be someone bigger and badder than them on the food chain."

I've never thought about it that way, but she's right.

I shake my head to dislodge the thought. Doesn't matter right now. If she's going to monologue, I need to focus. Not let her distract me. I can still see her shadow, but I can't tell what she's going to do. What she's got up her sleeve.

"Not like women," she continues. "We know what it's like to be the victim. We're born into watching our back at all times, accepting that we can be victimized at any moment. Groomed for it, really. Every day of our lives is an opportunity to be a victim unless we do something about it."

I move along the wall a bit. My weapon has maybe a foot of wiggle room, but I want to be able to come at her with some force when she's close enough.

"You're a real cliché, you know that?" I say, then I change my tone so it's a whiny, mocking voice. It's an act, but I have to nail it because it's my only idea. "Poor me, such a victim. I'm going to make myself feel good by hurting others. But I'm not the monster! No, I can only ever be the victim." I drop the mocking tone. "Honestly, Reva? Boring. I expected more from you."

"I never said I wasn't a monster."

"Reva? What's going on?" a man says from directly across the room. He's groggy like he's only just now waking up. It must be Colin.

If I take a step closer, Reva's within my reach.

I see the shadow of her hair swing as she glances over at Colin.

I slide closer and swing the hook at her back. It lands deep in the flesh of her shoulder.

I'm so shocked to land the hit that I don't move at first.

She wails and reaches around to pull it out, but she can't quite get it.

*Run, you idiot!*

I listen to myself and sprint out of the dungeon.

Pain ricochets through my skull, but I fucking run as best as I can out of that room and through the dark corridors. Each socked foot on the ground is a name in my mind.

*Cash and Shane. Cash and Shane. Cash and Shane. Cash.*

I have to get to them.

# SHANE

**BACK IN THE** kitchen, I go down the basement stairs to find what must be a doorway. It's the only thing here, so I go through it, and before me is the darkest hallway I've ever seen in my life. But then I hear something.

Soft feet padding concrete.

Breath, in and out. Gasping.

It's getting louder like someone is running toward me.

Should I say something or hide?

No time to decide before a body charges into me and sends me sailing against the wall. The gun that's strapped across my back hits first, torquing my spine. I cry out in pain.

"Shane?"

"Dalice! Are you all right?" I ask, bringing her into a hug.

"Cash," she says, out of breath.

"He's safe. I sent him to Hank and Brandy's with Gina."

"Oh God, thank you. Thank you so much!" She sobs at first, then collapses in my arms like a puppet dropped on the floor.

I pull her up and sling her arm around my shoulders. We have to get the hell out of here.

"Reva. She's down there," Dalice mumbles as we climb the steps. "Tried to kill me. Killed Renee. Probably Colin. Others, too. So many of them." She cries.

*Joel and Carissa.*

*Steve.*

That must be what happened to them, too. The reason I couldn't ever find them.

My knees start to buckle, but I purse my lips and force myself to keep going. How could I have missed this?

"You're safe now," I say, trying to keep the tears out of my voice.

"She's coming. Are there any other cars we can take?" Dalice asks.

"Gina said Reva took their keys. It's a miracle you had the foresight to leave yours in the car."

"So we're stuck here."

"We'll find a way out."

I take Dalice to the second floor, the nursery. Set her on the couch and load her up with blankets so she's warm enough. "Stay here. Rest."

She tries to stand up but moans and touches her forehead. She whispers, "Don't leave me."

I have to leave her.

I absolutely positively have to leave her, because I'm going after Reva. Dalice isn't well, for one, and I'm worried about that already. She needs to recover as much as possible. But also, I can't be trying to protect her from Reva *while* I'm confronting Reva. It's too much. I may be able to convince Reva I'm on her side, but not if Dalice is with me. Not with what Dalice knows about her.

I clench my teeth and clear my throat. Make my voice as hard as I can.

"I have to. You're too weak and you'll get in the way."

It hurts to say these words, but I know this woman, and it's the only thing that might give her pause. Because she believes it, even though it's so far from the truth.

She nods, pulls a blanket up to her chin. I rub her back. "I love you. I'll come back for you. Stay hidden."

# SHANE

**I PASS BY** the room closest to the stairs. A weak cry comes from it, and since the door is open a crack, I grip the rifle and go inside. Like everywhere else in the house, it's dark in here.

I say nothing, and step as quietly as possible.

"Shane? Is that you?"

Michaela's voice.

"Michaela. Are you okay?" I set the gun against the wall. As my eyes adjust, I see she's on the bed.

"I can't move."

I reach for her hand to help her up, but there's nothing.

Just a stump, and it's soaking wet.

Blood.

Michaela's hand is gone. Cut off.

*What the hell.*

"What happened?" I finally say, looking for a blanket, or pillow. Anything to stop the bleeding.

"Have you seen...Juniper?"

"Yes. She's safe. I sent her with Gina in Dalice's car. She's not here."

Michaela sobs. There's joy there, but it's overpowered by hopelessness and a sense of finality. I don't like the sound of it. It feels like that was all she was holding on for.

"You're going to be fine," I say as I wrap her wrist.

I'm lying. So much blood has soaked into the bed now that it's a miracle she's even alive. The pit in my stomach pulverizes me.

Michaela's other hand finds my cheek. I can only see the outline of her, but she's shaking. So weak.

"I'm glad for our friendship," she whispers.

"Let's get you out of here."

"Juniper. Take care of her...for...me."

Then nothing.

I shake her gently, but she's gone. Her body is empty. Her soul—or whatever the fuck it is—isn't there.

I spend a minute crying, brushing her hair off her face.

I brought her into this.

Her death is on me. All their deaths are on me. How can I live with myself?

Light shines from behind me, so I wheel around to see who it is.

"You always could find the good ones," Reva says, holding a lantern. There's a thin kitchen towel wrapped around her shoulder and under her armpit. Blood-saturated.

Dalice got her somehow. Pride blooms for a second, but quickly dissipates.

My gun. It's right beside Reva. No way I can reach it.

Why the hell did I set it down?

Reva looks at the gun, too. "It's not like you have the balls to use that thing anyway." She walks toward the dresser to set the lantern down, but it's still not enough distance for me to lunge for the gun.

Reva comes closer to me. Her hands are gold.

I could take her. Easy. She's tiny. But not with those hands.

"You're so skittish. You think I'm going to hurt you? Why would I do that? You're my person."

I step back, but space is tight. Not many steps back left.

"You're a murderer," I say.

"Oh, come on. You know I'm not. I'm like anyone else, doing what needs done to survive."

"Killing people? That's how you survive?"

"It's them or me."

She's still coming. Soon, I'll be trapped between the bed where Michaela's body lies, the wall, and Reva.

"Turn off the gold hands. Let's talk," I say.

She shrugs. "Can't. I've never been able to control it."

"You're lying. Turn it off."

Reva closes the distance between us. I'm going to have to take her down. But while I'm considering it, she leaps forward and her hands are on my face.

They're freezing cold, and I try to shake them off, but I'm getting weak too fast.

She wraps her fingers around my neck.

I consider pushing back, but I'm too slow, and Reva pulls me onto the bed next to Michaela like I weigh nothing.

Lying on my back, I can hardly breathe, but I feel around as best as I can. Hands searching for something, anything to use as a weapon.

Reva straddles my waist, carelessly nudging Michaela's body with her knee in the process, like she's merely a pillow in the way.

"Let's leave," she whispers, removing her hands from me. "You and me. Tonight. We can start over somewhere else. Help people again. It's what we were made for."

I can't even push her scant weight off me because I'm so weak. But I muster some strength to speak. "No. Never... again. You'll have to...kill me."

"Oh Shane, you know I wouldn't. Come on."

"I'll...kill you."

Reva cocks her head to the side. "Hilarious. How would you do that? One of your best qualities is that soft heart of yours. Besides, you'll die soon unless I heal you. And I won't heal you until you agree to come with me. I'm holding all the cards."

"You...always...do."

Reva climbs off me, goes across the room, and does something at the dresser with her back to me. I'm freezing cold, but trying to focus. I can hear her strike a match. Then a soft glow of light. She's lighting candles. Her back is red—blood. Like someone dumped a bucket of paint down her left shoulder.

I move my head and study Michaela again. Her eyes are open, and her hair hangs loose all around.

That pen she always wears. I swear she had it in her hair today. Where is it?

I feel around like it's the last thing I'll do. It's here somewhere, and I must find it while Reva's back is turned, but it's hard to move.

My knuckle brushes cold plastic.

I wrap my fist around the pen while Reva finishes lighting candles, illuminating the room even more. I bring it close to my side so she can't see.

She climbs on me again, this time sitting right on my ribs so it's even harder to breathe.

"I own you," she hisses.

Despite my foggy mind, that I can't move how I want to, I get a clear vision of the past. Like other times when I see things, it's a quick flash.

Reva in our old basement with Mom. Taking away her strength, just like this. Killing her.

Warm tears run down my temples and into my ears when I finally realize it all, even though somewhere deep down, I must have known.

"You killed…Mom," I whisper.

"She hurt me. Don't you remember?"

"You're…worse…than her."

Reva's face is dark, backlit by the candles. I can't see her expression, but anger radiates. It's like she dipped the world's biggest ladle into an ocean of rage and she's about to pour it out.

I squeeze the pen, make sure it's still in my hand. I use all my strength to force the sharp tip into Reva's side.

She screams and shuffles off me, trying to remove the pen. She falls on the floor in the effort, and I can't see her anymore. I try to pull myself to sit, but I can't even lift my head. My heart pounds, and I'm too dizzy to move.

A bloody hand grips the edge of the bed, and Reva's face rises slowly.

"Is your mind set?" she pushes out.

"Yes. Would...rather die...than be with...you."

Reva sighs. She's slow, weakened from the wound on her side, but not as bad off as me. She pulls herself to standing, holding her right side where I stabbed her. Blood stains the gown to match the gore on her back.

"And your girlfriend? Would you rather she die, too? Or is it worth it for you to come with me if it means she gets to live? Sacrifice or control, Shane. Which will it be this time?"

"No more lame-ass choices." Dalice breaks into the conversation from the doorway.

*No. She can't be here. I can't lose her.*

But when I strain to see around Reva, the only thing in view is the barrel of Dad's old .22, pointed right at Reva.

# DALICE

REVA PUTS A hand on Shane's chest, and he yells out. His voice is weak. Too weak.

"Get off him, bitch," I say, cocking the gun.

"What are you going to do? Shoot me? I doubt you even know how to use that thing."

I pull the trigger, sending a bullet into her left leg.

She screams and pulls her hands from Shane, puts them up in surrender, and sucks air through her teeth.

But now he's not moving.

A flood of emotion threatens to knock me over, but I steel myself.

Shane blinks. I've never been so happy to see someone blink before.

"Heal him," I demand.

Reva laughs. "I don't take orders."

That's when I snap. No idea why it happens now, but it's like everything I've been through with Cash, the way Reva strung me along about his healing, seeing the dungeon, all that death, the corpse hands, it mounts into a pressure I can't resist.

She doesn't get to hurt Shane anymore.

I shoot her again. This time in the stomach. She falls onto her back and doesn't move.

*No!*

That was a clumsy shot. I still need her to heal Shane.

I shove the panic down, trying to keep my voice even as I approach. "You will heal your brother. You owe it to him."

"I'm too weak," she says, trying to move around.

My mind races. I don't know the rules of this game, and she does. What if I try to force her to heal Shane, but she takes instead of gives and he dies?

"I didn't mean for it to go like this," Reva whispers.

"How the hell did you think it would go?"

"I wanted to help people. But doing that hurts me. I'd die like our uncle did if I only healed and never took life back from anyone. This is the only way I can fulfill God's will. He meant for me to choose sacrifice over control. But I found a way to have both."

"You've sacrificed nothing. Look at yourself. What you've become."

Her dead eyes find mine, and she growls, "You have no clue what my life was like."

*Shit.* This isn't helping. I need a fresh approach.

"You care about Shane, I know you do," I say, forcing my voice to be soft. I'm going for it, because, despite all of this, I think she loves him in her weird, twisted way.

It works.

Her eyebrows go up and she lets out a little cry. "Always have. I need him."

"Reva, he needs *you* right now." The words are totally gross coming out of my mouth, but this seems like it's working, and I have to keep pressing. "You're the only one who can help him. I can't. Nobody else can. Only you."

She blinks slowly, and it's like I can see the wheels in her mind turning even as her life wanes.

"I'm going to pull him to the floor, and you're going to lay those gold hands on him. Heal him," I say.

"How do you know I won't heal myself instead?"

I lower the gun a little. "I don't. It's a sacrifice to trust you to come through for Shane just this once. But it's up to you."

*And I'll end you if you hurt him, so there's that.*

"Gun's out of bullets."

Damn it, she's right. I turn the rifle around and lift it over my head like a club. "I don't need bullets. I'd rather not hurt you again, but I will."

*I want to hurt you. Please give me the chance.*

Her breathing slows, and her eyelids grow heavy, like she's struggling to open them.

I'm running out of time.

I set the gun down well out of anyone's reach and pull Shane off the bed by gripping his underarms. He's incredibly heavy. All dead weight. His head rests against my chest, and I move slowly until his boots hit the floor. I lay him down next to her so his feet are right by her head.

"You should know he never changes his mind once it's made up," Reva says. "That's one of his best qualities." She stops talking, struggles to breathe. "He tried to protect me. Always put me first."

Reva closes her eyes.

God, I don't need a soap opera death right now. I need her to heal Shane.

"Reva?" I say. Her eyes open into half slits. "Your turn to choose. Sacrifice or control?"

I should be terrified. She could easily lay hands on him and kill him, then kill me when her strength is back. While I shouldn't trust my gut because it has led me astray so many times, I do anyway.

Reva doesn't look at me. She stares at the ceiling, tears making pathways down the sides of her face, soaking her red hair.

"What would you ask of me?" she whispers to nobody.

"Heal Shane. Let him live."

Her hand comes off the floor by centimeters, but it's enough effort to read her intention. I grip her forearm and place her warm hand on Shane's chest.

Reva closes her eyes. Her breath slows to a quiet stop.

Shane opens his eyes and gasps for air.

# DALICE

**HE'S BACK. HE'S** alive, and I absolutely lose it, falling on him, crying.

He sits up and sees Reva, whose open, dead eyes are still fixed on the ceiling.

"Oh God," he whispers.

"I'm sorry, I had to do it."

"I know. I was going to do it myself, but..." He wipes a tear.

When Shane comes out of the moment of sadness, we find my phone and call the cops.

Then Shane goes down to the dungeon—nobody is alive. Reva killed them all.

He checks upstairs. Holly, Jonah, Colin's son, and a few others are dead in their rooms. I can't do anything but grip a blanket tight around me. And cry.

The storm hasn't died down, but the news of a dungeon full of corpses in the woods is motivation enough for the police to brave the weather.

No missed calls from Seattle, thank God. I call Brandy.

"Oh God, Dal. I've been calling you for hours. I assumed you didn't have service."

"Cash?" I choke out.

"Yes, your friend Gina made it to our house. Cash is here, and Juniper. Everyone is warm and fed. The kids are napping."

I put my hand over the phone and let out a cry. Shane's eyes are wide. He's trying to read into my reaction.

"She has the kids. They made it over there."

Shane exhales, and a tear slips down his face. I wipe it with my thumb and turn my attention back to the phone.

"I'll be in touch, but we'll probably stay here until the storm passes," I say.

I don't tell Brandy about the dead bodies we get to hunker down with. I don't tell her about how Shane almost died. How I could have too. That Reva is dead. I tell her something else completely.

"Bran, I'm sorry for everything. For how hard our relationship has been. Thank you for the survival box. The walkie-talkie literally saved Cash's life."

Brandy lets out a little sob. "Me too. I'm so sorry. I'll do better going forward."

"How did our wires get crossed so badly? I thought you were mad at me for making bad decisions."

"I know. I tried to convince you that wasn't how I felt, but over the past year, you wouldn't listen, so I gave up trying. You're so goddamn stubborn that it sent me into anger. Sometimes people will become what you think they are, even if you're wrong. It's too exhausting to keep trying."

"That's really profound, Bran, but I'm wiped out and sort of wish I hadn't asked. Can we dissect this later?"

Brandy laughs. She actually laughs. I made my sister laugh.

I pull the phone away from my ear so Shane can hear it. I point at the phone. He shakes his head and smiles.

I say goodbye to Brandy and allow my weight to fall against Shane. He wraps his arms around me.

But my phone rings, and this time, it's a Seattle area code.

# TEN YEARS LATER

# DALICE

**TONIGHT IS CHRISTMAS** Eve. Shane and I love to decorate the living room for Christmas. It's kind of our thing. We live at Reva's house, but we've made it our own. I know it's weird, but I'll get to that.

Every year we transform this room into an absolute twinkle-light disaster, stringing them all across the cathedral ceiling and around the insides of windows.

Think: dorm room meets outdoor patio. That's our vibe.

This year, Cash talked us into doing colored lights. I'm a little sad because I love the white lights, but the color is magical. Reminds me of being a kid and opening my bedroom blinds at night to watch the Christmas lights on our house hanging from the eaves above my window. Of falling asleep to the thought of Christmas morning. All that hope and promise of joy.

When I got the call from Seattle on the same day everything happened, we moved into action. It was a lot of drama, because at first, it didn't seem like we could get a flight out of Spokane. But there was a break in the storm, and we made it in time. Cash's heart transplant went off without a hitch.

Now he's thirteen, and he's fine.

As fine as a transplant patient can be, because life is never *normal* in the sense of other thirteen-year-olds whose original hearts still work. But Cash has nothing to compare his life to, and Shane and I try to treat him as normally as possible, without kid gloves. And like me and Shane, he's had lots of therapy. More, actually. Occupational, speech, physical, play—you name it, he's had it. He's about as normal of a teenager as you can imagine. So, yeah, lots of hiding out in his bedroom, playing video games, mouthing off. That sort of thing.

When he's not being super sweet and helping us with his nine-year-old sister, that is.

Yep, little sister.

Guess who got surprise-pregnant again? I was probably even pregnant the night everything went down, but really early. Like, baby-the-size-of-a-poppy-seed level.

Her name is Sera. She has Shane's brown hair and thick lashes, but my brown eyes. I was a basket case early in the pregnancy. So much stress from everything that was happening with the investigation and plagued by fears that her heart could be like Cash's. We were fresh from Cash's transplant when I finally figured out that I didn't have a month-long bout of the flu. The timing was overwhelming, but I wanted the baby.

I wanted a little-Shane, something good to come out of the nightmare we had survived.

As soon as it was possible to tell, my doctor did a scan to confirm the condition of the heart.

Four chambers.

Valves and arteries doing their goddamn job.

I thought I was a crier before, but holy shit, I filled that room with tears of relief.

So, why do we still live in this godforsaken house?

After the investigation, after all the reporters looking for interviews stopped calling, we realized there was no way in hell we'd be able to sell the estate. Nobody would buy it. Nobody would even list it for us. And that had been the initial plan.

Shane inherited everything, so yeah, why not sell it? Move to Hawaii. Or the Oregon Coast, or goddamn anywhere but Spokane. Turns out Reva had a non-murdery side gig healing people for cash, so he's loaded. We didn't need the money from a sale. We could abandon it here in the woods.

He wasn't as keen on the idea of being an origin story for some future haunted house, and I had nothing left in my arsenal of resistance. Truth is, I came to realize, like Shane had, that despite what we went through here, it was also where we found love. (Thanks, Rhianna.)

The fire roars while Shane and the kids hunt in the backyard/forest for a Christmas tree. I sip coffee and put my feet up on the end table.

Besides the fact that we couldn't sell this place, I tell myself it's not the house's fault it got stuck in a cult. Had it known what was happening, it never would have joined. It's an innocent victim in all of this too, and the house deserves to be loved just like any other victim.

It's not bad or unintelligent houses that become sites for cult activity. It's good, smart houses too. All houses want to be accepted, to be a part of something, and that's why they end up hosting cults.

Okay, okay, I'm not talking about houses anymore. I'm talking about us.

People can't comprehend why I joined in the first place, and why I didn't leave sooner, but I can't explain the sheer panic of having a child who might die. If you haven't been there, you don't know. It's one thing to fear your child dying, another to face the real possibility. I'm so grateful that I never had to go through it. So many heart moms have.

The other thing is that *anyone* can be blindsided when they want to believe in someone or something. If you think you're an exception, you're probably more susceptible than most.

Cash and Sera yell at each other out front, so I set my mug down to go open the door for them.

At first, I only see a tree, a huge trunk aimed right at me like a ramming rod, followed by Shane's face, covered in a black and silver goatee, separated by his giant smile. He carries the tree toward me.

"Better watch out, coming through," he says.

I stand back, deeper into the foyer, and watch him stomp snow off on the porch. He slips his Sorels off and comes inside.

I grab the boots and line them against the wall. The kids hold the other end of the tree, hence all the fighting.

"Cash is hogging all the space."

"Sera's too small to help anyway."

I wish I could say that life as a referee of my offspring is pure bliss. But when they argue like this, it's less than bliss. My solution? Sip the coffee. Pour the bourbon. Be grateful to be alive to witness it. So far, so good.

The kids walk past me, their boots still on. They didn't even stomp them out on the porch. I pull in my lips, trying not to laugh while I watch all the snow track in, covering the hardwood floors.

"Psst! Kids," I whisper.

Shane gets distracted trying to fit the trunk into the tree stand by the front window.

They come over to me.

"Boots, dudes. You *trying* to get a lecture from Dad?"

Surprise on their faces because they forgot. They take them off and fling them into the foyer.

"Nope," I say. "Try again."

They slouch over and line the boots up next to Shane's. I hand them towels and make them mop up the water.

It's dark by the time we have all our ornaments on the enormous tree and we're sitting in the fire room, lit by the blaze plus five trillion colored lights.

Once we've had all the eggnog (mixed with bourbon for the adults), and all the cookies, leaving only two and a half for Santa, there's a knock at the door.

It's Brandy and Hank.

Brandy puts on Christmas music first thing, which I forgot to do. She's been blaring it since October. One of *those* people. I love her for it.

Cash and Sera settle on the floor in front of the Christmas tree. They're opening their one Christmas Eve present.

It's pajamas.

They know it's pajamas.

Everyone knows it's pajamas, but it's fun how they still get excited.

Cash holds up his green- and red-striped long john jammies and Sera tears into hers. Also green and red stripes. What can I say? I'm a sucker for matchy shit.

Shane pets my hair and holds it in a low ponytail. It's long now, and I finally let it be blonde. He tickles my neck softly, and I lay my head on his shoulder. He smells like pine.

"Hey Mom?" I faintly hear Sera's voice, but her back is to me.

"Hey Mom?" Sera repeats, louder this time, and spins around. She stands facing me in front of the tree. Cash stares at her. There's total silence, and then all eyes are on Shane and me.

"I have Christmas on my hands," Sera says, holding them up.

Her palms are covered in gold.

# GET SHANE'S PLAYLIST ON SPOTIFY

**SCAN THE QR** code and sign up for my newsletter to get over two hours of tunes I know Shane would approve of. And don't worry, I only send emails once a month (or less, if I'm being particularly lazy). Of course, you're also welcome to get the link to the playlist and then unsubscribe. No judgment!

# AUTHOR'S NOTE

**AT MY TWENTY-WEEK** ultrasound in 2008, I got the news that my second child would be a girl and that she had a major congenital heart defect. She would require three open-heart surgeries within the first few years of her life, the first one taking place immediately after birth.

It was a whirlwind of grappling with this new reality during the last half of my pregnancy, finding out about insurance coverage, and then learning that I had to deliver in Palo Alto, CA. Idaho didn't have a pediatric heart surgeon.

My baby's name was Evelyn Hope.

She lived for thirteen days. I got to hold her twice, and both times she was heavily sedated.

My story with Evelyn didn't end as happily as Cash's story. Once she was born, the doctor found seven other major heart and pulmonary defects. Any one of them would be an enormous challenge to face, but altogether this meant that she couldn't survive off life support, and there wasn't a surgery in the world that could save her.

As you might imagine, there's a lot more to this story—ups and downs, moments where it seemed like things might just work out, and moments where we knew it wouldn't. I won't get into that here, but I can't seem to get away from it whenever I sit down to write. It pours out onto the page as what we call "grief horror," even though as of publication of this book, I'm fifteen years beyond the experience. I've found that the cliche is right: Time heals all wounds. But what's also true is those wounds change us and form us into who we are today. So far, I've found it impossible to sidestep processing my experience with loss when I write a story. I've given up trying.

This is my journey, and every family with a heart baby has a unique journey. There's no cookie-cutter experience. Some have endings like mine. Others don't. Regardless, there's inherent grief over losses of all kinds, even if the child survives and lives a happy life. Things the child misses because of so much time spent recovering from procedures. Needing to stay isolated during sick season and missing out on fun, sometimes meaningful activities. Some children experience developmental and learning delays. There's regret as a parent too, even when you're doing everything you can. There's guilt over past decisions and outcomes; no matter how unwarranted, you still wonder if you'd chosen something different about their care, would XYZ now be different?

This story about Cash is a fantasy. Selfishly, I wanted to experience what it would have been like to have a child survive an impossible heart condition as a way of creating something different from what I experienced. My deepest hope is that in doing that I haven't trivialized anyone else's experience with a loved one who has a severe heart condition. It's likely that despite my best efforts, I got a few things wrong in my fictionalization, and I hope you'll forgive me.

If you're in the heart-parent category, I want to tell you that I see you and I'm in awe of you. I'm sure you're so grateful for your child, just as I am intensely grateful for Evelyn's life, even if it was very short. But I also know there are things hidden from sight that you experience all alone because people forget the hard things others go through once the crisis subsides. Life moves on for everyone else. But you? You show up every day for your child. You're doing an amazing job and you're a wonderful mom. (Or you're a wonderful dad.)

# AUTHOR'S NOTE

I don't know how to end this on a cheerful note except to reassure you that I am doing so well. I have two beautiful, healthy children with me, and that's so much more than I could have hoped for.

Now I've typed and deleted fifteen million things to make this less heavy, but none of them land right, so I'm just going to say thank you for reading.

—XO, Steph

# ACKNOWLEDGMENTS

**THANK YOU TO** everyone who had a hand in inspiring this story and helping me bring it to life:

To Noelle Ihli, my first reader and sounding board. I'm so grateful for your friendship and publishing guidance.

To the phenomenal beta readers who poked holes and gave me a temperature read on this story before I put it into the world: Anna Gamel, Faith Gardner, Kelsey Zedwick, Jeanne Allen, Chris Nelson, and my lovely sister, Rebekah Dresback.

To my dear friend Heidi Hildebrand, who let me pick her brain about life with a CHD child.

To Barbara Drake, who read the book early and gave me feedback from a current medical mama's point of view. (Priceless!)

To all the Booktokers and Bookstagrammers whose excitement for books is infectious. Thank you for reading and sharing my books on social media.

To my publisher at Dark Matter INK, Rob Carroll, for continually believing in my stories and my career as an author.

To Maddy Leary, such a talented editor and a wonderful person too. That combination is more rare than it should be. So grateful for your eyes on this (and your suggestions to make Shane's playlist sing).

To Phil McLaughlin, who reads everything I write and offers so much encouragement about the potential my books might have on the big or small screen.

To Olly Jeavons, one of the most amazing cover artists working right now. I'm a fan and I can't believe I have a cover with your art on it! (Fangirl moment.)

And of course, to you! For picking up this story and spending time in my world. Thank you so much!

—Steph Nelson

# ABOUT THE AUTHOR

**A LIFELONG PNW** girl, Steph currently lives in Idaho, and when she's not working on her next story, she's devouring horror, thriller, and romance books.

## Also Available or Coming Soon from Dark Matter INK

*Human Monsters: A Horror Anthology*
Edited by Sadie Hartmann & Ashley Saywers
ISBN 978-1-958598-00-9

*Zero Dark Thirty: The 30 Darkest Stories from Dark Matter Magazine, 2021–'22* Edited by Rob Carroll
ISBN 978-1-958598-16-0

*Linghun* by Ai Jiang
ISBN 978-1-958598-02-3

*Monstrous Futures: A Sci-Fi Horror Anthology*
Edited by Alex Woodroe
ISBN 978-1-958598-07-8

*Our Love Will Devour Us* by R. L. Meza
ISBN 978-1-958598-17-7

*Haunted Reels: Stories from the Minds of Professional Filmmakers* Curated by David Lawson
ISBN 978-1-958598-13-9

*The Vein* by Steph Nelson
ISBN 978-1-958598-15-3

*Other Minds* by Eliane Boey
ISBN 978-1-958598-19-1

*Monster Lairs: A Dark Fantasy Horror Anthology*
Edited by Anna Madden
ISBN 978-1-958598-08-5

*Frost Bite* by Angela Sylvaine
ISBN 978-1-958598-03-0

*Free Burn* by Drew Huff
ISBN 978-1-958598-26-9

*The House at the End of Lacelean Street*
by Catherine McCarthy
ISBN 978-1-958598-23-8

*When the Gods Are Away* by Robert E. Harpold
ISBN 978-1-958598-47-4

*The Dead Spot: Stories of Lost Girls*
by Angela Sylvaine
ISBN 978-1-958598-27-6

*Grim Root* by Bonnie Jo Stufflebeam
ISBN 978-1-958598-36-8

*Voracious* by Belicia Rhea
ISBN 978-1-958598-25-2

*The Bleed* by Stephen S. Schreffler
ISBN 978-1-958598-11-5

*Chopping Spree* by Angela Sylvaine
ISBN 978-1-958598-31-3

*Saturday Fright at the Movies*
by Amanda Cecelia Lang
ISBN 978-1-958598-75-7

*The Off-Season: An Anthology of Coastal New Weird*
Edited by Marissa van Uden
ISBN 978-1-958598-24-5

*Club Contango* by Eliane Boey
ISBN 978-1-958598-57-3

*The Divine Flesh* by Drew Huff
ISBN 978-1-958598-59-7

*Psychopomp* by Maria Dong
ISBN 978-1-958598-52-8

*Disgraced Return of the Kap's Needle*
by Renan Bernardo
ISBN 978-1-958598-74-0

*Haunted Reels 2: More Stories from the Minds of Professional Filmmakers* Curated by David Lawson
ISBN 978-1-958598-53-5

*Dark Circuitry* by Kirk Bueckert
ISBN 978-1-958598-48-1

*Soul Couriers* by Caleb Stephens
ISBN 978-1-958598-76-4

*Abducted* by Patrick Barb
ISBN 978-1-958598-37-5

*Cyanide Constellations and Other Stories*
by Sara Tantlinger
ISBN 978-1-958598-81-8

*Little Red Flags: Stories of Cults, Cons, and Control*
Edited by Noelle W. Ihli & Steph Nelson
ISBN 978-1-958598-54-2

*Frost Bite 2* by Angela Sylvaine
ISBN 978-1-958598-55-9

*The Starship, from a Distance* by Robert E. Harpold
ISBN 978-1-958598-82-5

*Dark Matter Presents: Fear City*
ISBN 978-1-958598-90-0

## Part of the Dark Hart Collection

*Rootwork* by Tracy Cross
ISBN 978-1-958598-01-6

*Mosaic* by Catherine McCarthy
ISBN 978-1-958598-06-1

*Apparitions* by Adam Pottle
ISBN 978-1-958598-18-4

*I Can See Your Lies* by Izzy Lee
ISBN 978-1-958598-28-3

*A Gathering of Weapons* by Tracy Cross
ISBN 978-1-958598-38-2

Milton Keynes UK
Ingram Content Group UK Ltd.
UKHW040641271124
3169UKWH00040B/202

# PRAISE FOR THE THRESHING FLOOR

"Heart in my throat, jaw on the floor. This thriller will stay with me for a very long time. Steph Nelson is a master of heartfelt page-turners, and this book is no exception."

—Noelle W. Ihli, author of *Ask for Andrea*

"Full of desperation, love, and loss, *The Threshing Floor* is an absolutely chilling read. Few books have so thoroughly captivated me."

—Caleb Stephens, author of *If You Lie*

"This gripping, chilling, and utterly addictive book is a must-read for thriller fans. *The Threshing Floor* is both horrifying and hopeful. I loved it."

—Faith Gardner, author of *Like It Never Was*

"*The Threshing Floor* is a whirlwind of a novel that'll whisk you into its vortex from the very first page and keep you spinning to the very last. A supernatural cult thriller, full of twists and turns, but one which has a powerful moral dilemma at its core—How far would you go to save your child?"

—Catherine McCarthy, author of *Mosaic* and *The House at the End of Lacelean Street*